Unlawful Attachment

Unlawful Attachment

The Mackenney Family Saga Book Three

by Caz May

Unlawful Attachment

First Published 2020
Paperback ISBN 9780648853428

Published by Caz May

To anyone who has taken a chance on an old love.

Also by Caz May

The Mackenney Family Saga

Bk 1-Country Secrets

Bk 2-Doctor Attraction

Always Only You Series

Bk 1-Roommates Don't Kiss & Tell

Bk 2-Friends Don't Say Goodbye

Bk 3-Feelings Don't Play Fair

Bk 4-Hearts Don't Steer Us Wrong

A Holiday Romance Duet

Bk 1-Take Flight

My Girl Duet

Bk 1-Not my Girl

Bk 2-Still my Girl

Trigger Warning

Please be aware this story contains some content including scenes of sexual abuse and other dark themes including BDSM which may be triggering for some readers.

(Prologue) Quentin

Watching someone you've loved desperately for so long walk down the aisle of a church to marry someone else whilst your in the pews is like being in hell.

It's an uncanny feeling, being in a church and feeling like I'm in hell. She walks in, her arm linked with her father's, wearing an off white gown that clings to her curves and extenuates her ample cleavage. From her hips the fabric flows down to her feet and swishes around her legs as she walks. She's so elated the grin won't leave her face. She doesn't even glance at me for a moment and my heart sinks. She can't even acknowledge me with a nod after we'd slept together a year or so ago and she'd torn my heart out by rejecting me.

My stomach is in knots, as all the memories come crashing into my mind and all I really want to do is squeeze past whoever is next to me to race out the door of the church and run away like I'd done in the past, when I couldn't be with her.

But this time the pain is even more raw, more real, as this time she's actually marrying someone else.

She isn't in love with my older brother anymore, and she isn't in love with me, no matter how much I want her to be.

As she approaches the altar, I turn to look at my ex-girlfriend sitting a few rows back. Her eyes look sad, but her lips upturn in a scowl when she catches me looking at her. If we weren't in a church with most of the town around I think she'd have flipped me off.

I hadn't meant to break her heart, but no matter how much I'd wanted to I couldn't make myself fall in love with her, like she'd fallen for me.

My older brother was a little taken aback and worried about me when I'd told him we'd broken up. Telling him it was because I'm still in love with Addison is only half of the reason and now that Addison is marrying Zane, as difficult as it's going to be I need to tell my brother the real reason.

Unlawful Attachment

I need to move on from Addison and I need to stop thinking about how my past has fucked me up when it comes to love.

It's time to let go of the darkness completely, and step one is telling Hunter that I'm not the innocent flirtatious little brother he thinks I am.

❧

As soon as I enter the pub for Addison's cocktail style wedding reception, I grab a champagne from the waitress walking around with a tray load of glasses of the pale yellow gold. Downing it in one gulp I put it back on the tray before she even steps away. She gives me a smile, and queries, "Rough day Constable Mackenney?"

I squint at her name badge, intrigued as to how she knows me. "You could say that Mary."

Holding a up another glass to me, she says, "Have another, I won't tell anyone."

And walking away she winks at me flirtatiously.

It's gonna be one long arse night, and there's no way champagne is going to cut it. Getting blind drunk probably isn't the best idea, but it's the only thing that's going to dull the ache in my heart.

Samantha walks in, showing a little more confidence than she would have a year ago. Her brown hair falls over her shoulders and her dress shows off her sweet body that's usually hidden under her boyish work uniform.

I still feel guilty for breaking up with her, but her innocence damn near became my undoing. It not only brought the dark desires from my past crashing back, it made me crave them and with her.

Her sweet nature couldn't handle what I'd wanted from her but it didn't stop me from missing her though, as it had been nice to be with someone again.

Again I scan the room for anyone else I know, actually hoping to find that Hunter has arrived so I can steal him away from his wife and my nephew who's always stuck to his fathers side like glue, for just a moment to speak to him.

Seeing him walk in about twenty minutes later, I grab his arm and ask, "Hey Hunt, do you think we could talk about something?"

"Yeah Quent, just give me a minute to find Savannah and I'll meet you outside."

He crosses the room, seeing Savannah talking to some local women. After whispering in her ear, she nods and picks River up to hold him against her hip. Hunter comes back over to me and he follows me outside to sit on the bench seat by the pub doors.

Reassuringly when we sit down he touches my arm, asking, "So what's up little brother?"

"It was so fucking hard Hunt, watching her get married you know."

"I know it was hard Quent, but I'm sure your happy ending is right around the corner," he says, a soothing tone in his voice.

"Thanks Hunter, but I'm not so sure about that."

"Why Quentin? What makes you think that?" he asks, his tone concerned.

"I don't know…I just feel broken."

"Broken? I don't get you."

"Yeah, broken and I need to tell you something about my past."

He nods, rubbing his hand comfortingly up and down my arm.

"You can tell me anything Quent."

"I know, but it's bad Hunter," I say, dipping my head in shame.

"Quentin, you're my brother. I love you no matter what."

"I know…and well it's kinda actually about why Sam and I broke up too."

"Ok, so what really happened then?" he asks, nodding.

The knot in my stomach feels like it's being pulled by an invisible rope, and my heart is pounding hard but I have to tell him.

I have to tell someone.

"I…um…I drove her away…because I wanted too much from her."

"What do you mean Quent?"

"She was too innocent for me," I declare, feeling like a weight has lifted off my shoulders.

"I'm sorry I'm not following Quent."

"With sex, Hunter," I blurt out, feeling a blush rise up my cheeks.
Shock crosses his face, and I pull my arm back, cursing myself for even thinking that sharing this with him was a good idea, but I had to. When he doesn't reply I force myself to continue, "It started when I was at the Police Academy. I kinda just fucked anyone willing and got into some darker things."

"Like what Quentin?" he asks, a hint of what sounds like anger in his voice.

"Like wanting to control women to pleasure them as well as make them feel pain."

Again the shock crosses his face, at hearing the words I can't believe I've just said to my older brother.

"Whoah Quentin! Tell me why you'd even want to get into that stuff?"
And there it is, the million dollar question and the answer to that question has plagued me since I'd left Ridgehope for the police academy years ago.

"Because I couldn't have Addison."

"But why that stuff Quent?"

"I don't know. It was like a way of punishing myself...like I felt not good enough for her and you were."

"Quentin, honestly I'm sorry but you and I both know that neither of us can really be with Addison, regardless of the fact that she's found Zane and I've found Savannah."

"I know Hunter and I'm so glad she's happy, and you're to but I don't want to go down that dark path again and I feel like I am."

"Oh Quent," he says soothingly, before continuing with a question, "Is that the only reason you broke up with Sam?"

"No, I really liked her, but her being so innocent I don't know I just couldn't fall in love with her."

"I get it Quentin. You can't help who you fall in love with."
I laugh, wondering when my brother got so wise.

"Yeah, I just want what you have with Savannah, that kind of love."

"I know Quent, but do you still love Addison though?"

"No, I don't actually," I admit, feeling the weight of acknowledging it lifted from me. "Being with Sam kinda helped me get over Addison, even though I'm not in love with Sam."

"Yeah, I'm sure your someone is out there Quentin."

"Maybe, but I'm not counting on it."

"Oh, Quent, maybe you need to get out of Ridgehope for a while again."

I shake my head frantically. "Fuck no brother! I'm not leaving you, Savannah and River! You guys are my everything!"

"I know Quentin. You're the most amazing uncle but I just want to see you happy."

"I know that Hunter, but I'd rather stay forever single than leave."

"Oh Quent, I don't know. I don't want you to be lonely."

"I'm not Hunter, I have you guys and my mates. Hugh and Mark don't let a man drink alone," I say reassuringly, not completely convinced of my words.

I can't help but notice that he gulped hard when I'd mentioned my mates as though he's hiding something he wants to say.

Shrugging he speaks, "Yeah but you deserve to be happy Quentin. That's all I'm saying."

"I know Hunter and being here with you and your little family makes me happy."

"Really Quentin? Even if you can't have all you desire?"

Laughing, and running a hand through my hair, I say, "Yes desire and happiness are two very different things Hunter."

Again he speaks with words that seem wise beyond his years, "Are you going to be able to deal without giving into those desires though Quentin?"

"I'm not saying it's going to be easy Hunter, but yes I'm going to try to suppress those desires again."

He doesn't reply, urging me to continue, as though he knows I have more to say.

"Sam brought them back, but she also took them away again."

"Yeah I guess I see what you're saying. I'm never going to completely understand that side of you, but if it makes you happy then I'm all for it Quent."

I sigh deeply, laughing. "That's enough of this sap. I need a hard drink!"

He slaps a hand against my back when we stand up. "Sounds like a great idea."

Heading back inside the pub, the whole place is abuzz with chatter and music. Hunter walks up to the bar and orders two whiskeys straight up. Looking straight at me, he takes his glass from the bar top and clinks his glass against mine in a toast, "To happiness brother."

We both down the whiskey, slamming the glasses down on the bar top. Hunter then wraps an arm around my waist, pulling me closer to his side in a brotherly hug, and whispers in my ear, "Love you little brother."

Those words mean the world as the fact that he still loves me after what I'd just told him, makes my heart happy and confirms that leaving Ridgehope is something I'll never be able to do again.

It's home. And I'll never believe the saying that, *'home is where the heart is'* because even though I don't have love from a woman in my heart I have so much more.

Ridgehope, my Mum, my brother and his family are my heart and my home.

(1) Samantha

3 months earlier

Quentin lies down next to me, after we've just had sex for the third time. We haven't really even defined our relationship, but I honestly feel as though he's my boyfriend.

I've fallen hard for him, but haven't told him how I feel, except for giving into between the sheets of his bed.

It was a big deal for me to sleep with him once, let alone more than once.

But I can't explain how he makes me feel, or even try to resist him when he smiles at me. Before he kisses me, a devilish smile crosses his face and it never fails to make me melt.

But as much as I love being with him, there's a darker side to him that really gets to me.

He pulls me against him now—holding up a set of handcuffs—spinning them around on his finger so close to my face I'm afraid they're going to hit me square in the nose.

It's partly the fact I'm naked and vulnerable in his bed, but it's mainly the way he drawls at me, "Come on Sam, I really want to do this."

I try to roll away, but his arm wraps around my bare midriff pulling me even closer against his body that's eager for another round.

Feeling the cold metal of the handcuffs against my sensitive skin I whimper. "I can't Quentin. I don't like this side of you."

He stifles a laugh, and I try desperately to hold back the tears stinging my eyes. His tone when he speaks again is carnal, "I'm not going to hurt you. I promise you'll enjoy it."

The devilish smirk is on his face again, but instead of making me melt, it makes my stomach constrict in a knot.

"How do you know that?" I ask, watching his eyes and the anger that rises in them.

Sitting up on the bed, he runs a hand through his hair, not caring that the sheet falls away from around his body and he's completely exposed.

"For fucks sake Sam I thought you got over the fear when I tied you up with the scarfs."

I hesitate, not sure what I should reply, as I had kind of liked the thrill of being tied up the first time, but now something feels different.

"A scarf is very different to real handcuffs, Quentin."

"That's true Sam, but you know I won't hurt you."

Sitting up myself, I pull the sheets up to cover myself, stupidly feeling ashamed of my nakedness.

"I know Quentin, but I just can't ok."

He appears to get upset, clutching the sheets in his fisted hands.

The tears are still stinging my eyes and I sniff them back.

"God, Sam, I thought you liked me!"

"No, Quentin I don't like you! I love you!" I scream, instantly regretting the words the moment they've left my lips. There's no way he returns my feelings. He's still in love with her.

"Fuck Sam, I don't know. How can you say that?"

Tears are dripping down my cheeks now and wiping one away with my thumb I meekly reply, "Because it's true and that's why I can't do those things with you. It makes me feel like you don't love me." I pause wiping the tears away with my arm this time, carefully to not let the sheets slip before I continue, "Well don't feel anything for me and just want to use me for sex."

He shakes his head, and lightly touches my arm. "You know that's not true Sam. I can't not be me."

"Why though Quentin? Why do you want to do those things to me?"

He hangs his head, not able to meet my eyes that are trying to find an answer in his.

"I don't know Sam. I wish I could tell you." In that moment he seems vulnerable, ashamed for being himself and I want that Quentin so much.

"Yeah me too, but tonight I just need you, Quentin."

"I guess I can deal with that."

Leaning closer to him, not caring that the sheet falls, I press a soft kiss to his lips. I try to fill the kiss with emotion but he makes it carnal, biting my lip so hard he draws blood and I whimper when I pull away. Standing up I yank the sheets away to cover myself.

"I think I'm going to go home. I need to think about us."

He crawls across the bed, trying to stop me when I turn away.

"Please Sam, I'm sorry. I need you."

"Stop Quentin please!" I beg.

"Are we breaking up?" He asks shocking my ears with the odd question.

Spinning around I look straight at him. "I don't know. Was I ever really your girlfriend anyway?"

"Yes, Sam, you're my girlfriend!"

"Well, then maybe we are breaking up!" I snap at him, picking up my discarded clothes from the floor and tugging my skirt and t-shirt back on as I race out of his room.

Looking back at him, it's clear to see the shock on his face, but he doesn't move or say a word when I leave. And my heart shatters when I slam the door behind me.

How could I have been so stupid?

I can't believe I'd put myself out there, let him take my innocence away and fallen in love with him. I'm so stupid and I want to go home. Home to Adelaide, away from the hell of Ridgehope and the dark desires of Quentin Mackenney.

(2) Caleb

I'd fucked up, getting involved in the dark world of the Adelaide underworld. Putting my wife and daughter in danger had never been part of the plan, and merely escaping with my life I knew the only way we'd be safe was to get as far away from the city as possible and assume a new identity in a new life.

მ

We've been driving for close to five hours and still don't appear to be getting anywhere. Emilie is dozing in the passenger seat, suddenly stirring when I drive over the white line at the edge of the road. The rumbling sound—that makes you want to block your ears—reverberates through the car.

"Huh, what?" she mumbles in a daze.

"Sorry, baby, just went over the line a bit."

She sits up in the seat, touching my thigh with her hand.

"Are you tired?" She asks softly, running her small hand comfortingly on my thigh.

"No, no I'm fine. Just distracted."

She doesn't reply, turning away to look out the window at the endless bush, rows and rows of trees that are passing by the car windows.

"We're going to be safe, Emilie."

When she turns back towards me, I look at her out of the corner of my eye. She bites her lip before she speaks, "But you didn't pay him Caleb. He's going to come after us. You don't cross Vlad Manning." Her tone is one of warning and she turns her gaze to our daughter in the back of the car; latched into her car seat.

Not looking back at me, Emilie speaks again, concern in her tone, "I don't want Ember to get hurt or to know about what you were involved in."

Shaking my head, I try to soothe her with my words, "She's not going to Emilie. I never would have done it, if I thought either of you were going to be hurt, but we needed the money."

She lets out a little sob, as though she's trying to hold back tears.

"I'm scared though Caleb," She says, shivering even though it isn't cold.

"Me too Emi, but we'll be fine once we get far enough away from the city. We can start over," I say with more conviction than I feel, because as I gaze into the rear view mirror a small but ominous looking truck appears to be advancing on us; fast.

Clenching my grip on the steering wheel I try to focus on my breathing, to calm my racing heart.

There's no way it's a Manning family truck. It's just paranoia.

"Caleb, what's wrong?" Emi demands, sensing my visible sudden unease.

"That...t...t...truck behind us...is going really fast," I stammer, a little breathless from the anxiety rising in my chest.

Emilie turns back to look through the back window, her eyes boggling when she demands, "Speed up Caleb!"

Her request is idiotic, especially on a back country highway I've never driven down before—but if I don't speed up—the truck will end up behind me, too close for comfort and too close for it to pass me safely.

"Caleb!" Emilie demands again when I press my foot hard on the accelerator pedal and the car lurches forward; the speedo climbing.

My speedo now reads a hundred and fifty, a dangerous speed for any road, but out here it's practically a death sentence.

Looking back I can still see the truck, seeming like it's still coming closer.

Emilie is gripping the sides of her seat tightly and stupidly I close my eyes for a second, hoping that when I open them I've been imagining the truck still coming closer. Edging my foot a little off the accelerator when I open them I feel the impact against the boot of the car, the screech of metal scraping against metal and the wretched crying scream of my daughter.

Unlawful Attachment

Emilie turns back to soothe her, comforting her in the way only a mother can.

My mind goes blank for a moment, watching the truck now hanging back behind us. Gazing in the rear view mirror again I try to focus on getting a good view of the driver, but the tinted windows block my view.

As my speed has lowered, I'm waiting for the moment the impatient prick will pass. And I don't have to wait long, as mere minutes pass before he moves into the right lane, passing on a double line as though he has a death wish.

Again I have to cross the white line—the whole car rumbling—and again the piercing sound of metal scraping against metal fills my ears. The bastard is trying to run us off the road, the weight of his truck edging the car closer to the gravel on side of the road.

Moving the car back over when he finally passes, the mirror has ripped off, crashing to the ground behind us. The sounds are ear splitting, metal scraping, the shatter of the glass from the mirror and the inconsolable crying screams of my daughter.

Taking a few deep breaths I slow the car down, softly pressing my foot to the brake. Comfortingly I place a hand on Emilie's knee. Her breaths are shallow. "Calm down baby. We're fine. It's gonna be ok."

She nods and smiles at me. Her sweet smile, that always melts my heart and now I inwardly curse myself for putting her in danger.

The deal in the city should have been an easy one—get the goods, exchange the money and be in the clear, but it hadn't gone as planned and having a gun pressed to my head, tied up in some abandoned warehouse my life had flashed before my eyes. I'd not given them any information, and they know I'm not going to give it up now, so they let me go with a warning. A warning that had me so scared for my life and my family's that I raced home to Emilie, telling her we had to leave now or Vlad Manning was going to come after us. And now I get the sense that I hadn't been wrong.

The truck had driven off, but barely ten minutes has passed before I see it again on the other side of the road, coming back towards us.

Caz May

Rubbing my eyes, convinced I'm seeing things I slam my foot on the brake when the truck swerves across the double line in the middle of the road. It's gaining on us again—swerving side to side—crossing the white line over and over.

Getting closer to passing me again it careens into my door, pushing the door in against my arm that's tightly gripping the steering wheel. I hear a snap sound when a shot of pain runs up my arm, an ache present from then on. Trying to get my feet to work on the pedals is futile and in a panic I let go of the steering wheel, the car heading towards the gravel on the side of the road.

Again the truck is behind us—ramming into the back—sending the car spinning as I find my feet and slam on the accelerator to try and get away.

It hits a second time, sending the car down the embankment towards a barb wire fence and a row of large foreboding gum trees. Closing my eyes, I take my feet of the pedals for a moment to try and think of what to do. I've lost all control of the car now, all control of my life and my family is in danger of losing their lives.

Looking across at Emilie it's clear she's passed out; the shock hitting her. All I can hear is Ember screaming and it's breaking my heart that I'd put her in this situation.

In the rear view mirror I see the truck again, speeding up behind us on the edge of the embankment. Colliding with the side of the car for another hit against my side, it involuntarily causes my foot to press on the accelerator. The car lurches forward again—crashing through the fence—coming to a crushing stop against a tall thin gumtree. The sounds again are ear splitting, the whole front of the car crushed against the tree.

Emilie's head has jerked forward and all the airbags have deployed; except mine.

Panicking I unlatch my seatbelt, taking a look back at my daughter in the back seat. She's still crying and screaming, even when I speak softly, "My beautiful baby girl. Daddy loves you."

Unlawful Attachment

Her screaming is the last thing I hear before the splintering crack of the gum tree splitting down the middle from the impact. My eyes boggle watching the branches fall towards the windscreen, cracking through the glass and straight for me.

My breath catches in my lungs, when a large branch pushes straight into my chest, pinning me against the seat-back. The pain is so unbearable, I can't even think of a word to describe it. But I try to block it out, hoping that the fact my life is again flashing before my eyes doesn't mean that this time it's really goodbye.

Goodbye to my family, because I'd made a few moronic decisions and put their lives in danger.

(3) *Quentin*

Things have been relatively quiet in Ridgehope for months, just a few petty crimes and patrol duty filled my days, so getting a radio call out for a serious accident an hour away down Viewmain highway has me a little apprehensive. An ambulance and fire truck have been dispatched as well and I have to take the patrol car out to investigate. Unfortunately I've barely even spoken to Sam since she up and left after our last bedroom session. I'd tried to do things her way but it's becoming harder to suppress what I really want to do. And now she's sitting next to me in the patrol car—giving me a dirty look—opening and shutting her mouth like she's about to say something but doesn't really have the words.

"Have you ever been to an accident scene?" I ask her, trying to break the tension between us.

"No," she snaps back.

So that's how it's going to be, one word answers to drive me crazy.

"Well, it may be pretty confronting," I state, reaching over to grab her hand in mine.

I try to press a kiss to it, but she snatches it back.

"I'm a big girl Quentin. I'm sure I can handle it."

"I um..."

"Just shut it ok," she warns.

Her impoliteness makes desire run through me. I want to pull over on the side of the highway and fuck her in the back seat of the patrol car, but of course that isn't possible in an emergency situation.

She continues the opening and closing of her mouth, biting down on her lip occasionally. Even though what faces us now we've arrived at the accident scene is more horrific than I thought I've never been more glad to be in the thick of an emergency situation.

Unlawful Attachment

Jumping straight out of the car, leaving the lights flashing I race up to the car, my eyes taking in the carnage of the scene. The one vehicle pressed up against a spilt gumtree still has people inside.

Hugh is at the driver's door, attaching the jaws of life to open the badly damaged door.

The screaming of a child can be heard above everything, and it makes my heart ache because the child sounds around the same age as River. Sam is now standing beside me, and grabs my hand to calm herself.

"Quentin, it's horrible."

"I know. Could you maybe check the child in the backseat?"

"Ok," she says softly, running around the back of the car towards the backseat. Watching her comfort the little girl makes my heart swell with a strange feeling I can't describe. I love being an uncle more than anything, but the thought of having kids of my own has never really crossed my mind.

It isn't something I've thought about—or desired in my life—but in that moment, time stops and my heart goes out to the little girl who could quite possibly be an orphan.

Sam continues to comfort the little girl, holding her close to her chest and taking her to the ambulance.

Beckoning me over, she's filling Mark in whilst he checks her for injuries.

"Hey sweetie, whats your name?" Sam softly asks.

"Ember...Emberr Grracce," the little girl says through sobs.

"Thats a pretty name," Sam replies sweetly.

Ember doesn't reply but just smiles, and softly I say to her, "Ember I'm going to help Mark here get your mummy out now ok? Can you be a brave girl and stay with Sam here?"

"Okies," she coos nodding.

"Good girl," I reply, grabbing the neck brace Mark hands me as the stretcher is wheeled to the side of the car.

Yanking the front passenger door open is quite a feat, it seeming a hundred times heavier than it should be. Mark checks her for a pulse, leaning his head against her chest to listen for a breath.

Caz May

I know it's wrong, but I'm completely taken aback by her beauty, despite the multiple cuts and bruises she has all over her face and down her arms. Her dark brown hair cascades down her shoulders, a sweet wavy texture to it and her features are sweet and delicate.
I feel a pang of attraction to her, but it's something else as well that I can't place, a feeling as though I've seen her somewhere before.
Shaking it aside I help Mark lift her out of the car—onto the stretcher —and follow him and the other ambulance officer over to slide her into the back of the ambulance.
Ember has tears in her eyes, and tries to free herself from Sam's embrace to launch herself at her mother. My heart is pounding so hard in my chest, aching and breaking for this sweet little girl.
She's a spitting image of her mother, brown curls that bounce around her sweet chubby face and I want to hold her in my arms and tell her it's all going to be okay, even though those words feel like an empty promise.
"Ember, sweetie your mummy has to go to the hospital to get better," I sooth.
Breaking my moment Hugh calls me over to the driver.
"Hey Quent, man," He says holding out his hand for me to shake in greeting.
"Hey Hugh, so what's your gut feeling with the driver?" I ask looking at the tree branch wedged below his breast bone. The seat is stained with blood, and my eyes sting with hot tears at how graphic it really is.
"Well, to be honest man, he has a slight pulse but the blood loss is significant and from where the branch has gone in I'm sure his lungs are punctured. His breathing is quite shallow."
Nodding I reply, "I'll get on the radio to dispatch another ambo."
Turning to walk away he calls out, "Quentin mate, dispatch the coroner too. I don't think he's got much time."
Sitting in the patrol car, I press the radio button.
"Sarge Ryan, are you on channel? Over."
"On channel, I read you Quentin. Over."

"One vehicle. Three occupants. Male driver. Female passenger and minor. Over."

"Status of occupants. Over."

"Female, stable. Minor, fine. Male critical, dispatch ambo and coroner. Over."

"No worries Quentin. I'll head out to clear the scene. Head back in with the minor. Over."

Heading back to the ambulance I sigh trying to focus on blocking out Ember's wretched crying.

Sam is hugging her still, stroking her hair.

"Sarge wants us to head back. He's dispatching another ambo and the coroner." I choke on my last words.

Mark pats my back. "You ok mate?"

"Yeah, I just don't want to see someone become an orphan," I whisper to him, not wanting Ember to hear, even though she wouldn't understand.

"I don't think that's going to happen."

"I hope so man," I say running a hand through my hair.

"Me too. We'll see you back at emergency then?"

"Yeah, I'll follow you. Sirens and one forty if all clear."

He nods, shutting the door of the ambulance behind him.

On the drive back to town, Ember will not stop crying, screaming out, "Mummy, Mummy, I want my Mummy," through her sobs.

Sam pulls her close, soothing her by rubbing her hair and holding her close. I can't make out the words she's saying, but Ember's breathing slows and her tears become less wretched as we approach the hospital emergency bay behind the ambulance. We wait until her mother has been taken into an emergency bay. I'm pleased that both Addison and Zane are on duty, as they're both great doctors. Zane begins checking over the woman, checking her vitals as Mark fills him in on the scene. Sam takes Ember to Addison and I can't help but smile at how loving Addison is being towards her. Since she'd finally let herself fall for Zane, she's changed and seems a lot happier.

I kinda miss our friendly, teasing drunken nights out but I know she's happy and that's the most important thing. My thoughts are broken when Sam appears at my side.

"Ready to get back to the station?" I ask, as we walk back through the emergency department.

"Am I ever. That was seriously full on," she replies, pushing the double doors open. I'd taken a step back to look back at the woman, trying to think of where I know her from, but I still can't place her. Shaking my head, I slide into the drivers seat, turning to look at Sam when I reverse out of the emergency bay to take the car back to the station just down the street.

"You were really sweet with little Ember."

"Yeah I have two younger siblings," she replies nonchalantly.

"You've never spoken about your family," I question her, a little intrigued.

"You've never seemed to care Quentin," she points out, folding her arms across her chest defiantly.

"I'm sorry," I mutter, feeling guilty that I haven't really taken the time to get to know her before I'd had her in my bed.

"It's ok. It's just after the other day I'm not sure if I want to be with you anymore," she remarks.

My heart lurches in my chest, her words feeling like I'm being stabbed. She'd confessed that she's in love with me and now doesn't want me. I hate admitting to myself that her words hurt like a bitch, but they do. I don't love her, but I still want to be with her.

We're at the station, but when she goes to get out of the car I grab her arm, begging, "Sam please give me one more chance."

"I don't know if I can Quentin."

"Please Sam, just let me do what I want with you and if its not good for you then I promise I'll let you go."

She smiles slightly, before biting her lip, and replying, "Ok, my place, Saturday night, 8pm."

Unlawful Attachment

I nod, wanting desperately to lean over and kiss her but she unlatches the door, sauntering into the police station before I even have a second to process what she'd just said.

I've never been to her house and my mind starts wandering to what her bed looks like and how much she's hopefully going to enjoy giving into the pleasure and pain I'm craving to share with her.

Saturday can't come soon enough.

(4) Emilie

Opening my eyes, scanning the surroundings my breath hitches and panic rises in my chest. Trying to scream, no sound escapes my lips, as though they're bound shut. Touching them lightly with my finger all seems normal, but still the trepidation fills me.

This is not my bed. And I feel a sense of loss that something is missing. Caleb is sitting on the edge of the bed, in this the strange white walled room. His finger brushes my lips, stifling the scream I want to let out. His lips then brush mine in a soft kiss.

"Caleb why does your kiss feel weird?"

"We're in heaven baby."

"But, what, we're dead?" I ask, feeling a weird sensation of calm wash over me.

"Yeah," he says, almost elated.

"What about Ember?"

"I don't know who you're talking about baby."

Panic fills me, my heart aching.

"Our daughter Caleb," I snap at him.

"Daughter?" he questions, brushing my cheek with his hand, "You're delusional baby."

Delusional, no, I'm not delusional. I have a beautiful daughter, my Ember Grace, my world, my everything.

Shaking my head to try and block out the thoughts of dread that fill me at my husbands words I close my eyes again, to hopefully slip away from the nightmare that I'm clearly in. There's no way my Ember is gone.

Opening my eyes, I find Caleb still sitting on the bed. The small hospital room I'm in has a bedside table and large white cabinet with

medication behind it's glass doors. Panic fills me when I address him,
"Caleb you're here."

"Yeah, where else would I be baby?" he asks, laughing softly.

"Um, dead," I reply, slapping my hand over my mouth the moment I
utter the word, *'dead'*.

"No, baby, I'm right here."

"Where's Ember?" I ask, a frantic tone evident in my voice.

"Down the hall. I've already seen her. She's ok."

"What happened Caleb?"

"We had a car accident baby. A truck driver ran us off the road. Don't
you remember?"

Shaking my head I reply, "No the last thing I..."

My words are cut off when a doctor enters the room, giving me an odd
look as though I'm talking to myself.

"How are you feeling Mrs Buccianti?" he asks.

I answer in short bursts, pausing between my words, "I'm...fine."

"Any pain?" the doctor asks.

"No...um," I start, pausing and taking a deep breath. "I want to see my
daughter."

He nods at me. "I assure you Mrs Buccianti, she's fine, but your
husband..."

*I want to scream out that my husband is fine, he's right here next to me
isn't he?*

(5) Zane

The moment I say, *'husband'* her expression changes and it has me deeply concerned for her. Her words shock me more, "He's okay. He's here now."

"I'm sorry Mrs Buccianti but your husband isn't here. He sadly passed at the scene."

Violently she begins shaking her head, her hands in her hair as she screams out agonisingly. "No! He's here! He was right here on the bed, and he was fine."

"I'm sorry Mrs Buccianti, but you need to calm down," I sooth, hoping that those words will be enough.

"No! He's not dead! He's here. He can't be dead," she screams out again, waving her hands in the air as though she's touching something or someone.

She lets out an agonising scream, before breaking down into frenzied tears. Grabbing at the I.V in her arm she starts to try and rip the tape off. Her tears are wretched and before I can stop her she swings her feet off the bed.

I have to think fast, to try and calm her. Crossing the room I stand by the bed, placing my hands on her shoulders to steady her as she tries to stand up.

Gently I push her back down to a seating position, but still her tears are wretched. Her fists beat against my chest, and I know the only thing to do is press the red panic button behind the bed.

With one hand still on her shoulder I press the panic button with my palm, hoping that someone comes quickly as I'm not sure how long I can try and keep her calm.

Addison comes rushing in, and instantly I direct her, "Hey, hun can you get a sedative shot asap?"

"Sure hun," Addison replies, leaving the room to go and grab it.

Unlawful Attachment

"Mrs Buccianti, I'm going to give you something to help you get some rest. Please lie back down," I direct her, taking deep breaths in and out. Again I gently push her body back down onto the bed, which is no easy task when her whole body is shaking in anguish at the thought of her husband being gone.

Addison enters the room again, holding the shot in her hand.

"I'll hold her still, if you can give her the shot in the upper arm."

"Ok," Addison replies, moving to the other side of the bed, and pressing the needle against the skin of Mrs Buccianti's arm.

She flinches at the contact, as Addison draws the needle.

"Thanks hun. Do you mind going to check on her daughter? I'm just going to stay with her until she calms down."

Addison smiles at me and kisses my cheek. "No worries hun. I'll see you at lunch," she says before walking out.

My heart is pounding in my chest, watching my fiancee walk out the door, and looking down at Mrs Buccianti as she's beginning to calm down. I can't imagine what she must be feeling, hearing that the love of your life is gone. It's breaking my heart and I'm not experiencing the pain of such a cruel reality.

Sitting in the chair by the bed, I thank my lucky stars that I have Addison in my life and watch as my patient falls asleep, hoping that when she wakes up again she'll be calmer and able to come to terms with the reality of losing her husband. This is always by far the worst part of the job, other than actually losing a life when it's your job to save it.

Walking out of the room to go grab some lunch, I think about her little girl and I'm so glad she's not hurt, as I could not face having to deal with saving a child's life again. That pain would never leave me.

(6) Quentin

Sarge had decided to assign me the case of investigating the car accident much to my objection. I didn't want to tell him my suspicions that I knew a person involved, as it was scary to admit to myself where I thought I knew her from.

But I have to bite the bullet and face up to doing my job, which is going to start with a trip to the hospital to find out if she knows anything about the accident.

Walking into the hospital always gives me the oddest feeling, a sick feeling as stupid as that sounds and an overwhelming sense of déjà vu. Sauntering up to the desk, I slap my hands on the counter.

"Hey Maggie, I'm here to talk to the car accident patient."

She gives me a sweet smile, still the ever flirtatious old biddy.

"Yes, Quentin, dear, she's in room four."

"Thanks, Maggie." I smile back at her, laughing at her giggle when she watches me walk away.

Knocking on the door of room four, I wait a moment for a response and hear a meek, *'Come in'*.

She's sitting up in the bed, but still looks a little dazed. Her face has a scratch across her right cheek, and a large purple bruise on her forehead.

Down her left arm is also another bruise but other than those injuries —if you could even call them that—she seems perfectly fine.

Pulling up the chair next to the bed, I inhale a deep breath, regretting it when I cough, the bleach smell of the hospital hitting my throat.

Looking at her, it's evident she's waiting for me to speak but I'm to taken by how gorgeous she is. She opens her mouth to try speaking, and my wicked mind wanders to kissing her, even though I know it's wrong.

Unlawful Attachment

When she snaps it closed again, I bite my lip and open my own mouth to speak, "Mrs Buccianti, I need to talk to you about the car accident you were involved in."

Her sweet chocolate brown eyes look directly at me, confusion plaguing them and it makes me feel like melting.

"What accident? I haven't been in a car accident."

"Yes, Mrs Buccianti, you have and I need you to talk to me about it."

"I don't know you. You're not my Caleb."

"No, I'm not, I'm Constable Mackenney, but if it makes you feel calmer you can call me Quentin."

She sighs deeply, then says, "Quentin," pausing a moment to take a deep breath, "I have no idea what you're talking about."

The way she says my name sends a strange rush of warmth through my body. She obviously doesn't remember me—or if she does she's blocking it out—but it seems as though she's lost part of her memory and that's going to make finding answers about the accident even harder than I initially thought.

"Thanks for your time Mrs Buccianti," I say standing up to leave the room.

She doesn't say another word, only lets out a soft and delicious murmur when I lean down to brush a hand across her cheek.

"I'm sorry about your husband."

Leaving her be I decide to go and find Addison in the hope that she'll have some answers about her condition when she came in, or a reason as to why she can't remember the accident.

Walking towards the offices at the back of the hospital I can't remember which one is Addison's. But I don't need to worry, as in my haste I bump into Zane, who's reading a patient chart whilst he walks toward me.

"Hey Zane, I was just trying to get some info from Mrs Buccianti."

"Yeah, not much to tell."

"So you haven't got any details you can tell me?"

"No, we really don't know much at all."

"Oh ok," I say, shuffling a foot across the floor, not able to meet his eyes.

"Is something else up Quentin?"

"Yeah kinda man," I state, feeling a little odd to be talking to him as though he's a friend.

"Do you want to talk about it?" he asks with friendly concern in his tone.

"Only if you gotta minute," I say, taking a deep breath.

"Sure, come into my office," he says, reaching out to open the door behind him.

"Thanks," I croak feeling my mouth go a little dry.

Following Zane into his office, he gestures for me to take a seat in the tub chair in front of the large wooden desk, but I feel too nervous and the whole foreboding nature of the desk and chairs makes it feel a little awkward like I'm speaking to my high school principal.

Zane stops, standing behind his desk, and sensing my nervousness he says, "You don't have to tell me Quentin, I get it , I'm marrying Addison."

"Nah it's cool. I've not even talked to Hunter about it, actually," I say, again shuffling my feet against the carpet.

"Oh really?" he questions, looking at me worried, "well um, I'm here if you need a listening ear."

His response seems really genuine and I can see why Addison had fallen for him. He seems to have a way of making you feel comfortable when talking to him.

"Thanks, it's just um, Sam and I are kinda having issues."

"What kinda issues?" he questions.

"Bedroom ones," I state, hating to admit it because it makes me feel immature.

"Oh shit man that sucks," he affirms, completely understanding how I'm feeling.

"Yeah, I think our breakup is inevitable."

"I'm sorry to hear that man. She seems like a sweet girl."

"Yeah that's the problem," I complain.

"Oh right , so is that all that's bothering you man?" he asks again, like he can sense something else is getting under my skin.

"Yeah, but this car accident is pretty crazy."

"Yeah, something is odd about it. She keeps telling us her husband is here."

"What?" I spit in shock. "But he died at the scene, didn't he?"

"Well, yeah he was brought in but the tree branch went straight through. He had no chance."

I feel heartbroken for her, because her love for her husband is evident and she can't face the possibility that he's gone.

"That's so sad," I confess, feeling a sense of longing and sadness wash through me.

"Yeah it is."

"And their little girl? Is she doing okay?" I ask, hopeful for an answer that's positive.

"Yeah, barely a scratch on her. The curtain airbags took the impact."

"That's really good," I start, nervous to ask my question, "So you don't know much about the wife?"

It felt strange to say, *'wife'* considering that I feel an odd, almost consuming attraction to her. It's more than attraction though, it's longing.

Zane, again obviously sensing my weird signals asks, "Quentin man, are you asking as a police officer or..."

He stops mid sentence, laughing softly.

"Ok, you got me man." I laugh, before admitting, "I think she's fucking beautiful but it's wrong on so many levels."

Nodding, his reply isn't what I expect, "Yeah, well I gotta go to rounds. I'll let you know if I have case news."

"Ok thanks, I'd appreciate it."

"No worries, Quentin. No hard feelings about Addison yeah?"

"Definitely not Zane," I say when he leaves his office and I follow him out.

It takes a lot of willpower to resist the temptation of going back into her room. For the sake of my job, I need to keep my distance from her.

Because the fact she's turned up in my world, is my past colliding with my present and with things not going well with Sam, I'm truly scared my darker side is going to now be even harder to suppress.

(7) Samantha

Inviting Quentin over wasn't my best idea. He'd only been to my house a couple of times since we'd been together and I'd not showed him any rooms other than the kitchen, bathroom and lounge. He'd not set foot in my bedroom, and I was happy that we'd not had sex in my bed, but now that is most likely going to change.
Thinking about what he wants to do with me, and looking at my double bed in the centre of my room I feel trepidation rising in my chest. The simple cast iron frame I love is probably perfect for what he desires and I'm worried.

Just tell him no, Sam, you're a big girl, use some words.

Words will most likely fail me, as soon as I see him. I've fallen hard for him; every time I see him or he smiles at me with his devilish smirk I just melt and words are difficult to come by.
Slipping some track pants up my legs, I panic hearing the doorbell ring. I don't even have time to grab a bra, instead frantically shrug a jumper on before sliding down the hallway in my bare feet to answer the door.
Opening the door, he's standing there—right in front of my eyes— wearing black jeans that hang low on his hips, with a flannel shirt unbuttoned exposing his bare chest. The smirk on his face as usual makes me giddy.
Running a hand through his hair, he murmurs deeply, "Hey Sam."
"Hey Quentin," I blurt out, feeling myself blush.
Stretching up on my tippy toes, I press a soft sweet kiss to his lips. He tries to deepen it by licking my lip teasingly, but I pull back and edge backwards across the floor.
"Come on Sam, let me in baby," he taunts.

"Don't call me that Quentin, you know I hate it!" I spit at him, wiping the smirk right off his face.

"Ok, ok, can I least come inside, it's fucking cold out here."

Not replying, I step back from the door, pressing my back against it and gulping hard when he picks up the gym bag from by his feet.

When he follows me inside, the trepidation about what is inside that bag is making my heart pound.

"What's in the bag?" I stammer, not able to look at him, instead searching the floor for an answer.

Touching my cheek, he lifts my head to look at him and again he's smirking.

"You know what's in the bag, Sam."

Biting my lip, I meekly say, "But Quentin I don't know if I can do that."

Letting out a deep laugh, with his free hand he grabs me by the waist, pulling me close, so close that his face is just a whisper from mine.

"You promised me Sam."

You shouldn't make promises you don't intend to keep Sam, you silly girl.

Words of regret, of wanting to take back my promise are caught on the tip of my tongue and I don't have a moment to collect myself when he kisses me hard.

His kiss is desperate and carnal, and he temptingly licks across my lower lip with his tongue, biting it between his teeth, making us both moan before he pulls away.

I can't deny that I'd actually enjoyed that kiss, as I do like knowing that he wants me. There's lust evident in his eyes now and he grabs my wrists—forcing me to hold my hands above my head—when he lifts my jumper over my head.

He seems happy to find I'm braless, the grin on his face and his lower body giving away his excitement.

"Fuck Sam!" he drawls, taking one of my nipples in his mouth—teasing it with his tongue—whilst cupping and teasing the other with his hand.

My body betrays me, letting out soft moans at his sweet torture.

When he pulls back a moment, about to swap sides he instead grabs the waistband of my track pants plunging them to the floor in a pool at my feet.

Again his smirk spreads across his face, loving my choice of underwear, that I'm cursing myself for not changing out of.

"Why do you torture me Sam? You're fucking gorgeous!"

"Um...I thought you'd like them," I muse, even though I'm cursing myself for wearing the only g-string I own.

"Like them?" he questions, before continuing when I nod. "Are you fucking kidding me? I love them! And I'm..."

He stops mid sentence, afraid to say what he wants to do.

Biting down on my lip again, I warn him, "No Quentin."

Shocking me, he reaches his hand up to my cheek caressing it softly, his other hand wandering down towards my g-string and teasingly he runs a finger across the lace.

His gaze locks on mine and he murmurs, "Sam you promised me."

"I know," I reply against my better judgement, but his touch is making my body respond no matter how much I don't want it to.

"So can I show you what you make me want to do?" he asks.

Come on Sam, say no, you have to tell him you don't want this, it's now or...

"Yes," I reply.

"Then show me where your bedroom is."

This time I don't reply, instead grab his hand from my cheek and lace his fingers with mine. Leading him down the hallway—after he's slung his menacing gym bag over his shoulder—I'm scared.

My whole body is shaking, not from cold, but fear that I'm about to go down a path I'll never be able to take back.

But I'm in love with Quentin Mackenney and what he's about to do with me is all part of loving him. I want to give him that, in the hope that he'll fall in love with me too.

(8) Quentin

Sam is leading me down the hallway to her bedroom, shaking like a leaf whilst she clutches my hand. Part of me wants to just pull her close into a hug, and tell her she doesn't have to go ahead if she doesn't want to, but the darker side, the desire in my pants is still the winning side.

And that desire is begging to have its way when reaching her bedroom my eyes lock on her cast iron bed in the middle of the room.

I have to marvel at how perfect it is for what I want to do. I suppress the urge to say it's perfect, as she surely knows that fact.

Instead I drop my gym bag on the edge of the bed and pull her close for a kiss, that's hot and hard.

Demanding entrance I moan against her mouth, my hand wandering down to touch her sweet folds through her lacy g-string.

Her hips buck a little, showing me that she's enjoying my touch and her moans against my mouth as I kiss her are making my desire rise.

Pulling back from kissing her for a moment I revel in the desire that's evident in her eyes. It makes me feel even hotter knowing that I have such an effect on her.

Shrugging off my shirt I ask her ," Are you ready, Sam?"

She nods in response.

"No, Sam you need to tell me with words," I order her.

"Yes..." she replies in a raspy tone, further driving my desire up a notch.

Pushing her back on the bed, I grab out the handcuffs—my very real police handcuffs—from my bag.

Holding them up I ask her, "Do you trust me Sam?"

"Yes," she says, the same raspy tone in her voice, hinted with a sense of panic as well.

I grab her arms by the wrists , stretching them up behind her head towards the bed head. When I cuff her to it, she whimpers sweetly, and then a little deeper when I grab her legs by the ankles, pulling her down the bed a little. This time she gasps, as though she's kinda in pain but then her body rocks in a shiver of pleasure too.

Stretching over her I kiss her hard, biting her lips, craving taking her mouth all for myself.

Desire is rushing through me, after consuming her with a hot kiss. Pulling back from her mouth I begin trailing kisses down her body, over her collarbone, towards her delicious breasts, taking a moment to bite and lick each nipple as my kisses trail further down her body.

She's writhing beneath my tongue, her body responding to the pleasure.

Reaching the sexy lace g-string I kiss along the edge, running my tongue across the sensitive skin of her hips, before taking the lace in-between my teeth. Looking up at her, with the lace still in my teeth I slide them down her legs, marvelling when the lace rips. Her sweet folds are exposed to me now and I laugh devilishly before licking her without warning.

Her hips buck to meet my mouth on her. Tasting her want is like nothing before, a sweet nectar all for me.

"God Sam, you taste so fucking awesome," I moan against her, still licking her folds and biting her clit, sending a moan escaping her sweet mouth.

It's time to take it up a notch.

It's time to show her how I really want to fuck her.

Grabbing the spreader bar from my bag, I feel a pang of worry when her sweet eyes take it in, wondering what on earth I'm going to do with the contraption I'm holding.

Carefully, I lift her ankles into the leather cuffs, buckling them just enough so they can't come undone. Putting two hands on the bar in the middle, I yank them apart to spread her legs wide. She gasps at the sensation.

"Ok Sam?"

She nods making slight anger rise in me.

"Words Sam," I demand.

"Yes," she says raspy again.

Running a hand down her side I tell her, "If you want me to stop you need to say, 'Red', is that clear?"

Again she nods at me.

"Sam," I grunt angrily.

"Yes, Red, yes."

Again I lean over her body, kissing her hard, and teasing between her spread legs with my fingers.

Breaking the kiss I ask her, "Are you still okay?"

"Yes," is her breathless reply.

Reaching back into my bag I grab a condom out, before awkwardly yanking my jeans and boxers to my knees. Sliding the condom on, I look at her biting her lips.

Grabbing the spreader bar in my hands I drive my throbbing arousal into her, hard and deep.

She gasps at the sudden contact, but her hips buck up meeting my thrust into her at first. She drives me wild, and I thrust harder, pulling and raising the spreader bar.

Her whimpers turn to moans and I pull out to spread the bar wider. But when I'm about to drive into her again I see the tears in her eyes.

"Sam, am I hurting you?" I ask, feeling like a right tool.

"No," she replies meekly.

"Do you want to stop?"

"No," she replies again.

I don't ask her again, instead push myself inside her again, grabbing the spreader bar. She gasps again, my thrust into her deeper than ever before and she screams out, "Red ,Quentin,Red."

Without saying a word I withdraw myself from her body, reaching up to un-cuff her. Gently I rub her wrists with my thumb for a moment, before releasing her ankles from the spreader bar.

Yanking my pants back up I sit next to her, and she recoils into herself, clutching her knees against her chest.

"I'm sorry Sam. Please speak to me."

"I c...c...can't."

"I didn't want to hurt you Sam."

"But you did!" She screams at me.

I reach out to touch her cheek, but she slaps it away with her hand.

"No, don't touch me!" she seethes, before calmly asking, "how can you like doing that to me?"

The look in her eyes is pleading me for an answer that I'm really not sure of, as though she's asking me to lie to her. It makes me wonder if I should tell her why I have the desire to take her like that.

"Because having that control over your pleasure turns me on Sam, so fucking bad."

"But it wasn't pleasure, Quentin."

"I'm sorry," I say meekly, not sure of what else I can say or what she wants to hear.

It's stupid, but I lean closer to her to try and kiss her. She turns her head away, snapping loudly at me, "Get out! Leave me alone Quentin!"

"Please Sam, you don't mean that," I argue.

"Yes, I do! Just fucking leave my house now!" she pleads breaking into tears.

This time I don't respond. There's nothing to say.

Instead I grab the spreader bar, forcing it closed and shoving it back in my bag. Picking up my discarded shirt, wrapping it around my shoulders I slip my arms into the sleeves and ask her one last time,

"Are you sure Sam? You really want me to leave?"

"Yes, just get the fuck out!" she screams.

Turning to leave her bedroom, I feel the pillow she throws at me hit my back, a wild angry grunt escaping her mouth when she hurls it across the room at me.

She's still sobbing when I leave, walking out her front door into the cold night air.

Unlawful Attachment

Tugging at my shirt I wrap it tighter to get some warmth for the walk back to my house.
When my feet hit the red dirt, the guilt hits me hard in the chest.
I've fucked up so bad, pushing her too fast into my dark desires and it's now going to be the end of us.
And that's the last thing I want.
I'm scared.
I let my darker side take over and can't fall in love with her.
And I'm scared now I'll never be able to love someone again without the darker desires taking over.

(9) Samantha

After Quentin leaves—slamming the door behind him—I grab my checkered pyjama top and shrug it on without buttoning it up.
I slip some comfy plain white cotton knickers on as well, not wanting to even look at lace ones or a g-string again in my life.
And stupidly I run out to the kitchen to grab my phone from the kitchen counter, to call someone I probably shouldn't.
I've not spoken to him in years, and hope he hasn't changed his number. I need to speak to someone, and for some reason he's the first person who came to mind.
Plonking myself on the couch, I scroll through my contacts and tentatively dial his number.
He answers almost straight away. "Hey Sam, why are you calling me?"

Ok, that hurt a little, hang up now Sam, it was stupid to call him.

"I screwed up Seth," I admit, feeling the tears beginning to run down my cheeks again.
"Are you crying?"
"Yeah."
"What happened Sam?"
"I don't know where to start."
"Sam, you called me, so something's definitely up. We've barely spoken these last few years," he says, a hint of sadness and regret in his tone.
"I know and I'm sorry," I apologise.
"It's ok, so what's got you so upset?"
"I fell in love with someone," I state, sighing through my sobs.
"How's that bad Sam?" he asks with a concerned tone.

"Because he doesn't love me back and he's..." I sob again, drawing in a deep breath.

"Sam did he hurt you?"

"Yes."

"How? Did he force you to fuck him?"

"No, he didn't force me but he hurt me."

"So hang on, you wanted to fuck him?"

"Yes, but he's into some kinky stuff," I admit, not believing the words I'm admitting to my ex-boyfriend.

"What do you mean?"

"Fifty shades kinda stuff Seth."

"Oh shit Sam, that's fucked up."

"I know and it really hurt."

"So, um, are you still together?"

"Well, yes...um, no I don't think so."

"Oh ok," he says, kinda sounding happy.

"I can't be with him if it's like that all the time."

"Yeah I get you," he pauses a moment, "um Sam?"

"Yeah Seth?" I question.

"I miss you and I'm sorry for what happened with us."

"It's ok, you don't need to apologise. I was stupid and naive."

"Oh Sam, you're not stupid," he muses, a tone in his voice that confuses me.

"I wish I could go back and have my first time with you."

"Awww Sam, don't say that yeah?"

"Why?" I ask, confused by his emotional tone.

"Do you want the truth?"

"Yeah of course."

"I haven't been with anyone since you left."

"What? Seriously?" I spit into the phone, absolutely shocked.

"Yeah I'm not over you Sam."

It seems crazy to ask, but I have to know.

"So, um...are you telling me you're still a virgin?"

"Sadly yes," he admits.

"Fuck Seth, I don't know what to say."

"There's nothing to say. I'm an idiot."

"You're not an idiot Seth."

There's silence on the line for a moment and thinking he hung up, I take the phone from my ear to check if the call has ended, but he's still on the line.

"Sam, can I come visit you soon?"

"You can do something better."

"What's that?" he asks, sounding like he's smirking.

"I have to stay here for another couple of months, but after that could you come pick me up to take me home?" I ask, my heart pounding at what his answer might be.

I can hear him take a deep breath before he answers, "Yeah sure babe, anything for you."

"Thanks Seth. I really am sorry for what happened between us."

"No hard feelings, Sam. I really have grown up a lot since then, though not as much as you," he says with a slight laugh.

I have to laugh though, as being with Quentin made me grow up a lot.

"Yeah , so I'll text you in the meantime."

"Sounds great. I love you Sam,I can't wait to see you."

My heart leaps, hearing him say, *'I love you'*.

I'd not heard someone say that for years and it makes me feel giddy, even though it's Seth saying it and not Quentin like I want.

"I can't wait to see you too," I admit sighing.

"Bye babe," he says making a kissing sound into the phone.

"Bye Seth," I say softly, hanging up before he can say anything else.

I think about just getting a bus back home straight away, but I need to make sure I don't leave anything unfinished here and stupidly I open messages on my phone to text Quentin.

Sam: Sorry about tonight. But I can't be with you anymore. I've made plans to head home soon so until then please just leave me be. Your handcuffs will be on your desk Monday morning. I love you Quentin and I'm sorry I can't be the girl you need me to be. I don't regret being with you though. You opened my eyes. Sorry...

Putting my phone down, I trudge back to my bedroom, climbing into bed and pulling the sheets up , clutching them my chest.
Tears start to fall into the pillow, and feeling the handcuffs hit the top of my head I think back to the first time I slept with Quentin; my first time.

I was laying beside Quentin on the couch, as he stroked a finger up and down my arm. The simple touch sending a shiver through me.
Looking up at him, I said softly, "Quentin I'm ready."
"Sam, please I can't take advantage of you. Are you really sure?"
"Yes, I want my first time to be with you."
He let out a deep long sigh, and pressed a soft kiss to my lips, gentle and caring, not like he usually kissed me. Pulling back, he stood up, lifting me into his arms and carrying me to his bedroom.
Placing me on the bed, he lifted his shirt over his head and as I edged back on the bed he stretched over me, kissing me with the same sweet loving kiss.
I couldn't help but let out a moan, and he pulled back again, "God, Sam you're gorgeous."
Feeling brazen I lifted my nightie over my head, and his eyes took in my nakedness. He then ran his hands down my body , heating my skin at the simple touch and sending desire pooling in my cotton knickers.
Reaching them, he touched me through the fabric, licking his lips and uttering a simple 'mmm' that sounded so illicit and full of longing.
Again he stretched over my body to take my mouth in a kiss that was a little deeper and sent my desire higher. Being with Seth had never made me feel so aroused.
As he kissed me, he slipped a finger inside the cotton knickers, touching me teasingly for a moment before pushing the soaked cotton off, down my legs.

"Are you really sure Sam?"

"Yes, Quentin, please, now," I begged.

Reaching into the drawer beside the bed he grabbed a condom out, holding it between his teeth for a moment, as he plunged his track pants and boxers to the floor. I let out a gasp seeing his erection, wondering how he'd even fit inside me.

Ripping open the packet he slid the condom on and knelt on the edge of the bed, leaning against me.

He kissed me softly again, and all could feel was his erection grazing the edge of my aroused body. Pulling away from the kiss, he brushed a sway hair from my cheek and slowly slid inside me.

At first, it was painful, and I let out a slight whimper.

"You ok, Sam?" he asked, as he increased the pace a little of his in and out thrust.

"Mmm...y...y...yeah," I murmured.

The pain had seemed to disappear and my hips rose to meet his, as he thrust in and out of me a little harder.

"Oh God, Sam!" he cried out, as I felt the warmth of his release filling the condom.

Pulling out he discarded the condom in the bin beside the bed and lay down next to me.

"I'm sorry Sam."

"What for? That was amazing."

"I'm sorry you didn't get to come."

"It was still amazing Quentin."

"Yeah, well next time I'm going to make you come."

"Ok, and you'll show me what you really want to do to me."

"Soon Sam, yes," he stated pulling me close for a deep, teasing kiss.

Clutching the pillow close to my face I take in a deep breath, wishing I could go back and share that first time with him again. It deeply upsets me that sex with him can't be like that all the time.

Unlawful Attachment

My body is aching just thinking about it and I reach down to touch myself as I fall asleep, thinking about making love to Quentin because I know now I'll never get to be with him again.

(10) Emilie

Waking up again in the hospital bed excruciating pain is shooting up and down my leg, causing an agonising scream to escape my lips.
Caleb is sitting in the chair by the bed again and comfortingly touches my arm. "What's wrong baby?" He asks.
"My leg!" I practically scream out.
"Is it broken baby?"
"Yes, yes it's...oh it hurts Caleb!" I scream out grabbing the sheets in my fist and pulling them back to look at my leg.
Touching it gently, I yelp in pain when the door cracks open from hearing my screams.
"Mrs Buccianti, What's wrong?" he asks, concern on his face.
"My leg, it's agony," I shriek as another shot of pain runs down it.
The doctor looks down at my leg then, letting out an audible, *'Fuck'*, obviously hoping I didn't hear him being so unprofessional.
It's evident he's angry for not knowing sooner, as it's clear now with my leg being so bruised and swollen from the ankle to my knee.
"Mrs Buccianti, we need to get an x-ray done on that as soon as possible," he says a little more calmly than his sudden curse word outburst before.
"No, it's fine. I'll be fine," I try to demand.
"I'm sorry, but it's not a choice!" he yells at me.
I feel tears stinging my eyes. "Just give me some more painkillers," I suggest.
"After the x-ray you may be able to have some more."
"Fine," I say, pouting like an uncooperative child.
From the corner of the room, he grabs a wheelchair, grabbing me by the waist to help me out of the bed.
Gently he sits me in the wheelchair and wheels me out of the room down the small hospital hallways to an x-ray room.

Unlawful Attachment

I hate feeling so helpless, not being able to use my legs and being in a wheelchair is like torture. I've never had to use a wheelchair, even when I'd gone into labour with Ember and they'd tried to put me in one at Adelaide general I refused, stumbling in like an elephant instead.

Now in the x-ray room the Doctor and some nurses are helping lift me up onto the bench, gently touching my leg to move it into the right spot.

When I again wince in pain, a sweet older nurse ask, "You ok dear?"

"Y...yess," I hiss out, trying not to wince in pain again.

Taking a deep breath when they start to prepare to walk out to complete the x-ray I feel a hand grab mine, looking up to see Caleb standing next to me.

About to tell him to leave the room, he speaks softly, "It'll be ok, baby. I'm not going anywhere."

Closing my eyes I wait for the x-ray to be completed, and open my eyes when the doctor walks back into the room.

"Excuse me Doctor Rivnay?"

"Yes, Mrs Buccianti?"

"Why didn't you make my husband leave the room?"

He looks at me quizzically. "I'm sorry, but your husband isn't here."

And he's right, Caleb isn't by the bed anymore, and isn't holding my hand as the nurses again flit around me to help me back into the wheelchair.

He'd said he wasn't going anywhere, but he's gone and I'm starting to wonder if maybe he wasn't there to begin with just like everyone keeps telling me.

(11) Quentin

When feeling like shit, nothing beats going out with your mates to get blind at the pub.

Being at the pub isn't how I thought my Saturday night was going to go, however, leaving Sam's house I head straight there.

I grab a black T-shirt out of my gym bag, and put that on discarding my flannel shirt, shoving it down into my bag even though it's freezing.

Sauntering into the bar, I sit on a barstool and sigh deeply.

"Rough night Quentin?" Mike asks.

"Yeah, shoot me a whiskey."

Pouring the whiskey into the glass he questions me, "Want to talk about it?"

Downing the whiskey I reply, "Not really. I'd rather get blind and forget it ever happened."

He slides another whiskey to me, and about to down that just as quick I stop lifting it to my lips when I feel my phone buzz in my pocket with a message.

Extracting it there's a message from Sam, that tears at my damaged heart.

Sam: Sorry about tonight. But I can't be with you anymore. I've made plans to head home soon, so until then please just leave me be. Your handcuffs will be on your desk Monday morning. I love you Quentin and I'm sorry I can't be the girl you need me to be. I don't regret being with you though. You opened my eyes. Sorry...

Fuck, fuck, why'd I fucking show her the real me?

Unlawful Attachment

I can't stop glaring at the message, looking at the words, *'I love you'* makes me feel terrible. All I want is for someone to love me, but who I love doesn't love me back and I can't love someone who loves me. It's a mess.

"Mike, a beer please," I muse, putting my phone down on the bar top.

Zoning out for a few minutes I try to collect my thoughts, thinking about how I can possibly make it up to Sam when I hear the laughter of my mates coming into the pub.

Turning I look back when they come in the door and I can't help but notice that they appear to be sharing some private joke about something, a strange closeness between them.

Hugh upon seeing me, waltzes up to the bar, signalling Mike for a beer when he sits down next to me.

I don't look at him, instead pick up my phone to look at Sam's message again.

"What's up with you man?" he asks, a hint of concern in his tone.

"Sam," I muse, taking a long gulp of my beer.

"You whipped man?" he inquires, jokingly.

"Nah, far from that!"

"What? You break up?"

"Yeah, read this," I demand, handing him my phone with Sam's message open.

He takes a moment to read it, his expression unreadable.

Handing it back to me, he declares, "Oh shit man! You fucked up big time."

Running a hand through my hair, I reply, "I know man. I've lost Addison and now Sam."

He laughs, and I feel a bit hurt for a moment.

"Maybe you should switch teams," he suggests winking at me.

"Not a chance mate," I spit back, my mind wondering for a moment if there's something behind those words.

Gulping down the rest of my beer I contemplate Hugh's past behaviour when it came to women, and it makes me wonder a bit, as he never seems interested in the countless local women that have tried to get it on with him. He's a well built, attractive guy but I sometimes do wonder if he's batting for the other side, especially with the snide comments like he just made.

When I don't reply, he grabs another beer and heads over to a booth with Mark, sitting down and looking rather cozy.

I shrug it off when my phone rings. The number isn't in my contacts but I answer anyway.

"Hey man," a familiar voice says into the phone.

"Hey Zane, whats going on?" I question.

"I need to speak to you about Mrs Buccianti," he states, his tone direct.

"Ok, so you have some info about the accident?"

"No, not exactly," he says sounding defeated.

"So what's up then?"

"She has badly broken leg we didn't notice at first because of her high dose painkillers."

I'm silent for a moment, wondering how a good doctor like Zane could miss something concerning a patients care. As though sensing my thoughts he continues, "And the bruising and swelling hadn't flared up at the time she came in."

Finding my voice I blurt out, "Shit man, thats not good."

"Definitely not, but Quentin we have a problem."

"Whats that?"

"We'd like to keep her in for a few weeks as it starts to heal, especially with her apparent psychiatric condition as well."

"Yeah I get you. So what can I do to assist?" I ask, my mind coming up blank.

"There's the matter of her daughter, we can't keep her in any longer," he starts, taking a deep breath in, "And her mother at the moment is not fit to care for her."

"Ok Zane, I'll um, speak to Sarge Ryan and get back to you," I say trying to not sound negative in my tone.

"Thanks Quentin, I'll speak to you soon," he says, hanging up the phone.

Standing up, I walk a little closer to the booth Hugh and Mark are sitting at.

"Guys, I'm out. Got something I need to take care of."

"No worries mate, hope you sort shit out with Sam," Hugh says when I walk out.

Sitting on the bench outside, with my phone in my hand I'm staring at the screen, unsure of what I need to say to Sarge. Things like this don't happen normally in Ridgehope and there isn't anywhere for the little girl to go.

Hesitantly I dial Sarge's number, hating to bother him so late on a Saturday night.

"Hello Quentin, is there something wrong?"

"Well, um, I just got a phone call from Zane about the accident victim."

"Oh right, anything we can use?"

"No, the mother has a broken leg and they can no longer keep the daughter in hospital. Is there something I could do? Take her in maybe?" I suggest, hardly believing what I'm suggesting.

"Oh right, um yeah it's not normal protocol, but we probably can't get a DHS case worker out until mid next week."

"So I'm all clear to have her at mine until they arrive?" I ask, feeling a little panicked.

"Yes, and you can have the next week off too."

"Ok, thanks Sarge, I'll let Zane know," I declare, "and can you let me know when you've spoken to DHS on Monday?"

"Will do. Have a great weekend Quentin."

"Bye Sarge, you too," I say hanging up the phone, dropping it on the bench beside me.

Fuck, I'm gonna have to look after a kid!

(12) Hunter

Hearing about the terrible accident a month or so earlier had really shaken me, thinking back to when Savannah arrived in town. It could very well have been something that could have happened to her and my heart couldn't handle thinking about such things.

I'd not heard from Quentin since it happened either, not that he was really able to tell me anything regardless, but I was still a little worried about him as I got the sense things weren't going well with him and Samantha and I'm sure the stress of a such a dramatic emergency situation would have to take it's toll.

Surprisingly, as though his ears are burning, knowing I'm thinking of him my phone rings with his picture flashing on the screen.

"Hey little brother," I answer.

"Hey Hunter," He says, an odd tone in his voice.

"Quent, what's up? You sound..." I pause a moment, just listening to his heavy breathing, "I don't know...scared?"

He takes a deep breath in, exhaling loudly. "Well, yeah kinda...I need some advice," he states.

"Yeah, sure I guess," I advise, my interest piqued at what he'd want to ask my advice on considering the scared tone in his voice.

"Um...I...um...need to," he mutters, taking another deep breath in, exhaling it harder, before blurting out,"to look after a kid...for a few days." It's as though he can't believe the words he's saying.

"What?" I spit into the phone, completely shocked.

"Yeah I um...have to look after the little girl from the accident."

"Um...Yeah ok, but why?" I ask, a little confused.

"Sarge can't get onto DHS until Monday and they take forever to come out."

"Shit Quentin. Um, so you could bring her here if you want. Savannah could look after her," I suggest, trying to sound supportive and not utterly worried.

"No can do brother. She has to stay with me. It's a police clearance thing."

His words make sense, but it doesn't help quell the uneasiness I feel.

I love my younger brother, and he's a great uncle, but having a kid full time in your care is a completely different thing.

One that I'm not sure my carefree younger brother is ready for.

"Oh right ok," I start ,thinking for a moment, "Well I guess we could give you some clothes and stuff like toys."

"That would be great."

"How old is she?" I ask hesitantly.

"Not sure, but I'm guessing Riv's age."

"Ok no worries."

He's breathing heavy again, hesitance in his tone, "But Hunter, I'm scared."

I completely understand, and even though I know he isn't ready to face it, I say, "You'll be fine Quentin, you're a natural with kids."

"Yeah I don't think so big brother," he says sounding truly scared again.

It's against my better judgement but I have to reassure him and be supportive.

"Come on Quentin...River adores you."

"Yeah but this is kinda different," he states, nervously.

"Yes, but just make sure you feed her, bathe her and tell her a bedtime story. You'll be fine."

"I hope so," he sighs, "she seems so sweet and what she's been through with the accident it's just so traumatic."

I don't have a good reply, one that will reassure him that despite my reaction it's going to be ok, instead I can only say, "Yeah it is but um, Quentin I gotta go, it's my night for bath and bedtime story with River."

"Um, yeah ok."

"But how about you bring her along to Lee's all ages gig on Tuesday night," I suggest happily.

"Yeah? Are you going with River?" He asks, seeming a little perkier in his tone.

"Yeah of course. You know River, he's a born Lee Kernaghan lover," I reply laughing.

"Ok, I'll see you all then. It'll probably be good for her to meet someone her own age," he replies.

"Exactly Quentin.Don't stress and let me know if you need anything ok?"

"Thanks Hunter, you're the best big brother."

"Awww, thanks Quentin. I love you too. Night yeah?"

"Night, Hunter. Give River a big kiss from Uncle Quent."

"Will do, bye," I reply hearing him hang the phone.

I think about the whole predicament more when I walk to the kitchen to grab River for his bath. I have to trust my brother, but it's still getting to me. He's never really shown an interest in having his own kids, and I'm not sure if that's purely an age thing, the fact he's never really had a serious girlfriend or if he just doesn't want his own kids.

In the kitchen I scoop River up into my arms from the booster seat at the kitchen table. Savannah is at the sink washing dishes and turns to smile back at me when I say to River, "I've got something for you buddy."

"Wha Daddy?"

I don't reply straight away, instead kiss his forehead first. "Kisses from Uncle Quentin."

A smile spreads across his face when I kiss his nose, then each cheek and finally a soft kiss on his lips.

He lets out a cheeky giggle and asks, "Ca e kis im Daddy?"

"Well, no, not now sweetie but you can on Tuesday when we go to the Lee Kernaghan concert."

"Es, Daddy, e xsited," he tries to say getting his words mixed up again.

"Excited, baby, yeah?" I correct him.

"xsited," he says again, running the x and s together.

"Oh River, you make me laugh baby," I muse, kissing his forehead again when we start walking to the bathroom.

Putting him down once we reach the bathroom, I start the taps, squeezing in a little too much bubble bath. River stands still, lifting his arms up for me to take off his t-shirt.

As soon as I've yanked his pants and underwear down, he steps out of them and starts to run around the room, excitedly singing, *'boy fom ush, on't iv in, on't ack onw.'*

I can't help but cack myself laughing at his craziness.

"Come here you!" I say, grabbing him and tickling him, making him erupt into a fit of giggles. I turn off the taps and pick him up, putting him into the warm bath.

He's still singing when I grab a face washer, running it over his skin. Washing his hair is a challenge—to not get soap in his eyes—as he's wiggling his body, never able to keep still and splashing water everywhere.

Grabbing a towel from the rack next to the bath, I pull the plug when he stands up, ready for me to wrap the towel around him.

A hand around his tiny waist, I carry him to his bedroom, putting him down by his toddler bed. He again starts to wiggle, dancing on the spot whilst I dry his body with the towel.

"River Alexander, you need to calm down. It's bedtime!"

"Soe, Daddy."

"It's ok sweetie, put your pyjamas on buddy," I direct, opening the drawer behind me to grab a pair of jocks out for him.

Holding them out, he steps into them before holding his arms up for me to put on his pyjama top. Lastly he steps into the pants, laughing sweetly when the elastic snaps across his belly.

Pulling back the covers of his toddler bed, I pat the edge, directing him, "Jump in buddy."

Whilst I'm tucking him in, pulling the sheets up to his chin he asks, "Daddy, ell me stoei of mummy an oo?"

"You've heard that before buddy," I reply with a laugh.

"Me ike it."

"Ok River," I start, kneeling down next to his bed. "Once upon a few years ago there was a lonely farmer, who found a beautiful woman hurt in his house. He took her to the hospital to help her get better," I pause, smiling at my son, asking him, "What happens next River?"

"He ells in wuv wi mi Mummy."

"Yeah buddy, I fell in love with your mummy."

He's now smiling so wide his whole face is full with his grin and he's looking towards his bedroom door.

Turning towards the door myself I find Savannah standing in the door jamb. River's eyes light up and he calls out, "Mummy!"

Savannah comes into the room then, bending down to press a soft goodnight kiss to his lips.

Before standing up I do the same. "Goodnight River, love you buddy."

"Nite Daddy, nite Mummy, wuv oo."

Following Savannah out of the room, I grab her hand just outside River's door, pulling her back to me to kiss her, deep and lovingly.

Pulling back—a little breathless—I lift her t-shirt up and press a kiss to her bulging belly.

"I love you Savannah and my babies."

She lets out a sweet giggle when I kiss her again, sweetly before I speak again, "I'm the luckiest man alive to have such an amazing family."

This time she cups my cheeks in her palms, kissing me hard but sweet.

"No, I'm the lucky one Hunter and I love you more than anything."

She takes my hand in hers again, smiling wickedly at me as she leads me back down the hallway to our bedroom.

I can't help but honestly feel like the luckiest man alive, she loves me, has given me the most gorgeous son and her belly is swelling because she's pregnant again, with twins who I have no doubts are going to turn our world upside down.

I'm most definitely lucky and loved.

(13) Zane

My heart has found the past few weeks pretty hard to deal with. Losing anyone in the hospital makes my heart ache and these past weeks have been particularly difficult with the accident victim. When Mr Buccianti had been brought in barely clinging to life, with the tree branch through his chest it took so much willpower to not get straight in there and yank it out of his chest.

The thought did cross my mind of taking him into surgery, but we didn't really have the equipment on hand to cut the branch quickly enough to save his life.

Sitting at my desk I'm contemplating the guilty feeling it left me with, and getting things organised for Embers discharge, when the door cracks open and Addison comes in.

"Hey hun, you look like someone died?"

She walks closer to my desk, coming around to my side. I swivel my chair around to face her, and she sits on my lap.

"Oh, hun, you know I wanted to save his life."

"Who hun?"

"Mr Buccianti," I say trying to hold back the tears.

"Hun, there was nothing you could have done. Please don't beat yourself up about it."

"I know hun, but you know I can't deal with anyone dying on my watch."

She doesn't reply, instead presses her lips to mine in a sweet kiss, that sets my insides fluttering. It's still hard to believe I'm going to be marrying her in a couple months.

Pulling back from her kiss I whisper in her ear, "I love you Addison, and..."

Her eyes lock on mine, my heart pounding in my chest, hoping she's finally going to say that she loves me too but instead she says teasingly, "And what hun?"

I laugh, thinking back to the first day I met her, and the moment I first sat in the very chair I'm in now.

"The first day I came here and sat in this chair, I wondered what it would be like to fuck someone in it," I tell her, my eyes not leaving hers.

Her eyes sparkle at my suggestion and she taunts, "Oh really?"

"Yep, it was just after I'd seen you for the first time and I might have thought about it being you," I tell her, not able to fight the blush that rises up my cheeks.

"Well, hun, I'm not wearing any knickers under my scrubs today," she teases, making my dick rise to attention instantly.

Without saying a word, she jumps off my lap, slipping her scrub pants off and stepping out of them. Bending over me, she kisses me hard, teasingly as she undoes my belt, and frees my throbbing dick from my pants.

She runs her hands up and down my length for a moment, whilst I touch and tease her clit with my fingers.

"Seriously, Addison...I never thought we'd fuck at work, but damn."

She doesn't reply, instead straddles me, pinning me to the chair.

When she slides her hot body down onto me I push my arse back into the chair, making the back recline.

Thrusting up into her, she lets out a delicious moan, loving the rhythm of riding me.

Grabbing her around the neck I pull her down to me for a hot, consuming kiss, licking and biting her lips, her body still pumping up and down on me.

Pulling back from the kiss, she murmurs in my ear, "Zane, I'm going to come so hard."

She sits up then—looking straight down at me—gazing into my eyes, sliding almost completely off my dick, before she takes me into her folds again, screaming out, "Oh fuck Zane, fuck!"

Her release around me, and the pounding knock at the door make me explode hard into her body, filling her as I try to stifle my, 'Oh fuck!' unsuccessfully.

She presses a quick kiss to my lips, jumping off and pulling her scrub pants back on.

"Can I come in?" a voice asks from outside my office door.

"Just a minute," I call out, standing up to do up my pants.

I grab Addison by the waist, pulling her close for a quick kiss.

"Hun, that was fucking awesome."

"I know hun, I'll see you later," she replies walking to the door, opening it to Quentin.

He eyes her up and down—both of them blushing—Addison knowing she's been caught fucking me and Quentin knowing that he'd caught us.

He enters the room as she leaves and gives me a wink.

"Sorry I didn't mean to interrupt," he apologises.

"All good man," I say feeling a little guilty, but so satisfied at the same time.

"So, I'm...um...here to discharge the little girl from the accident."

"Yes, I'm just finalising the paperwork now. Her name is Ember by the way," I inform him, shuffling the papers on my desk.

"That's sweet, so what do I...um...need to know?" he asks nervously.

"You sure you're ok with this Quentin?"

"Yeah, just a little nervous about looking after a kid, but all good."

"Ok, well let me know if you need anything."

"Will do," he says a little more confidently when I hand him the discharge papers.

"So, you need to sign this on your way out, and thats pretty much it."

"She doesn't have any like special things I need to know about?"

"Like what exactly?"

"You know, like food and stuff?"

"Not that we know off," I tell him when we head to the door, "Follow me and we can get it all sorted."

Caz May

Leaving my office, we walk in silence to the room she's in at the back of the hospital.

He looks at her sitting on the bed, clutching a pink teddy bear to her chest and smiles wide, as though he's fallen in love with her on the spot.

He may have doubts about looking after her for a while, but I know he'll be just fine.

(14) Quentin

Looking at the sweet little girl sitting on the large hospital bed, clutching her pink teddy bear to her chest both shatters my heart and makes it swell with a strange loving feeling.

Never before have I wanted to protect someone so much.

Zane steps closer to her, softly speaking, "Hello Ember."

She lets out a whimper, so scared it tugs at my shattering heart more.

"Are you ready to go home with Constable Mackenney?" he asks her, making her whimper again and shake her head.

Nudging Zane, I say, "Maybe it's best I tell her my name."

"You're probably right," he muses when I step closer to the edge of the bed, tentatively.

Sitting on the edge I softly speak, "Hi Ember, I'm Quentin."

She whimpers again and touching the top of her pink teddy bears head I ask, "And who do you have here?"

Her little face looks up at me, her mouth opening and shutting a moment.

"It's ok Ember," I say softly again, soothingly.

"Inky," she declares suddenly, a tentative smile crossing her mouth.

"That's a cute name," I say leaning closer to her and mouthing, *'hello Inky'*.

She lets out a little giggle that warms my heart a little.

"So Ember and Inky, are you ready to get out of here?"

She shakes her head. "N...n...no...ss..ared."

"You're scared?" I ask her.

This time she nods.

"Why are you scared?"

"Mummy."

"You don't want to leave your mummy here?"

Her little nods are so sweet.

"How about firstly we go see your Mummy so you know she'll be safe here with Doctor Rivnay?"

"Ok, an en we o?"

"Yes, sweetie," I say hesitating at my use of an endearing word. "I might have some lollies for you to if you're a good girl and you know what else?"

"Wh?"

"I have a cat at my house, do you like cats?"

"Me wuv kitays," she says sweetly.

"Thats great, he'll love meeting you. Are you ready to go see Mummy now?"

She nods again and I stand up, a little unsure of what to do when she stretches out an arm towards me.

"Upsies."

Without a second thought, strangely knowing exactly what she means I scoop her up, holding her against my hip like I do with River.

Outside the door I put her down, and she grabs my hand with her small one.

With Zane leading the way we follow him down the hallway towards the room her mother Emilie is in. Lifting her up to peer through the door we can see she's asleep.

"Mummy, goed oo?" Ember asks sadly.

"No Ember, your Mummy is just sleeping," Zane says calmly. "How about you go with Quentin and come back to see Mummy tomorrow?"

"Okies, she no eep en?"

"Hopefully sweet girl," I tell her, putting her back down on the floor.

She holds my hand tightly in hers, waiting patiently whilst I speak to Zane, "So I just sign the papers on behalf of Emilie?"

"Yes, if you could put your ranking and the station details under your signature that will be great."

"Ok, no problems, and um Zane..."

"Yeah?"

"Again I'm sorry about earlier but also thanks for your support."

Unlawful Attachment

"You're welcome Quentin and you don't need to be sorry, but yeah it wasn't my wisest moment," he says a little ashamed.

"Your secret rendezvous is safe with me," I tease, winking at him.

"Thanks, I hope we can maybe be friends."

"Yeah, I could do with another friend," I start, pausing a moment before asking, "Um, do you think there might be some clothes for her in the lost and found?"

"Yeah probably, take whatever you need and call me if you need anything else."

"I will, thanks for the confidence boost Zane."

He doesn't reply, only smiles before turning to walk back to his office.

With Ember's hand still clutching mine I go to the nurses station, sign the discharge papers and ask about some clothes for her.

Moments later a nurse brings out a 'my little pony' nightie that looks a touch too big, and a sweet frilly pink tutu dress, that looks like the most perfect outfit for her.

"Thanks, ladies," I say, taking the clothes and tucking them under my arm.

"No worries Quentin, look after this sweetie," Maggie tells me, giving me a wink that's a confidence boost too.

I'm ready.

Ready to make the life of the sweet little girl clutching my hand just a little happier, after what she's experienced.

***

The moment we walk in the door of my house, Ember spots Tiberius, running straight up to him.

Dropping 'Inky' on the floor, she uses both arms to scoop Tiberius up, crushing him against her chest squealing.

I laugh, looking at the utter disgust plastered on Tiberius's face like he's inwardly cursing and asking, *'what fresh hell is this?'*

"Be careful Ember," I warn. "He might bite."

"Ike im," she squeals excitedly, turning to look at me when I walk towards the kitchen.

Take a deep breath Quentin, you can do this, she's just a sweet little girl, remember what Hunter said, food, bath, bedtime story, you can do it, grow up!

"That's good, so are you hungry?" I ask.

"Yea," she says squeaking and clapping her hands together.

"What do you like to eat?"

"Cees!"

"Cheese?" I question, not understanding her baby words.

Again she claps her hands excitedly, confirming the answer to my question.

"How about Mac & Cheese then?" I suggest, hoping she knows what that is.

Her excited claps echo again, making me feel so out of depth.

"Ok, I'll make you some then," I say, thinking about what she can do whilst I'm in the kitchen. "Do you want to watch cartoons?"

"Ipee!" she coos, starting to dance on the spot.

She follows me over to the lounge, tottering slowly towards me when I flick on the TV with the remote, changing the channel to the ABC and finding the excruciatingly annoying singing of the Wiggles blaring out.

"Is this ok?" I ask her.

She doesn't speak or look at me, instead starts to bob up and down in the weird kid like dancing way that always makes me laugh.

Walking back to the kitchen, still able to see her across the room I laugh harder watching her dance and hearing her attempt at singing, 'ot atao, ot atao'.

Starting to make the Mac & Cheese, I watch her, thinking about her mother holed up in the hospital. Something is definitely unsettling me about the beautiful Emilie and I'm not sure of what the feeling is.

I've seen her before, and where I'd seen her had been a during a time in life I want to block out of my mind, because it makes those dark desires come crashing back even more so than my whole relationship with Sam.

If she's still involved with that world, despite the fact she's the mother of this sweet little girl dancing to the Wiggles in my lounge room, then I'm in big trouble.

The darkness of my past threatened my career then—before it even began—and now I'm in danger of that darkness coming back to destroy my career again.

It truly scares me, but I want to get to know Emilie and confront the darkness in hope that maybe she'll be the one to take away the need and the craving to take control.

And the first step in doing that is finding out some answers about the car accident, and also finding out if she remembers me as well.

Smiling I look over at Ember—pouring the Mac & Cheese into a bowl—deciding that I will take her to visit her mother first thing in the morning and demand she tell me something about her literal crash into my world again.

(15) Emilie

Waking up in the hospital bed again is beginning to feel like a sick cruel case of déjà vu. I'm almost at the point of hurtling myself out of the bed and stumbling down the hallways just to get outside to gulp in some fresh air, but having a cast on my leg from my ankle to my knee makes that need impossible to fulfil.

But opening my eyes this time I can feel the bed moving and can hear it creaking, as well as a sweet little voice practically singing, "Mummy, ake up, mummy!"

Standing over me on the bed, with her stubby little legs either side of my waist is my baby girl.

Pulling her down against my chest I envelope her tiny body in a hug.

"Hey baby girl, I've missed you," I tell her, kissing her bouncing brown curls.

"I viss oo to Mummy."

Letting out a sigh I kiss her forehead and look up at the other person in the room.

He speaks deeply, "Hello Mrs Buccianti."

I try to think for a moment—forgetting who he is—so meekly I mutter, "Um hi."

"I'm constable Mackenney remember," he reminds me.

I nod, but don't speak.

"But well you can call me Quentin," he says nervously.

I smile at him a moment, before I spit harshly, "I don't know why you keep coming here to ask me things. I don't know what happened."

A frown crosses his face at my vicious tone, but I'm not lying when I say I have no idea how I've ended up in the hospital bed.

His next words however are nothing to do with that and confuse me more.

"I know, I actually just brought Ember in to see you."

"Sorry? Why?" I start confused, scanning the room with my eyes for my husband, seeing him in the chair beside the bed.

"She should be with her Dad."

"Mrs Buccianti, you know your husband is deceased," he says apologetically.

"No! He's not! He's been in to see me!"

"I'm sorry, but that's not possible," he says with the same apologetic tone that's making me feel like bursting into tears.

Pointing at the chair beside the bed I confidently say, "He's here now though, in the seat just here."

"No, he's not I'm afraid," he says, shaking his head.

I look down at Ember laying against my chest, touching her soft chubby cheek to get her look at me.

"Ember baby, you can see Daddy in the chair yeah?"

My sweet baby girl shakes her head at me. "No's daddy ot ear mummy."

The words coming out of my sweet baby's mouth can't be true. She loves her Dad with all her heart and if she can't see him, then maybe it's true that he's not here.

But I don't want to believe that's true.

Caleb had been my rock, taking me away from the pain that was my life. I'd not been in love with him at first, but he was gentle and caring in everything.

I'd started to fall for him and now he's been ripped out of my life.

All I have left of him now is the sweet baby girl leaning over my chest who looks just like her gorgeous daddy, and it makes my heart ache.

Hugging her close again, I lock my eyes on Caleb sitting in the chair for a moment, before closing them tightly and inhaling a deep breath.

Tears are stinging my eyes, forcing me to open them and face reality.

Reality meaning that Caleb isn't there in the chair like I thought.

"He's gone really?" I ask, turning my gaze to Quentin on the opposite side of the room.

"Yes, Mrs Buccianti, he is, I'm sorry."

The tears turn to sobs then, and I take in another deep breath.

"Please don't call me that," I snap.

"I'm sorry I didn't mean to upset you," he says in his usual apologetic tone that's beginning to irritate me a little.

"No, no, it...it just hurts hearing that, so um call me Emilie please."

"Ok Emilie it is then," he says with a perky tone.

I think about the way he's just said my name, how it almost sounded illicit coming from his lips and I can't help but look him up and down. His physique isn't overly muscular, but he's still manly. And his face is boyish, but handsome; his strong jaw is covered in a healthy five o'clock shadow that makes his lips look plump.

I stifle a gasp, thinking for a moment about what it would be like to kiss him, but I shake the thought away as the unnerving thought of seeing him somewhere before surfaces in my mind again.

I can't work it out, so shaking it away, I ask him, "So how come Ember isn't in here anymore?"

"I've been taking care of her since yesterday because DHS can't come out until later in the week."

Oh God no, they can't take my Ember away, not like they tried to last time, no, no, no!

"No, no, please don't get docs involved," I say panicky.

"We don't have a choice Emilie," he pleads, once again causing my stomach to flip flop when he says my name.

I open my mouth to speak, but can't utter a word and his next words hurt a little, despite them being true.

"In your current state you can't care for her."

"But can't she stay here?"

"No, the hospital is not able to care for her like that."

Again I kiss Ember's hair, holding her so close, not wanting to let go. After thinking for a moment, I blurt out, "I want her to stay with you then."

"Emilie, I'm only able to do that temporarily."

"No please I..." I sob, breaking into tears.

Ember looks down at me. "On't tears mummy."

"Oh, Em, baby," I muse softly kissing her soft chubby cheek.

Quentin looks at me like his heart is breaking. "I'll see what I can do, but I'll likely need your written consent."

Nodding, I say, "Ok."

He now appears tongue tied like there's nothing else to say and he's thinking something he can't verbalise.

Grabbing Ember by the waist I sit her up on the edge of the bed, taking her little hand in mine. "Em baby, are you happy to go with Quentin again?"

"Es Mummy, e et me wat iggles."

"Ok baby, I'll see you soon ok?"

She stands up on the edge of the bed, faltering a little and falling into Quentin's arms. "Careful sweets," he says, pulling her against his hip.

"Thanks," I say softly, hoping he hears me.

"No problems Emilie," he replies turning to leave.

Watching my daughter wave back at me with a sweet smile on her face melts my heart. Quentin seems so caring in how he interacts with Ember and considering how I'm thinking about our possible past connection I'm wary.

But I have no choice because my whole world has changed and I have a feeling that I need Quentin to help me piece it back together.

(16) Quentin

With Ember clutching my leg, I have to stumble like a drunk into the pub for Lee's gig.

I've barely taken a step inside the door when River sees me and comes racing up to me.

Bending down and grabbing him by the waist I hug him tight and kiss his cheek.

"Hi Unci Kent," He says sweetly. It melts my heart that he can't say my name properly, always turning the q into a k.

Putting him down, I ruffle his hair, "Hey big boy, did you grow since I saw you last?"

He looks up at me, confused at my question, and tugs on Hunters pant leg when he walks over to me.

"Daddy id I grow?"

"A little bit River," Hunter says to his son, in an odd tone like he has a stick up his butt.

Ember is still hiding behind my legs, peering out to look at River standing between Hunter and I.

Bending down a little, with a hand on her back I urge her forward, closer to River.

His eyes light up when he looks at her.

"River, this is Ember. She is staying with me for a little bit whilst her mummy gets better in hospital."

A frown crosses his sweet face when he asks, "Why Unci Kent?"

"They had a car accident sweetie."

I smile when he takes her tiny hand in his, suddenly declaring, "She cute."

"Will you look after her tonight River?"

He nods. "Ep we ance oo Lee."

"Ok sweet boy, but first can I have my kisses back that Daddy gave you from me the other day?"

He drops Embers hand when I pick him up, holding him around the waist with his legs dangling.

He presses a kiss to my lips, and melts my heart with his words, "I wuv oo, Unci Kent."

"I love you too, River."

Putting him back down next to Ember he excitedly pulls her close into a hug. She shrieks, and steps back crashing into my legs.

I bend down to her, feeling my knees crack. "It's ok Ember," I sooth.

Her eyes look at me, tears in the corners. "Viss Mummy," she mutters through her sobs.

"I know sweetie," I tell her standing up, about to scoop her up in a hug when Savannah comes over and bends down to her level.

Ember seems to instantly like her; obviously a mother thing.

"Hi sweetie, what's wrong?" Savannah asks Ember softly.

Wiping her arm across her face Ember replies, "I viss my mummy."

"That's not good sweetie," Savannah says with a soothing tone.

The tears are still evident in Ember's eyes when Savannah picks her up and stands up with her against her hip.

"I'm Rivers mummy," Savannah says happily. "Maybe you can come sit with me and tell me about your mummy."

Ember nods, and they walk over to a booth to sit down.

Hunter is still standing next to me, and I can sense he wants to say something. He nudges me in the side. "Quent, you alright bro?"

I shake my head, responding , "Um yeah...it's just I...um..."

"What?"

"She's such a sweet little girl Hunter."

River claps his hands together at our feet, shrieking, "Ep I ike her."

Hunter looks down at his son, directing him authoritatively, "River, go sit with Ember and mummy please. I need to talk to Uncle Quentin about something."

"Okies Daddy," he replies running towards the booth Savannah is sitting in with Ember on her lap.

As soon as River is out of earshot my older brother speaks, "Quentin I'm not sure what to say but it seems like you're in too deep here."

"What do you mean?" I ask incredulously, feeling like he's just punched me in the stomach.

"You said DHS was being contacted yeah?"

"Yeah but..." I start, swallowing the rest of the words I want to say.

"But what?" He spits at me, a little too loudly, continuing when I swallow hard again without a reply. "Are you really going to let them take her?"

His question is a little confusing but I get what he means and reply with a hint of vengeance in my voice, "No Hunter I'm not, I promised her mother she'd stay with me."

"That's what I mean Quentin."

Again he's making me confused with his cryptic words.

"What Hunter?"

"Do you want to look after her, or has it got something to do with her mother?"

"I...can't tell you, but I.." I stammer, feeling as though my brother can see straight through me.

"Think about that sweet little girl Quentin. Do whats right for her, not what your dick tells you!" Those words are harsh, and I almost can't believe they came out of my older brothers mouth.

"Fuck Hunter, that fucking hurts that you'd think so low of me."

He scoffs, completely shocking me when he speaks again, "You think I don't know about you jerking off in my room when Addison slept over, Quentin, huh?"

"Wh...I...um," I stutter, having no idea what to say and feeling a blush rise in my cheeks.

"You've never been one to keep it in your pants."

Well, that fucking hit me where it hurts, especially coming from my older brother who I look up to.

Unlawful Attachment

I have no words to reply, utterly speechless at his harsh words. Not able to meet his intense gaze on me I walk away to the bar for a drink. Watching him when I gulp down my whiskey I feel a punch like feeling hit me in the heart and guts.

He bends down to kiss Savannah on the lips, smiling at her before he says something to River that makes him giggle.

I've always looked up to my older brother, and he's never hurt me before even with words said in anger.

Looking at him now though, with his little family and Ember I'm not just looking up to him anymore, but longing to have what he has with Savannah.

Love and a family of my own, and considering my dark past that is scary and most likely not ever possible.

(17) Savannah

Lee has started to set up and tune ready to start on the small stage near the front of the pub. But my eyes are darting between my brother in law crossing the pub to the bar and my husband coming back over to the booth I'm sitting in with the kids.

The conversation they'd just had clearly upset Quentin and it's not like Hunter to speak that way to anyone, especially his younger brother.

"Hunter Isaak Mackenney, what did you say to your little brother that's got him so upset?" I berate.

Putting his hands on the edge of the table, he looks straight at me.

"Nothing I shouldn't have said a long time ago."

"Baby that doesn't tell me anything."

"It was something to do with..." he starts, cutting short his words, looking at River and Ember, not able to say what he needs to with their little ears open to hearing the words.

River couldn't care less about what his Dad is going to say, because he's watching Lee on stage, and when he speaks his eyes light up.

"Hey Ridgehope, I'm Lee and I'm delighted to share tonight with you all. Shoutout to me at any point for requests but let's get started with a classic, hey!"

Lee starts the strum and classic beat of, *'Outback Club'.*

Cheers and applause fill the room, and the dance-floor erupts with people starting to kick up their heels, and wave their hats around, as well as doing some flashmob country dance that I don't know being a city girl originally.

River is jumping up and down on the seat , so Hunter grabs his hand and helps him down to head for the dance floor. River holds out his hand to Ember and she takes it in hers when he asks, "Ance wit mi?"

She nods and follows them both to the dance floor. Adorably, clutching each others hands they bob up and down in the cute kid like dancing way.

Not knowing the song, and also still worried that Quentin is still sitting at the bar about to down another drink I leave the booth to go and speak with him.

"Hey bro-in-law," I greet him.

"Hey sis-in-law," he replies in a happy tone, kissing me on the cheek.

"It's still weird saying that," he announces.

"Yeah I know right? So um...what did my husband say to you?"

"It's stupid, and he's right," he says sounding forlorn.

"What was it about?"

"That I can't look after her."

"Who? Ember?"

"Yeah I um...I...her mother," he stammers.

Reaching out I touch his arm comfortingly. "Quentin, you don't need to tell me. I saw you come in with her and right now despite what Hunter thinks, you're the best thing in that sweet little girls life."

"Really?"

"Yes, really," I reply, nodding.

"I don't want her to get hurt though, she just lost her father."

"Exactly, so be there for her. I can tell you're already falling for her sweet childlike charm."

"Thanks Savannah."

"I'll talk to Hunter as well."

"Thanks, I'd appreciate it, and yeah I am falling for her charm."

"She's definitely a sweetheart."

"Yeah, I never thought I wanted kids in my life, you know?"

"Yeah I know, but you're an amazing uncle, Quentin and you'll make an even better father."

"Aww thanks Savannah. I'm not so sure about that but still thanks."

"Anytime," I say, smiling at him. "Now let's go dance with those little charmers of ours."

He laughs then, following me to the dance-floor and taking Ember's hands to be a little silly with her.
She lets out delightful giggles, spinning in her pink tutu dress.
Stepping closer to Hunter, he says into my ear, "What were you talking about baby?"
"Nothing baby, but you should apologise to your brother later. He means well."
"I know baby."
Smiling, my amazing husband presses a kiss to my lips, a sweet kiss that shows everyone in the pub I'm his. Cheers and applause again fill the room and pulling back from the kiss when the song ends I laugh looking at Hunter as though the cheers were for us kissing.
Lee speaks again, *"That was a great start hey Ridgehope! Any requests out there!"*

There's silence in the pub when Quentin walks up to Lee, whispering something in his ear. Turning back he looks straight back at Hunter and I winking.
Hunter shrugs at me, both of us wondering what Quentin had said.

(18) Quentin

After whispering my request in Lee's ear I wink at Hunter and
Savannah, walking back to the middle of the dance-floor.
It makes me laugh out loud, looking at River staring wide eyed up at
Lee on the stage anticipating what he's going to sing next.
And my nephew's smile grows so wide when Lee speaks, *"Ok
Ridgehope! This next song 'Boys from the bush' goes out to my biggest
little fan here! River Mackenney, where you at little mate?"*

The crowd erupts into laughter watching when River races up to the
front of the stage eagerly, jumping up and down on the spot.
Lee bends down to speak to him. *"You ready to sing with me little
mate?"*
River can't stop jumping and down, squeaking out, "Mi frend oo."
"Of course little mate," Lee replies, looking out into the crowd.
Grabbing Ember's hand in mine I lead her up to the stage to stand next
to River.
"And who is your little friend here River?" Lee asks, leaning closer to
Ember to hear her.
The crowd is dead silent, and she mutters, "Ember."
River excitedly declares, "She fro sity."
The crowd laughs with Lee when he says, *"Well then River, you'll have
to teach her how to be a girl from the bush then little mate. So are you
all ready?"*
Again River does his little jig on the spot. "Es Lee!" he squeals
excitedly.
Lee starts playing 'Boys from the bush' and everyone starts singing
along, dancing together. Sliding across the dance-floor I elbow
Savannah in the side whilst she's dancing with Hunter.
"Look at them, they're so damn cute. It melts my hardened heart."

She laughs, as we watch River and Ember dancing, bobbing up and down, and spinning on the spot. River is singing at the top of his little lungs.

And when the song ends, my sweet little nephew leans forward and presses a kiss to Ember's cheek, giggling and smiling like a cheeky devil, before turning back to look at me.

I can't help but smile at his cheekiness, but partly hope he takes after his Dad, and not me when it comes to women in his life in the future.

*

After Lee has played a few more songs I notice Ember rubbing her eyes and wobbling a little from side to side like she's about to collapse and fall asleep on the floor any second.

Without another thought, picking her up, I hold her against my hip and she nuzzles into my chest.

Before walking out, I say to Hunter and Savannah, "I'm going to head off, get this one to bed."

"No worries, we'll be heading off soon too," Hunter says. "And Quentin I'm sorry for earlier."

"I know Hunter, I'll talk to you on the weekend," I tell him, walking away.

River waves at me when I leave and my heart melts.

*

Walking home, holding a child in my arms is more of a feat than stumbling home drunk.

The usual twenty minute walk seems to be dragging, but I don't dare put her down.

Her eyes are closed, she's not asleep but so close and if I were to put her down, asking her to walk it would take three times as long to get home and I'm afraid her tired little legs won't hold her up for a second.

Once at home, I carry her to the guest room she's been sleeping in the last couple of nights and sit her down on the edge of the bed.

"Bed," She says softly, opening her eyes to look at me.

Unlawful Attachment

"I know sweetie, lift your arms up so we can put your pyjamas on," I softly say.

She yawns, with her arms over her head and I take off the pink tutu dress, replacing it with the my little pony nightie.

Pulling back the sheets then, she crawls in and I tuck her little body in, smiling at how her little body in the middle of the double bed makes her look so small.

"Ok Ember, goodnight,"I say, kissing her forehead.

"No, stoi?"

"Aren't you too tired for a story?"

"No, ont stoi," she snaps defiantly.

"Ok, just a quick one," I suggest, sitting on the bed when she nods a response.

"So one night a little girl went to see a special concert, and she met a little boy who liked her a lot..." I stop as a smile spreads across her face.

"Ats ot a stoi." She giggles.

"Oh really? Did that happen?"

"Es, mi et iver nite."

"Yes, did you like River?"

"Es e ute."

"He thought you were cute too."

"I ike im."

"That's great sweetie, hopefully we can see him again soon."

"Air, an Mummy et im oo."

"Soon sweetie yeah? Time for sleep now ok?"

"Okie, nie kent," She says sweetly.

My heart is melting even more for her now, and when I press a kiss to her forehead and say, 'goodnight' I know there is no way I'm going to let docs take her away.

She's a charmer and it really makes me feel like I want a child of my own.

Walking out of the room, my phone vibrates in my pocket.

Yanking it out there's a message on the screen.

Hugh: hey man, how was the Lee gig? You still partying hard?
Quentin: not bad man, pretty sweet watching River and Ember dance...home now
Hugh: Ember? She the kid I heard about of yours?
Quentin: not my kid man. She's the little girl from the car accident
Hugh: oh right man, so why you looking after her?
Quentin: her mother is still in hospital and her father didn't survive his injuries
Hugh: oh shit man. Mark didn't tell me that. But man you with a kid
Quentin: what? Don't think I can handle a three year old?
Hugh: hey man I didn't say that...but you know you've been lucky so far to not end up with a kid and well...
Quentin: I know man...I've not even had the fun part of getting this one lol
Hugh: Haha Yeah
Quentin: but can I be honest man?
Hugh: yeah of course man
Quentin: I fucking want to with her mother...
Hugh: Quent man...be careful yeah? She'd be fucked in the head you know having lost her husband
Quentin: I know..I know...I'll keep 'it' in my pants
Hugh: prolly the best thing...catch ya later man
Quentin: yeah Sunday sesh still on?
Hugh: yeah but no kids haha
Quentin: haha man not funny...nite
Hugh: nite man...luv ya

Putting my phone down I sigh climbing into bed, not even bothering to get undressed.

I curse myself for even thinking about Emilie at all, let alone admitting to one of my best mates that I want to sleep with her.

It seems like Hunter was right about not being able to keep my dick in my pants.

Unlawful Attachment

I've not even kissed Emilie, not even touched her, or held her body against mine and yet she's all I can think about.

I want her to be mine, and for her and her little girl to be a part of my life.

Shutting my eyes though, I try to not think about that because falling for Emilie is wrong.

So wrong, my career could be over as a consequence.

(19) Emilie

The day to officially get out of the hospital has finally arrived. Six weeks holed up in a hospital bed has been literal hell.
Quentin had brought Ember in a few times to see me and he's just so sweet with her. I can tell she misses her daddy but Quentin is helping her get past his loss.
Every time I look at Quentin though a strange feeling stirs my insides, a feeling I'd never felt with Caleb and I'm not sure what to make of it.

Again Quentin is here, making my insides flutter just by looking at him, and the way his eyes focus on me when he bites down on his lips like he wants to say something. His dark eyes shine with lust when he looks at me too, and that has me both scared, and stirs up that feeling I've never felt before.
Awkwardly I stand up on one leg, trying not to crash my casted leg against the bed. Pain is still evident in it at times, and the doctor had informed me that I'll most likely have the cast on for another month. But I need out of the hospital, intent on fending for myself again and trying to leave Caleb's ghost behind in the hospital.
I know that now I'm going to be out of the hospital I'll have to face actually organising to stay 'goodbye' to him, arranging a funeral and getting all of our other affairs in order.
But to do that I need to talk to Quentin about what happened before the accident and my mind is coming up blank on most of it.
It's safe to say I've been lucky that they've not pushed me to organise things earlier, but I guess that's partly due to knowing his cause of death.

Breaking my thoughts Quentin puts his hands on my shoulders.
"Emilie, are you ok?" He asks softly.

Unlawful Attachment

"Yes, yes, my legs just feel like jelly," I mutter, feeling like my whole body is going to melt from his simple touch.

Stepping back he grabs some crutches, helping me prop them under my arms.

"Just take your time, I'll meet you at reception with Ember."

"Is she ok?"

"She's fine, the nurses are keeping her entertained."

He laughs deeply and it sends the same strange rush feeling through me.

He leaves the room then, leaving me to sort myself out. Taking a few deep breaths I stumble out of the room, out into the hallway.

Using crutches is a tad difficult, especially for someone as uncoordinated as me.

I'm not exactly sure which way reception is, but the sound of my daughters giggles wafts down the hallways and I follow the sound, cursing the pain that shoots through my body when I press my armpits against the crutches whilst I walk.

Reaching the reception, I find Quentin standing at the desk tickling Ember playfully.

Her little voice is protesting through her giggles, "Kent sop, sop!"

A wide smile spreads across my lips, watching them. Even though Ember is protesting she loves being tickled. It's something her Dad always did as a game.

Seeing me, Quentin looks up. "Hey, are you ready to get out of here?"

"Am I ever."

"Great, then we are all set," he says smiling at me, and sending that feeling rushing through me again.

He's right by my side when I hobble out of the hospital to the patrol car he's parked outside.

Opening the door for me, he takes the crutches, leaning them against the side of the car. I fall against him, and feel safe, but also feel a rush of warmth course through me.

With his hands on my hips, he helps me sit down on the car seat and lifts my legs, swinging them into the car before closing the door.

Even with clothes on and his hands no longer on me I can still feel them against my body and I'm scared to admit to myself what that might mean.

He helps Ember into the back seat of the car, buckling her in.

"Air ee o-ing Kent?" She asks him when he gets into the drivers seat and starts the engine.

"To your place sweetie."

I can't help but smile at him calling her sweetie. It seems evident that he cares for her, probably a lot more than he needs to purely for his jobs sake.

"But mi ont ive ere," She says sadly.

Moving the car away from the curb and turning out onto the main road, he speaks again, "I know Ember, but you're going to be living in a new house. Is that ok?" He looks back at her in the rear view mirror, to see her nod.

Only a few minutes pass, as we drive across town and stop outside a quaint cottage style house. It's well looked after and has a neatly kept garden at the front.

Quentin is out of the car almost immediately, opening up my door, grabbing the crutches and getting Ember out.

"I'm just going to head in and get Ember settled watching tv."

Handing me the crutches, he takes Ember's hand in his. "Meet us inside, and call out if you need me."

I watch as he goes inside the house and stumble in a few moments later to find he's sat Ember down on the couch to watch cartoons and he's in the small, homely kitchen about to make a coffee.

Seeing me at the door, clearly struggling with the crutches he comes straight over, taking them from me.

"Lean into me," he muses, his tone deep but sweet. He grabs my arm, putting it around his waist and wraps his arm around my shoulder.

Slowly we hobble like that, me hopping on one leg, leaning into his waist to the island bench in the kitchen.

Unlawful Attachment

On one side of the bench are three bar stools. Reaching them, he steps back, effortlessly lifting me up by the waist to sit on one. The heat of his touch on such a sensitive spot again lingers.

He's gone back to the other side of the island bench again, finding it difficult to look at me.

"Do you want a coffee?" he asks.

"Yes, please," I say, but shaking my head.

Just being in his presence has me so confused, because the way he's acting doesn't seem like he's just doing his job.

Waiting for the kettle to boil, he looks at me a little perplexed too, asking, "Whats wrong?"

"Why are you being so nice to me?"

"I'm just doing my job Mrs Buccianti," he says, matter of factly.

"Please, I told you to call me Emilie," I say a little harsher than I intended.

"I'm sorry, it's just I..." he starts, stopping to pour the hot water into the two cups on the bench.

"What?" I ask, when he doesn't continue speaking.

"I..." he stutters a little unsure of what to say. "It feels too personal to call you Emilie."

My heart leaps in my chest, pounding wildly suddenly when he says my name, and it rolls off his tongue so sweetly.

He hands me my coffee, and I inhale the aroma before taking a long sip. His eyes are locked on me, clearly looking at my lips when I lift the cup to my mouth again.

It partly has me feeling a little uneasy but it also makes me feel a little excited and makes me wonder what kissing him would be like.

Taking another sip of coffee I curse myself for thinking such things, as only a few weeks have passed since Caleb's death and I shouldn't be feeling anything for someone else so soon.

But if I'm being honest with myself I'd never felt the sense of attraction I feel for Quentin when I met Caleb. And I'm truly scared about what that means for me and for Ember.

Caz May

My mind starts to wonder back to the past when I take another sip of coffee.

As I finished applying my makeup, swiping a touch of mascara on my lashes I could feel his foreboding presence enter my dressing room. His requests when I was due to go on stage were becoming increasingly demanding and I cringed when he stepped up behind my chair at my dressing table.

"Emilie, are you ready?" he asked in a deep tone, his eyes looking into mine in the mirror.

"Yes, boss," I replied.

"I want you singing as well tonight Vixen," he demanded, using my stage name to imply that it was an order.

Still I protested, "Boss, it's really hard doing both."

"Emilie, you will do as I say , sing and strip or it's no pay tonight."

"Ok boss," I replied, as he turned to walk away.

Pursing my lips, I applied the bright red lipstick, before standing up and sighing, taking in my appearance in the mirror. Even though it was a burlesque club first and foremost, I never had to wear a fancy costume like the other girls. Being the star—the best girl—I had to dress like an everyday girl, as the customers liked to think I was attainable and more like a girlfriend, than some skank in a club they were paying to watch. Trepidation always hit hard as I left my dressing room, and tonight even more so as I needed to sing for my supper so to speak.

Peering out from between the backstage curtains I could see no seat or space near the stage was empty. The club was packed to the hilt, as if it ready to explode.

*My music started, rhythmic, slow and sensual. Sauntering up to the pole in the middle of the stage, I wrapt my body around it seductively, dancing sexily before opening my mouth to sing **'Come away with me into the night...'***

As I continued singing I slid down the pole, jumping away from it and taking off my white sweater exposing my barely there lacy bra.

Unlawful Attachment

Dropping to my knees, still singing the sensual words I crawled seductively out along the catwalk part of the stage.

When on the stage it was supposed to be a no touching place, and patrons were carefully watched to ensure they complied, but nearing the edge of the stage I felt a hand grab my thigh in a tight grip.

Looking into the crowd for the owner my eyes locked on a handsome stranger, who mouthed 'You're beautiful' to me. I was struggling to sing, shaken by his touch and the primal look in his dark eyes.

Shaking my leg I freed it from his grip, standing up to shimmy my white denim skirt over my hips.

I couldn't tear my eyes from his that were still locked on me, taking in my body as I striped. He licked his lips, and I gasped, faltering in my singing, feeling panic rise in my chest.

The sudden boos and taunts coming from the crowd made bile rise in my mouth and without thinking of the consequences I ran straight off the stage, tears in my eyes.

As soon as I burst through the backstage curtain I ran straight into the unforgiving arms of my boss, Vladimir Manning.

"Vixen, what the fuck are you doing?"

"I um...are...um.." I stammered.

"Vixen, you better fucking tell me what happened out there or it's no pay!"

"Someone touched me," I muttered softly.

"Vixen, that's nothing new."

Shaking my head I replied meekly, "No...but he told me I was beautiful."

"Well, we know that's true Vixen," he mused, before smashing his dry lips against mine, taking my mouth violently with his.

I pulled back, knowing I shouldn't and tried to protest, "Boss, please, not tonight...I can't."

He laughed deeply, mocking me.

"Vixen, you need to be punished for running off the stage."

This time I used his name instead of boss, hoping it might save me, "Vlad, no please, I'll do better...I'm your best girl," I begged, looking into his evil filled eyes.

"It's boss to you Emilie," he spat at me, saying my name harshly and grabbing a fist of my hair again kissing me so hard I gasped. When he pulled back breaking the kiss he spoke lustily, "And boss says you need to be punished."

I nodded, knowing that submission was my only option, "Yes boss, I need to be punished."

Without warning as soon as the words left my mouth, he growled, grabbing me by the waist and hoisting me over his shoulder.

Like a bear he sulked down the narrow back hallways of the club to the room at the back of the club, that only he had access to. The room that gave me both pleasure and pain, when my boss needed to punish me.

"So I can stay here as long as I need?" I ask Quentin, taking one last sip of my coffee and putting the cup on the island bench.

"Yes, everything is fully stocked..." he says, before taking a big sip of his own coffee.

"What?" I ask, knowing he wants to say something by his gaze not leaving mine over the rim of the cup.

"I'm only a phone call away if you need anything," he says, slightly suggestively.

I smile, and reply in a flirty tone, "A friend?"

"Emilie, I'm here for you..." he starts, gulping hard before continuing, "yes its my job but I..."

He stops again, words caught in his throat. He looks straight at me as I awkwardly stand up sans crutches, falling into him, against the hardness of his defined chest. His arms instinctively wrap around me in a tight hug, and I feel safer than I have in a long time. It isn't just the fact that he's a cop, as that probably should have me running scared considering what I've run from in the city, but it's him and his comforting presence.

Without letting me go, he speaks, "If you don't want to tell me anything that's ok, I get it."

Pulling back a little, slightly unnerved by what hugging him made me feel, but also by what he's implying with his words, I say, "I...I want to but I can't right now."

"Take your time, I'm here for you both," he says comfortingly.

Stepping back against the seat, leaning into it I reply calmly despite my heart pounding. "Thank you Quentin, for everything, this and how you took Ember in."

"I'm just doing my job, but Ember is a real sweetie."

"Yeah, she hasn't shut up you and someone called River." I laugh.

He laughs as well. "River is my nephew and he seems quite taken with her charm too."

"Oh," I gasp, taken aback by his statement.

Again he laughs. "Emilie, it's ok, he's three."

"Oh right," I reply laughing, feeling a little silly.

"Anyway, I have to get back to the station. Are you going to be ok here?"

"Yeah I'll be fine. I'll call you if I need anything."

"Ok, I'll just say bye to Ember and leave you to it then."

I can't help but look at his butt in his tight dress work pants and thoughts come to mind that most definitely shouldn't. He bends down to Ember on the couch pulling her into a hug that tugs at my heart.

She gives him a soft kiss on the cheek and he stands up to walk out.

"Bye Kent," she says softly.

He waves to me, and I meekly wave back, fighting the urge to run to hug him again. It's not like I could move that fast anyway.

After he closes the door behind him, I hobble over to the couch and sit down with Ember.

"You like Quentin don't you sweetie?"

"Es mummy, he een ice oo me."

"Yeah, come here sweetie, it's just you and me now."

She scoots across the couch next to me and snuggles against me.

Despite my words, I don't want it to just be Ember and I.

I want someone else to be sitting on the couch with me, and it scares me, because if he's connected to my past like I think he is, then getting involved with him would be hazardous to my heart.

I can see myself falling in love with Quentin Mackenney and I'm scared of that. I've never been in love before.

(20) Quentin

Walking out of the emergency house—after saying goodbye to Emilie —my heart is aching.

I know I have to keep away from her, if I want to fight the dark urges that haunt me when she looks at me, but when she'd hugged me a rush of desire coursed through me and it took a hell of a lot of restraint to not kiss her.

My mind has thought of nothing else since the accident and she's on my mind even more because she seems to be opening up to me a little. I get the impression that she's hiding something from me about the accident. But it's also more than that.

She looks at me the same way I look at her, with a hint of lust and a longing brought on by a possible past connection. That may be why she seems a little distant.

The only thing I can really do is throw myself into finding out about the accident but if I'm being honest I don't even know where to start with that.

&

Arriving at work on Monday morning I find my handcuffs on my desk, like Sam had said in her text .

Shoving them in the top drawer of my desk I sit in my chair and think about our breakup. I'd not meant to hurt her but I can't control how she makes me feel.

Her innocence reminds me a little of myself when I'd stumbled into the Burlesque club as a nineteen year old. And that experience had opened my eyes, drawn me into darker desires and ultimately left me feeling a little damaged.

Thinking about that at work though is not really appropriate, so instead I shake the thoughts away, turning to look towards Sam's desk.

She isn't there and for some reason I feel the need to go to ask Sarge where she is, getting the sense that something is amiss in the station. At Sarge's desk I stop, standing at the corner with a hand on my hip.

"Hey Sarge, where's Constable Prattman?"

"You don't know?" He asks, looking up at me over the rim of his glasses resting on the bridge of his nose.

"Um, no I've not been in this past week Sarge, you know that."

I get the sense sometimes that Sarge is possibly going a little crazy, having been on the force so long. He's forgetful sometimes and not as thorough in his work as he used to be.

"Yeah, that's right," he says, sighing and taking off his glasses.

"Um, well, she made a complaint against you."

"What?" I spit at him, shifting on my feet nervously and swallowing the lump that rises in my throat.

"Yes, Quentin. A sexual harassment complaint."

"Oh come on Sarge, you know she was my girlfriend," I protest defensively.

"Yes, I'm aware of that Quentin but we have to take these things seriously."

"You really think I'd jeopardise my career Sarge."

"No, Quentin, I don't, but I still need to follow the correct procedure."

"Oh, come on Sarge seriously? Are you going to ask me to have time off again?"

"No, I've let her have the week off to think about things."

"Oh for fucks sake Sarge, I don't know what to say. I could lose my job," I reply, angrily.

"I'm sure it won't come to that Quentin and right now you need to focus on your job of finding out more about the accident."

I don't reply, instead turn away from Sarge's fatherly gaze on me. He'd been close with my father, and it wouldn't have surprised me if he'd been told to keep an eye on me after Dad's death.

Unlawful Attachment

Back at my desk, my phone is staring at me on my desk and again sitting in my chair I think about Sam for a moment, letting Sarge's words sink in when I lean back into the chair.

Opening messages I type a text to Sam, taking out my anger with each word.

Quentin: How dare you Sam

Sam: I'm sorry but you hurt me

Quentin: Don't fucking start Sam. You went after my job

She doesn't respond to that, and the anger rises in me more.

I can tell a scowl is plastered on my face when I angrily type another message.

Quentin:Thats really spiteful Sam

Sam: I'm sorry

Quentin: Thats not going to cut it Sam

Sam: Well its all I have to say. I gave you all of me

Letting out a deep sigh, even though she won't hear it I think about how much I'd given her of me that I've never even thought to share with someone else and she ran from it.

Quentin: I gave you a part of me too Sam, that I'd not shown anyone else and you chose to walk away

Sam: I'd never have all of you Quentin

Quentin: You don't know that Sam

Sam: Yes I do. I know in my heart you'll never love me

Quentin: If I can't be me with you it makes it pretty hard to fall in love with you

Sam: I know. I'm sorry. I'll call Sarge & say I made it all up ok?

Quentin: you don't have to do that, I kinda did taunt you a little

Sam: no this is all on me cause I had a crush on you from the day I met you

Caz May

Quentin: really?
Sam: yes and I was the one who asked you out
Quentin: fair point, are you really leaving?
Sam: yeah after Addison's wedding. I need some space to decide if I chose the right path for me
Quentin: ok, well for what its worth I think you have the potential to be an amazing police officer
Sam: Thanks, I guess I'll see you @ work next week
Quentin: yeah. I'm not expecting you to speak to me Sam, but if you have any ideas about the accident then fire them @ me please
Sam: I will bye Quentin

Putting my phone down—conscious of Sarge staring at me—I run my hands through my hair to calm myself and sigh deeply.

I've fucked everything up again, pushing Sam too far before she was ready to see my darker side. I don't believe that she's right, that I'll never be able to fall in love with her. If she could accept that darker side, I'd fall for her .

But in some ways I know she's right, and to get back at me she's gone after the one thing she knows will get at me, my job.

Being a police officer is everything and one small thing could fuck that up.

The other thing on my mind though, the accident, the cause of it, and the devastatingly beautiful Emilie is more of a threat to my career.

Because even though I know it's best to keep my distance, I already feel like I'm in too deep and for some reason I'm feeling as though I could fall in love with Emilie Buccianti.

I already love her sweet daughter, Ember as though she's mine and that's a fucking scary thought.

I'm most definitely in too deep.

(21) *Samantha*

Why I can't just make a break for it with some dignity is all I thought about since I'd spoken to Sarge and filed the complaint against Quentin. It was stupid to think he wouldn't find out it was me and now I have to face him.

Walking into the police station with my head down I can't even look at him, knowing that he'll probably smile at me and I'll be a puddle at his feet. His darker side scares me, but it's because he's never told me why he has those desires and why he wants to take that control with me. Granted, I'm the naive idiot who fell in love with him, knowing that if I didn't let him in he'd never fall for me too.

Breaking down the walls that he'd built up from his past for me was futile. I'd wondered if I'd let him fully take control in the bedroom whether he'd have let me in and fallen for me too, but there's no point worrying about that now. He's never going to love me, and I only have a week or so left in Ridgehope so I need to suck it up to finish what I have to.

But sucking it up means speaking to Quentin about the accident and hoping I won't end up being a blubbering mess the moment I open my mouth. Speaking to him over text was easy, but standing next to him he still has the power to make me melt.

Taking in a deep breath I casually walk over to his desk, standing behind his chair and sighing heavily. He appears to be looking at something intently on his computer screen—an address of somewhere in Adelaide—that looks a little suspicious for him to be looking up at work.

About to turn away, he jumps in his seat sensing I'm standing there. He quickly minimises the screen and turns his chair to face me, his knees brushing mine.

Breathe Sam, breathe, fight the feeling that you're about to melt.
Stepping back from him a little, I put a hand against the edge of his desk to steady myself.

"Hey, um, I thought about the accident."

"Yeah, what is it?" he asks casually.

"I...um...has a full scene investigation been done?"

"As far as I know, yes."

"Oh ok, cause I just remembered seeing more than one set of tyre tracks on the road and one looked like a larger vehicle."

"Oh yeah, I think I recall that too. I'll look through the report Sarge did when tying up the scene."

"Ok well um..." I say, tongue tied now I don't have anything else work related to speak to him about.

He smiles at me then, and I can feel my body betraying me, melting and heating all over.

"Sam, are you ok?" he asks with a concerned tone in this voice.

"Yeah...I'm f...fine...I was just um wondering if we should go take another look at the car too?"

"Yeah I was thinking that too."

"Ok um so..." I mutter, again feeling completely tongue tied, hating that he still gets to me.

"Sam, please, you don't have to be nervous around me. Everything is good between us, no hard feelings."

It may be no hard feelings between us, but I still have feelings for him and suggesting to go to the wreckers isn't my best idea, but I have to do my job, so feelings aside that's what I'll do.

"So should we go grab some lunch and head to the wreckers?"

"Sounds good," he says happily, standing up and brushing his hands down his creased pant legs. "Have you spoken to Sarge yet about the complaint?"

I can't meet his eyes when I reply, "Yeah I'm dropping it all. It was stupid of me, but I was hurt."

"I get it Sam, I do, but I never meant to hurt you, believe me."

"I do, and thats why I told Sarge to let it go."
"Ok, enough talk of that, let's go grab that lunch," he says laughing to lighten the moment.
I walk towards my desk to grab my purse, with him only a step behind me. Reaching down to grab my bag, he touches my arm, urging me to stand up and look at him.
"Don't worry about your bag, lunch is on me."

(22) *Quentin*

After grabbing salad rolls from the bakery we've driven to sit outside the wreckers.

Sam still seems anxious, like she's regretting even suggesting to leave the police station together.

It's obvious she still has feelings for me, and I truly do feel bad that I can't return those feelings.

However I can't deny she's gorgeous, even more so when she's nervous.

Munching into her salad roll, she can't look at me. The silence between us is awkward, especially when I raise my eyebrows suggestively and see her eyes roll as she tries not to avert her gaze to me.

She licks her lips, before she laughs suddenly, her eyes then looking towards my lips.

"What?" I laugh.

"You've um..got lettuce on your um..." she stutters in her sweet nervous way.

"What? Where?" I ask, a hint of a tease in my tone.

I expect her to tell me that it's on my cheek, but she doesn't speak instead presses her thumb to the corner of my lip pulling it back with a tiny piece of lettuce stuck on it.

She holds it up. "Got it,"she coos and I take her thumb in my mouth, taking the piece of lettuce in between my teeth and licking the tip of her thumb with the end of my tongue. She gasps at the contact, her thumb grazing over my lip when she snatches it back.

"Um sorry Sam, I shouldn't have done that," I say apologetically but flirty.

"It's ok I..." she stammers, stopping to take a bite of her roll, again trying to hide her nervousness.

"Sam?"

She turns to look at me. "Yeah?"

"You have mayo on your mouth."

"Really?" She asks rhetorically, licking her lips and missing the mayo completely.

"Did I get it?"

"Um...no let me."

And without thinking that it's Sam, and for a second about what I'm doing, I lean across the console and kiss her hard, licking her lips to taste the mayo on them. To my surprise she responds to the kiss, letting out a sweet little moan.

Cursing myself, I pull back. "Fuck Sam. I'm sorry, I couldn't help myself."

Again taking me by surprise, she laughs sweetly. "I've missed kissing you, but we can't be together Quentin."

"I know Sam but I've missed kissing you too."

That I'm certainly not lying about. It's one of the things I'd liked about being with her, never knowing what type of kiss you were going to get. She blushes at my admission, her nerves rising again. "But I..."

"What Sam?"

"Let's just get this job done," she states, clearly wanting to say something else.

"Sam please tell me what you want to say," I suggest, touching her arm.

"I want to be with you one last time," she says, a blush colouring her cheeks more.

"What?" I spit back shocked. "But you broke up with me Sam."

"I know but I..."

"Tell me Sam," I demand, trying to curb my rising anger.

"I want to sleep with you like the first time...to remember how good it feels before I leave in a couple of weeks."

To say I'm shocked is an understatement. The words she's saying don't seem like something that would ever come out of her innocent mouth.

"Sam as much as I want to say yes to that, I can't do that to you."

"I want you to," she says with a flirty tone and a seductive smile, that sends a shot of lust straight to my pants.

Again I press a kiss to her lips, wanting to fulfil her want right there and then.

Breaking the too sweet kiss, I say, "Only if you're sure."

"I'm sure," she says sweetly.

"Ok, then meet me at mine after work to say goodbye," I say, my hand on the door latch.

Opening the door I get out of the car, but she doesn't follow, leaving me to go inside the wreckers to look at the car myself.

My mind is distracted by her request though. Part of me knows I shouldn't even entertain the idea, but a part of me is also hoping that maybe I'll be able to convince her to stay; because I need a distraction to stay away from Emilie.

(23) *Samantha*

Walking up to Quentin's door after work, I'm thinking about our day together, partly cursing myself for kissing him back and partly excited to be with him again.

His darker side still scares me, and I honestly don't want to be with him in a relationship as that darker side is bound to come out more than it already has.

All I want is to just be with him to remember what it feels like when he lets me in, when he takes his time and makes me feel special.

This night though I'm going to take control, make him feel how it is to be the one who's being teased. It's time to be brazen.

Opening the door to me, after I've softly rapped my hands on the door he stands before me wearing a blue stripy sweater and jeans that hug his hips as usual.

How dare he look so fucking gorgeous.

Not giving him a second to speak, I stand up on my tiptoes and press a hard kiss to his lips. I'm about to take the kiss further when he pulls back.

"Whoah Sam! I thought you wanted to take tonight slow."

Shaking my head slightly I reply, "Yes but I.."

He lets out a deep laugh at my sudden nervousness, it sending the desire for him running through me.

"Fuck, just kiss me Sam," he drawls out huskily.

Stepping a little closer to him, pressing my body against his I stretch up to kiss him again.

This kiss is a little deeper, and he grabs my waist, lifting my feet off the floor. Instinctively I wrap my legs and arms around him, clinging to him even when he pulls back from the kiss, asking gruffly, "Where to?"

"Bedroom," I say teasingly into his ear, starting to kiss down his neck. He lets out a growl, stumbling backwards down the hallway, still with me wrapped around him.

Reaching the bedroom, he gently places me against the bed, stretching over my body to kiss me, a little deeper than before.

Drawing him closer, bucking my hips up towards him I can feel his hardness pressing into my stomach when he deepens the kiss, pushing his tongue into my mouth.

Gasping I break the kiss, and he starts to speak against them, "Tell me what you want Sam."

"You," I tease, a raspy tone to my voice.

"Sam, please you don't want me; this is just goodbye sex."

"Well, in that case..." I stretch up to lean against him, my lips at his ear. I whisper, "I want to be on top."

A devilish grin spreads across his face, that I kiss away, fumbling with the button and zip of his jeans.

Pulling back from the kiss, he puts his fingers into the side of his pants about to plunge them to the floor, but I stop him, grabbing his wrist in my grasp.

"No clothes stay on," I demand, loving the odd 'what the fuck' look that shines in his dark eyes.

Giving in, he sighs when I run a hand over his already hard dick, freeing it through the hole in the front of his boxers.

Running my hands up and down his length I tease him more, loving the chance to take control.

"Oh Sam, why?" he drawls when I sit back on the bed, taking him into my mouth, teasing his hardness with my tongue, licking and sucking him.

He gasps. "Oh fuck Sam, please no, I can't do this to you," He says gruffly.

I can't help but smile around his dick, at the effect I'm having on him.

Unlawful Attachment

It feels amazing to take the control back.

(24) Quentin

There's no denying that having Sam's sweet lips around my cock is amazing. The way she's stripped me of any control and is teasing me is so arousing, it almost makes me lose myself. As much as I want to blow in her mouth, making her taste my cum when it slides down her throat, I can't do that to her.

It's a little strange that she all of a sudden wants to please me, so I grab her head between my palms and pull her mouth off my cock.

"Sam, as good as that feels, tonight is not about me."

Her eyes lock on mine, pleadingly, like she wants to say something but doesn't have the words.

Instead she crawls back on the bed, grabbing at the hem of my jumper to pull me down onto the bed with her.

Fiercely she kisses me then—taking charge again—and it definitely makes the desire run through me, but it's too little, too late.

Pulling back from the kiss I lay down next to her, sighing deeply.

My cock is screaming for release, but I'm not going to take charge now. Part of me is enjoying seeing this side of her, even if it's too late.

Without warning she climbs on top of me—straddling my hips— grinding against me when she leans down to kiss me again.

I laugh through the kiss. "Sam, are you wearing anything under your dress?"

"No," she laughs in reply, sliding herself suddenly onto my cock, gasping when she takes me in; deep.

Slowly she rocks her hips from side to side, pushing herself deeper onto me. Watching the sheer pleasure on her face is amazing and I call out, "Sam come for me! I want to see you come riding my cock!"

Slamming down hard on my cock, she shudders, her climax overtaking her body when she screams out, "Oh fuck!"

It excites me, hearing her scream out in release.

Unlawful Attachment

Without warning though, before I can reach my own end, she slides off me, taking my length into her mouth, again sucking and licking along my length like she can't get enough.

I can't control myself, and verbally hiss, "Oh god Sam, fuck!"

Taking me deeper, my tip touching the back of her throat I let go, exploding down her throat. I feel her swallow hard before she pulls herself off me.

Opening my mouth to speak in thanks, my words are stifled by her pressing a finger to my lips.

"Goodbye Quentin. I'll see you at Addison's wedding."

Leaving me dumbfounded, lying on my bed she's walking towards my bedroom door, stopping in the door jamb a moment.

"Sam, please, can you just come back to bed?" I beg, feeling hopeless and desperate to take some control back. "I'm sorry for everything."

"No, Quentin, mind-blowing sex doesn't change anything between us," she says shaking her head.

"So we're still breaking up?" I ask, kind of hoping her answer will be 'no'.

"Yes, I just needed to say goodbye in a way that would make you miss me."

My reply catches in my throat, watching her turn and walk out of my bedroom and straight out the front door, slamming it behind her.

Cursing I yank my jeans down my legs, throwing them on to floor by the bed, pulling the covers back to slide into bed. Tears—fucking tears—are stinging my eyes.

Come on Quentin, be a fucking man! You never loved her, so why the fuck are you crying like a wuss?

A miaow at the bedroom door announces Tiberius's presence before he jumps onto the bed. When he curls up next to me I stroke his silky soft fur. "Tib, I fucked up buddy," I say to him and he lets out a long miaow in response.

Even my cat knows how much I've fucked up with Sam.

Caz May

After her behaviour tonight I feel used, and the pain outweighed the
pleasure I'd felt.
I wish I'd never shown her my darker side, because now I'm dateless
for Addison's wedding, heartbroken and seriously fucked up.

(25) Emilie

It seems a little silly in my head because he's repeatedly told me that his kindness to me was him just doing his job, but I feel as though I need to repay Quentin somehow.

Plus, I just want to see him again, so plastering a smile on my face I walk up to his door with Ember by my side. Rapping on the door I wait for him to open it up, not exactly sure what I'm even going to say if he's home.

The door swings open, just as I'm about to turn away and I gasp seeing him in front of me again. He looks devilishly handsome, in navy dress pants, and white button shirt with bare feet peeking out.

In his mouth, he's holding a toothbrush, the foam of the toothpaste across his lips.

A slight smiles crosses his mouth, and he holds a finger up to me to say, *'wait a moment'* before he scoots down the hallway.

On his return a minute or so later—sans the toothbrush—he looks me up and down, smiling.

"Hey, sorry about that, I thought..." he pauses a moment, touching his clean shaven jaw. "Never-mind, whats up?" he says, casually.

His confused gaze turns to my leg, no longer in the cast .

"I, um...came to give you this, to thank you," I say meekly, handing him the bottle of whiskey I'm clutching under my arm.

"Thanks Emilie, but you don't need to thank me," he says casually taking it from me. "When did you get the cast off?"

"A few days ago," I tell him, feeling a little nervous.

"How? I could have taken you to the hospital."

"You did enough for me already. It's fine, Doctor Rivnay made a house call."

"Oh right ok..so um I can't really chat right now," he apologises.

"Yeah, I um...should have called first."

"Its ok, don't apologise. I've just been busy at work and..." He bites his lip, as though he's stopping himself from saying anything else.
The expression on his face gives me the impression he's hiding something from me.
"What?" he asks, looking straight into my eyes, making my insides stir a little.
"I get the impression your not telling me something Quentin."
"No, no, I'm just um...I need to finish getting ready for Addison's wedding."
"Oh right, that would explain the outfit," I say nodding.
"Yeah, look Emilie, I'm sorry if I gave you the impression there was something between us but..." He again bites his lip even harder than before as though what he's saying isn't the truth.
"What?" I spit. "I don't know what you're talking about."
"Emilie, please, you have to go. I have to go."
I feel a little taken aback by his sudden insolence—having no idea how to respond—a little hurt that he's just pushing me away.
He bends down to Ember at my side, who has a pout on her face.
"Sorry sweetie, you can come over another day to play with Tiberius ok?" he says, kissing her forehead.
Standing up he leans against the door, grabbing the handle in his grip.
My heart is pounding in my chest, taking him in and how sexy he looks just standing there staring at me.
I've barely been able to stop thinking about him, which is crazy considering it has only been a few months since Caleb's death, but I've never felt such an attraction to anyone before. It seems the only way to get Quentin to talk to me is to play dirty.
"I've um...remembered something about the accident," I drawl.
His eyes light up and I know that's the key to spending time with him.
"That's great, but I'll have to discuss that with you next week at the station."
"Ok, yes, I'm sorry. Have fun at the wedding," I say turning to walk away, looking back at him still standing against the doorway, so obviously still affected by my turning up on his doorstep.

Unlawful Attachment

Walking back to the car my mind wanders.

"Vixen?"

"Yes boss?" I asked sweetly, feeling as though something wasn't right.

"You're not going on stage tonight," he told me, a harsh tone in his voice.

"Why boss?" I asked, confused and scared.

"After your stunt the other day with a full house again I'm not risking it."

"So where do you want me then boss?"

"VIP room Vixen, lap dances in that sexy black lingerie please."

I cringed when he said please, hating every-time that word came out of his mouth, as he never meant it. He came closer to my chair, turning it around and grabbing me to force me to stand up.

With a hand on my hip, he pressed a hard kiss to my lips, untying my robe at the same time to expose my nakedness.

Stepping back and breaking the kiss a wicked smirk crossed his face, looking me up and down as he spoke, "This body Vixen is why our clients pay the big bucks."

I scoffed at his words, and he continued, "You know the rules Vixen yes?"

"Yes...no kissing...no penetration."

"Good girl Vixen, who owns this hot little body of yours?" he asked, plunging a finger inside my body.

Gasping at the contact I could only mutter, "You do boss."

Pulling his finger out of my body, he licked it as he walked away, slapping my butt through the robe.

"Mummy, wha ong?" Ember asks, sensing my obvious unease.

"Sorry sweetie, mummy was just thinking about home."

Ember has tears in her eyes, hearing my words. Picking her up, I hold her against my hip, to have her close when we walk inside our house.

"Is ot home Mummy," she says sadly.

"I know sweetie but it's our home now, ok?"

Ember nods when I put her down inside the front door.

"Is kent oing to be ere with us?" she asks me so sweetly, my heart breaking at what I have to respond to her.

"Sorry sweetie, but Quentin isn't part of our lives now."

"But we ust aw im."

"I know sweetie, but thats the last time you'll be seeing him."

Ember stomps her feet. "No! I ike im! He ice to me!"

I ignore her tantrum, feeling a little angry at Quentin for the love he's shown her.

Starting to make a coffee I try to shake the thoughts of him out of my head, but my thoughts wander back to him standing against the door jamb. The look in his eyes was raw, full of emotion that he couldn't hide.

The cup of coffee between my palms is warm, but thinking about Quentin is making my whole body feel warm. His eyes on me made me feel stripped bare.

And that thought crashing into my mind tells me exactly why I feel such a connection to him, why I'm so fixated on his eyes.

He has been in my world before, the night it all came crashing down.

My heart is pounding in my chest, my coffee cup crashing to the floor at my feet.

I'm in trouble, in deep and scared that now I'll not be able to keep away from him, because I'd wanted him that night and now I want him even more.

(26) Samantha

Sitting in a pew, in a church at wedding always makes me feel emotional. Tears are stinging my eyes, the emotions overtaking me a little. The last wedding I'd been to was my older sister's and the after events of that wedding always crush my heart when I think about it.

Quentin catches my eyes, looking back from closer to front of the church. He looks forlorn, utterly heartbroken and it hurts a little to see him feeling that way. Our breakup had to happen, but I still love him and feel a little regretful for the way I'd used him a week ago.
Saying goodbye was never going to be easy, but I need to protect my heart and taking a piece of his heart in a physical way is the best thing.
Scowling at him, I avert my eyes to focus more on the wedding. If I wasn't in a church though I would flip him the bird, anything to make him think I want nothing more to do with him.
The rest of the wedding passes by in a blur, and I try not to think about my sister, Alysha. Her wedding was beautiful and prestigious, so different to this quaint country town wedding.
Part of me isn't sure if going home—back to Adelaide—is the right thing to do now, but I need space from Quentin and the heartbreak he's caused me.

❧

Leaving the church the thoughts of Seth's arrival to pick me up surface in my mind. His confession of being in love with me and still being a virgin has puzzled me from the night I'd spoken to him on the phone. We'd only communicated via text since and he'd sent me kisses, always ending a conversation with, *'I love you.'*

I know he wants more, but he'd hurt me too and I don't feel that way about him anymore, having lost a major part of my innocence and given my heart to someone who doesn't want it.

Walking into the reception at the pub my phone pings with a text.

Seth: Babe, I'm here early. Couldn't wait to see you
Sam: At pub, for reception, ex here
Seth: I can come and get you now
Sam: Please do
Seth: Be there soon. I bet you look beautiful
Sam: cut the crap Seth. hurry up

Putting my phone back in my purse, I grab a champagne from the waitress walking around the room, gulping it down.
Involuntarily I look up at the door when Quentin walks through the door with Hunter. He looks so heartbroken. It takes a hell of lot of willpower to not walk over to him and hug him.
My heart hurts like hell.

(27) Seth

Trying to be casual I walk into the pub—puffing my jacket collar—partly hoping to confront Sam's ex-boyfriend and tell him he's a fucking tool for hurting her. I know he's a cop, so I'll probably not even have a chance against him, but god do I fucking want to knock the bastard out.

I've cursed myself everyday for the stupid words I'd said to Sam, the choices I made that night when we were nineteen. Being so naive and a horny teenager I'd thought only with my dick and now I'll not get to share Sam's first time with her like I desperately want to.

I'm still in love with her and she's fallen for someone else—giving him everything—now left with a broken heart.

Gazing around the room, the moment my eyes lock on Sam there is no one else in that pub.

She's clutching a champagne in her hand, a sad, when the fuck can I get out of here look on her face.

Walking up to her, I look at her outfit, my pants feeling a little tighter taking in the way her strapless ruby red dress hangs across her cleavage, her shoulders bare. Her legs are crossed and the short dress edges high on her thighs.

Swallowing hard to gain a quip of confidence I greet her, "Hey Sam."

Standing up she hugs me—innocent and friendly—before she pulls back, looking at me sweetly.

"Hey Seth," she coos at me, in a tone that seems like my innocent Sam is still here in front of me.

"I was right, you do look beautiful."

Playfully she slaps my arm in response, no words escaping her lips, like she'd always done when I teased her.

"Sorry, babe. So who's the ex?" I ask, glancing around the small pub.

Discreetly she lifts a pointed finger towards a ridiculously tall, dark haired guy standing at the back of the pub. He isn't as burly as I'd thought, but he has a presence that shows dominance for sure and he has a pretty boy, but bad boy look about him too.

"Oh right, well I guess I can kinda see why you fell for him," I acknowledge, my stomach lurching at the way her eyes shine looking at him.

"Yeah, he's um..." She swallows her words, turning to look at me again.

"You ready to go?" I ask.

"Yeah, I just need to say goodbye to Addison, and we can head back to my place, for my clothes and stuff."

I watch her when she walks over to a stunning blonde, in a figure hugging beige gown. Sam embraces her and says something to her, before returning to my side.

"The bride I'm presuming?"

"Yeah, it was a beautiful wedding...but well you know."

"Yeah Sam, I should have been here with you."

"Don't Seth, please, I don't want to think about it. Can we just go?"

"No worries babe," I reply, grabbing her hand to lead her outside to my car.

I'm surprised my little rust bucket car, the old as fuck Datsun 240z had made here in one piece, but thankfully it had and hopefully it will make it home too.

After sliding in, the memories of the early days of getting my licence flood my mind. Driving out into the Adelaide hills for the day together, just enjoying being in each other's company without a care in the world. But all that changed after her sister's wedding, before I'd gone and fucked things up when I should have been there for her and supported her choice to join the police force. No doubt if I'd thought more about our future, she'd still be my present.

Pointing directions at me for the short drive to her house, my heart is pounding thinking about the past, but also I'm drowning in the silence between us.

"Sam, please talk to me or going home tomorrow is going to be torture."

"I'm sorry, I just feel so stupid," she declares when we pull up in front of a quaint looking cottage.

She doesn't say another word, jumping out of the car, and gesturing for me to follow her inside.

Once through her front door—she kicks off her high heels—heading across the small room towards the lounge and an inviting brown couch, that I'm presuming will be my bed for the night.

"Why? You didn't do anything wrong Sam."

"Yes, I did. Getting involved with Quentin was stupid."

"You can't help it, you fell in love with him. He's the stupid one for not loving you back," I tell her sincerely, even though I want her to love me again.

"Hmm," she muses, falling to the couch and tucking her legs underneath her, the short dress edging further up her thighs than earlier at the pub.

Sitting down next to her, I sigh, words that I want to say caught in my throat. It hurts to see her hurting, and the hurt is evident when tears are stinging her eyes, dripping down her rosy cheeks.

Brushing them away with a thumb, she leans into my touch, almost begging me for something more. Part of me knows I shouldn't take advantage of her when she's hurting, but dammit I love her so much still and want to take away the pain he'd caused her.

Leaning forward—closer to her—closing the barely there distance between us on the couch, I kiss her, softly at first.

Damn, I've missed kissing her, but god, oh fuck, this kiss is...

Expecting her to pull away, I kiss her slowly, taking my time to taste her again. Her response to my lips on hers is new—carnal—and she licks them forcing her tongue into my mouth, teasing me and taking my mouth as hers. This kiss is more demanding and fierce than any kiss

I've ever had and I fucking loved it, revelling in how she's taking control over it, making me breathless.

Pulling back, starving for air, I pant, "Wow, Sam that was one hell of a kiss."

"Yeah, um Seth?" she asks blushing even more than her already rosy red complexion.

"Yeah Sam?"

"Are you ready?"

"For what Sam?" I ask, shocked when she grabs my hand putting it under the hem of her dress, practically between her thighs.

"Sam, what do you mean?" I ask, swallowing hard as my mind starts to race with thoughts about what her gesture is implying.

"Touch me Seth," she tempts.

"Oh Sam, I don't think I can. I don't know what to do," I say innocently, feeling myself blush.

A sweet as fuck smile spreads across her plump lips I'd only moment ago kissed. "I'll show you," she says in the same tempting voice.

"Ok, but tell me if I'm bad ok?"

Laughing she stands up from the couch, standing in front of my knees. "You won't be."

She steps out of her lacy knickers—seductively sliding them down her legs to the floor—before grabbing my hand again.

This time she guides me—taking my hand straight between her thighs —to touch the crevice between them. Feeling her intimate skin, on my fingertips I curse, "Oh fuck Sam."

Running my fingers over her body, even though I feel like I'm completely out of my depth. I can feel myself hardening, straining against my track pants.

Watching the sweet pleasure on her face, I whisper, "Sam I want to..."

"Say it Seth," she moans, my finger grazing over her clit.

"I want to make love to you, Sam."

The look in her eyes changes then—lust shining in them—and she pushes my back against the couch.

Unlawful Attachment

Instinctively I yank my track pants and boxers down, never happier to be free of the fabric restraining my dick.

"Sam, I don't have a condom."

Sitting on my lap then—her crotch against my straining groin—she leans over me to whisper in my ear, "Don't worry about it."

"But Sam, I don't think I'll be able to control myself, you know?"

She doesn't reply, instead kisses me with the same fierceness as before, grinding her pelvis against me, but not letting me slip inside even though it's clear from the slick wet feeling I can feel against my dick that she's more than ready to.

"Give me a minute," she says standing up.

Walking away she lifts her dress over her head, making my dick harden even more as her watch her bare arse wiggle when she walks down the hallway.

Waiting for her to hopefully return, I try to telling myself to breathe, that this is finally it, that I'm finally going to lose my v-card to her like I always wanted.

But the moment she enters the room again, my breath catches in my throat. In her hands, she's holding a condom but my eyes can only focus on her completely naked, having taken off her strapless bra as well. She'd always been beautiful, but part of Sam's innocence was the fact she'd been a bit a of late developer, not having even grown tits until like eighteen, but now fuck did she have a nice set, perfect for cupping in my hands.

Ok Seth, seriously down boy, breathe, let her take your v-card and think later.

Before I can think or say anything to her about how stunningly beautiful she is I find her straddling my lap again, sliding the condom on me effortlessly.

"Are you ready Seth?" she almost moans.

I mutter an, *'mmm'* biting my lip when she slides her body down on mine, starting to rise up and down on my dick.

Watching her perfect tits bounce a little I loudly moan, "Oh Sam, fuck that feels good."

It feels like mere moments when I can feel my dick starting to pulse, ready to release. Grabbing her cheeks in my palms I kiss her hard, pulling back and exploding my release into her, screaming out "Fuck, Sam, I love you."

Still buried within her, she rocks her hips a little before reaching her own climax.

Without a second thought, she climbs off my lap.

"Thanks for that Seth. I'll see you in the morning."

Walking away from me towards her bedroom, she doesn't turn back, leaving me completely dumbfounded. She'd literally just fucked me, and damn it was good—better than good—but my heart hurts bad, like she'd just fucked me to not think about him.

Sighing, I stand up, yanking my track pants back up, before I lay back down on the couch.

There's so many emotions rushing through me, yes, I'm happy to have lost my virginity but even though it was with Sam like I'd always wanted it was far from special.

All I really want though is to make Sam fall back in love with me, to have her in my arms again and be buried inside her again on my terms, not hers.

Even though my next decision is not the wisest, I stand up from the couch, stumbling through the dark house to find her bedroom.

It isn't hard to find—even in the dark—because I can hear her sobbing.

Reaching her bedroom, moonlight shines through the open curtains, basking her still naked body in light, a silhouette under the threadbare sheets she's clutching against her bare chest.

Sensing my presence in the room, her eyes open and look straight into mine in the darkness. Without speaking I enter the room, crossing to the other side to climb into the bed next to her.

Unlawful Attachment

She sniffs back the tears, about to speak but she shuts her mouth
when I pull her naked body against my clothed one.
Pressing a kiss to her hair, I muse softly, "Don't Sam, ok, just sleep."
She moans a little, turning her head towards me and pressing a soft
sweet kiss against my lips before closing her eyes, quickly slipping away
into sleep wrapped in my arms, right where I've wanted her ever since
we'd broken up.

(28) Quentin

When walking into Ridgehope supermarket at just after noon on a Monday you don't expect to see anyone but the checkout chick Annie in the store, so I'd hoped to slip in under the radar on my lunch break to grab some much needed groceries to feed my cupboard and fridge.

What I didn't expect was to turn down the far aisle and come face to face with Emilie with Ember standing next to trolley she has a number of grocery items in. I feel a pang of anger that she's buying groceries for the emergency house—without asking me—but shrug it off because I've been avoiding her for the past couple of weeks and have no right to intrude.

Since Addison's wedding, and Sam leaving town I'd decided to focus on work more, because it's clear that I'm going to be forever single, especially if I can't stop myself from craving the darker things I want to do.

They'd come crashing into my mind, a lot since Sam broke up with me. My head is constantly spinning with various emotions; anger and shame mostly.

I'd even contemplated taking a drive to Adelaide, and throwing myself back into the club scene—to pick up some random skank and have my wicked way—but it isn't going to heal my broken heart.

I've been working so much more now Sam has gone that there's barely a spare moment in my day to be in the supermarket like I am now, let-alone drive six hours to Adelaide for a night of drunken debauchery.

Now standing in the supermarket in front of Emilie, I try not to stare at her, feeling a little lost for words.

It's Ember who speaks first, looking up at me sweetly. "Hi Kent."

The look in Emilie's eyes is unreadable, she bites down on her lip as though she wants to speak but isn't sure what to say.

Unlawful Attachment

The words I want to say are tumbling in my head, the words of apology for not speaking to her after she turned up unannounced on my doorstep a few weeks earlier when I was getting ready for Addison's wedding.

Instead of speaking to Emilie, I scoop Ember into my arms, hugging her tight, spinning her legs around.

"Hey sweet girl, I missed you," I coo at her.

She presses a soft kiss to my cheek. "I miss oo too Kent."

I hear Emilie's breath hitch in her chest when I put Ember back down and without thinking about what I'm doing I pull her close to me in a hug as well.

A shot of warmth runs through me, an almost electric feeling at having her so close. She practically melts into my arms, leaning her head against my heart that's beating way harder than normal.

I pull back from our embrace—feeling Annie's eyes glaring at us from the front of the store—finding my voice. "Emilie, are you ok?"

"Yes," she replies meekly, hanging her head a little when tears threaten to spill from her eyes.

Tentatively, I caress her cheek, a thumb under her chin to lift her face to look at me when I speak, "Emilie, you don't look ok. What's going on?"

"I...I c..can't tell you."

"Is it about the accident?"

"No...well yes kind of," she mutters, her gaze turning away from mine again.

"Is this all you need?" I ask, gesturing towards the items in her trolley.

"I just need some milk, but yes that's all."

"Let me get these for you and I'll take you home," I offer, genuinely concerned for how she's expecting to walk home with a trolley load of groceries.

"You don't have to do that Quentin, please."

"I'm not taking 'no' for an answer, please Emilie, it's the least I can do."

"Thank you, I honestly don't know why you've been so kind to me."

Lightly, I brush her arm, as she wheels the trolley to the fridge at the back of the supermarket to grab some milk.

"It's my job Emilie," I say, looking straight at her.

The rush of cold air from the fridge hits me right in the face, making me take a deep breath in.

Ember is tugging on my pant leg.

"Kent arry me," she asks.

Picking her up, I hold her against my hip when we walk to the register to check out.

Emilie unloads her groceries onto the conveyor belt, the awkward tension in the room is broken by Annie greeting me, "Hi Constable Mackenney." Her tone is like a giggling school girl even though she's like eighteen.

"Hi Annie, can you put this through on the station account?"

Emilie has finished unloading everything, and pushing the trolley aside she touches my arm, letting it linger on my bare wrist when she says, "Quentin, please I'll pay for it."

"It's fine Emilie." I wink at her, noticing the stupid grin that crosses Annie's face.

"Are you sure Constable Mackenney?" Annie asks with a concerned tone.

"Yes, Annie, I'm sure. This is Emilie Buccianti and her daughter Ember. They are staying in the emergency house at the moment."

"Oh, ok after that horrible accident?" Annie asks scanning the last item.

"Yes, so please show her every kindness when she comes in."

"No problem Constable," Annie replies, totalling the transaction and grabbing the printed receipt.

From the register drawer she pulls out an account slip, with a pen and shows me where to sign for putting it through under station expenses.

Emilie grabs the five full grocery bags, not showing any sign of struggling to carry them. Still holding Ember against my hip I follow her outside to my car.

"You won't get in trouble at work for this?"

"No, why would you think that?"

"I don't know, a hundred dollars is a lot to spend on food that's all," she says sadly, a deep set frown on her face.

I'm a little lost for words, worried about how much money Emilie has to her name to be so concerned about buying groceries.

I buckle Ember into the backseat behind the drivers seat, whilst Emilie puts the groceries onto the backseat next to Ember, before she gets into the car herself.

Driving back to her house, I can see tears stinging her eyes. The silence between us is killing me, and looking over at her in her vulnerable state my mind flashes back to the first night I'd gone into the burlesque club in the city.

Having downed countless whiskey's and a couple of light beers, I was pretty well baked, dancing suggestively with Britt. The desire was rising in my pants, with her plump arse grinding against me. Grabbing her by the waist I turned her to face me, and kissed her hard full of drunken rage. Forcefully she pushed her hands against my chest, not just breaking the kiss but pushing me away from her. "Seriously Quentin, why are you always trying to get with me."

"Oh I don't know Britt, maybe because you get blind and throw yourself at me."

"Oh come on Quentin, I did nothing of the sort."

"Yeah right, keep telling yourself that Britt. You're such a fucking cocktease."

She scoffed, storming off the dance floor, yelling back to me, "Fuck you Quentin!"

If only I could fuck her, like I wanted to and forget all about Addison losing her virginity to my older brother. Being flirtatious was fine, but so far it hadn't gotten me laid. I was a nineteen year old police officer in training, with no life experience at all.

Stalking out of the pub myself, the alcohol suddenly hitting my head, I stumbled down the street mesmerised by the lights of the nightclubs.

Caz May

One in particular caught my eye, the flashing neon sign of 'Bloom' was so bright and vivid in the blackness of the night.

Walking in, passing the front desk with a simple wave, happy to not pay yet another cover charge I was immediately drawn into the dimly lit club, captivated by the singing of a beautiful woman on the stage taking up most of the room. Surrounding the stage was men, ogling her, watching her sing and strip from the barely there clothes she had on.

Pushing my way through the crowd to get closer to the stage was near impossible but I needed to be closer to her, to see her beauty up close. She wasn't what I would normally find beautiful—dark haired, wavy and shoulder length—and dark eyes that looked troubled, as though she was hiding a painful secret.

Stepping closer to the stage, a tall male grabbed her leg as she crawled out onto the stage. Her body went tense, flinching at his touch, before she stood up continuing to strip. She sang for another moment or so abruptly faltering in her words and running off the stage clearly traumatised.

Without thinking I lunged at the guy who'd touched her leg, a hand on his shoulder forcing him to turn around and face me.

"What the fuck man? Get ya hands off me," he yelled accusingly.

Looking straight into his eyes, I could see nothing but carnal lust in them, that scared me, making me wonder what kind of place I'd set foot in.

"Sorry man, thought you were someone else," I apologised, walking away to check out the rest of the club.

Cursing, I grip the steering wheel tight, turning my knuckles white, the realisation hitting me hard.

Pulling up in front of Emilie's house she can sense my unease, looking over at me and breaking the silence that has enveloped us, "Quentin, whats wrong? You look like you've seen a ghost."

"You could say that."

"Did you see my husband? Is he here?"

Shaking my head, I look at her.

"No Emilie, he's not but we need to talk," I say, grabbing her hand in mine. "About the past."

Snatching her hand back without saying a word she jumps out of the car, obviously shocked by my words. She walks around to the driver's side, opening the door to grab Ember out and runs inside without even looking back at me.

"Fuck," I curse, slamming my fist into the steering wheel, making the loud honk of the horn reverberate through the silence outside.

Getting out of the car, I grab the groceries, carrying them to the doorstep. Stopping a moment, I contemplate just leaving them there and leaving Emilie be, but after what I've just realised I need to speak to Emilie more than anything.

Pounding on the door, I yell, "Emilie, please let me in."

"No! Go away! I don't want to talk to you about what I left behind," she yells at me through the door.

Clearly she's standing right on the other side because I can feel her words right in my face as though the wood of the door isn't between us.

"Please Emilie, it will help with following up on the accident," I beg, unsure of what else to say.

For a moment she's silent, before the door swings open.

"Fine, coffee first and you can start by telling me what you know about the accident."

"Sounds good," I beam, grabbing the bags to carry them inside.

Placing them on the bench I think for a moment about how forthright her tone was. So far she's seemed so meek, hiding behind the curtain of her husband being gone, afraid to let me in and find out her secrets.

My realisation about the first night I'd entered 'Bloom Burlesque' only makes me more curious about her past, her so called husband and why they essentially crashed into Ridgehope.

Her heart is guarded and even though I know it's wrong I want to break it down, hoping that she can break down the walls I've placed around my own heart.

She'd been a part of that dark world before, which means she'll understand what I crave so desperately.

I'm afraid that she'll want no part of it anymore, if she finds out about my past too, and likewise won't want me despite the sexual tension between us.

Hearing the bubbling of the boiling water in the kettle, I search through the bags for the milk, tossing the one litre carton between my hands like a ball as I walk over to hand it to her.

"So the past Emilie?" I enquire.

Pouring the hot water into the two cups on the bench her eyes lock on mine, and my heart leaps in my chest, hoping she has realised the connection between us and hoping that this time I'm going to be the one to save her from the past.

(29) Emilie

Just when I'm about to open my mouth to tell him I'm not sure about delving into the past tonight, Ember comes rushing up to him.

"Kent play dolls with me?" she pleads with him, tugging on his pant leg.

I watch as he follows her to the lounge room, taking in his confident stance and the way his arse moves beneath his dress pants.

I feel angry at myself for thinking that way about him, but the attraction I feel towards him is real and it has me scared to feel.

It's evident now he knows something about our past connection, but I'm not sure if I'm ready to tell him about what I've left behind.

Quickly I put the groceries away, glancing in the direction of the lounge room as my mind wanders.

Just about ready for the night, I was checking my makeup in the mirror, as I tugged on the tie around the waist of my silk robe.

Vlad came sauntering into the room, his presence making the room feel devoid of air.

"Vixen, you've been requested tonight."

"What for boss?" I asked, a pang of fear hitting me in the guts.

"A private lap dance, in a single VIP room."

"Boss, you know I hate being alone with the men that come in here," I pleaded.

"Yes, Vixen, but it is your job," he said coldly, "they pay for you, they get you."

Knowing that protesting was futile I followed him out of my dressing room, to the four single VIP rooms at the back of the club. They screamed opulence, one wall was lined with a plush black velour couch, the other displaying an array of various bondage and other sadistic equipment that clients were free to use as they wished. In the middle of the room were dining room type chairs, with hooks on them for bondage activities. Going into this room was my worst nightmare at the best of times but this night as I stepped up to the door with Vlad behind me just a step away I froze looking at the client who had requested me.

It was the guy who had grabbed my leg a few nights ago. Trying to make one last attempt to not have to face him I turned to face Vlad, looking at him, pleading my 'no' without words. He pushed a hand against my chest, forcing me to step back into the room, flicking the door lock closed from the outside as he said menacingly, "Twenty minutes Vixen, obey the rules."

"Hey," the stranger said to my back, in a tone to try and entice me. Turning to face him, still standing by the door I said as seductively as I could, "Hi, where do you want me?"

"Where don't I want you beautiful."

"There are rules sir," I said as forthright as I could, the nerves of having him so close after he'd invaded my personal space on the sanctuary of the stage.

"Sir, so official." He laughed, patting his knee. "Come sit on my lap beautiful."

Nodding I undid the tie of my silk robe, letting it drop to the floor, leaving me exposed in my lacy red bra and knickers.

Crossing the room I straddled him as he lent back into the chair. The look in his eyes was the same as the night he grabbed my leg, carnal 'I want to fuck you' now lust. It scared the absolute shit out of me, but still I started to grind my pelvis against his straining body beneath me. I had to do my job or the consequence of Vlad finding out would be far worse than what this stranger wanted from me.

As I continued grinding he grabbed my breast through the lace, kneading it and teasing my nipple, sending a shot of desire straight to my groin. My nipples being touched always made my desire pool, even when I didn't want it to.

"You like that Vixen?" he asks as I let out a moan.

"Tell me your name beautiful."

"I can't, there are rules."

"Fuck the rules Vixen," he drawls out huskily before smashing his lips to mine.

Slowly I start to kiss him back, shocked at myself as I know it's wrong, but liking the feel of his soft plump lips on mine, as opposed to the callous dryness of Vlad kissing me.

Breaking the kiss, his eyes lock on mine when he begs, "Come on beautiful, tell me your name."

I lean into his chest, knowing I shouldn't but feeling a strange connection to him after his sweet kiss.

"Emilie," I whisper into this ear.

"Fuck, even your name is beautiful," he whispers, kissing me again a little harder.

I bite my lip, cursing as I pull away when I hear the door unlatch.

I can feel Vlad's domineering presence enter the room, the scrape of his shoes on the floorboards as he gets closer, grabbing a fist of my hair and yanking me back from the stranger's lap.

I cower back a step, but Vlad's menacing eyes lock on mine before I close them, feeling the slap of his hand against my cheek, hearing the smack that will leave my cheek red raw.

The stranger stood up angrily, grabbing Vlad's arm.

"Fuck man, how dare you treat her this way," he seethed, before continuing a little calmer, "I. Kissed. Her."

Vlad appeared to get angrier, as though the blood was boiling inside him.

"Is this true Vixen?"

"Yes, but I just did what the client wanted," I pleaded, chastising myself, knowing that Vlad wouldn't care.

He didn't acknowledge my plea, instead turned to the stranger, his anger rising as he fisted his palms.

"If you set foot in here again and try to get with my girl again there will be consequences!" Vlad seethed.

The stranger shook his head, "Sorry man, I didn't know about the rules."

"Well, now you do. If you want to request her again you'll pay double and will not be alone with her."

"Ok, fuck man, you're a hard arse."

"Now tonight, you need to get the fuck out of my club. I'll be watching you," Vlad threatens as the stranger brushes past him leaving the room, seeming relatively calm given the situation that just happened.

Vlad looked back at me, his eyes gazing over my body as I put my robe back on.

"Playroom in ten Vixen. I can tell your wet and ready baby."

He turned to leave the room and tears broke through, seeping down my cheeks. Him calling me baby made me feel like a dirty whore, just the way he treated me.

I needed to do something to get out of this hell.

Pouring the milk into the coffee cups, I take one handle in each hand, walking carefully to the lounge room.

I nearly spill the hot liquid everywhere, laughing from hearing Quentin speaking with a girly tone. "Oh Ken you're so hot!"

Ember is giggling excitedly, loving him playing with her just like Caleb had done.

Quentin stops when I step closer, looking up at me and blushing.

The wide smile on his face makes my insides squirm with the same giddy feeling I get when he hugs me.

"Ember, mummy needs to speak to Quentin about some grownup things, can you take your dolls to your room?"

"Okies, mummy," she squeaks, picking them up and skipping down the hallway.

Quentin uses his hands to lift himself off the floor and sits back on the couch, as I hand him a coffee.

He takes a long sip, sighing deeply.

"So, Emilie, tell me what you remember about the accident?"

"Nothing," I lie, taking a sip of my own coffee to stop myself from biting down on my lip, making him realise I'm lying to his face.

Unlawful Attachment

I watch him over the rim of the cup, sitting down on the couch next to him.

I cross my legs under me, gasping when he touches my thigh.

Even through the fleecy fabric of my track pants I can feel his touch, like my thigh is on fire.

It sends a delicious shiver through me and I look straight at him, nervously.

"Emilie, don't lie to me. I know you remember something," he chastises me, seeing straight through me.

"Ok, I...I remember a truck following us."

"A truck? What kind of truck?" He enquires.

"Like you know, those small moving van type ones."

"Did it have any writing on it or anything?"

"Not that I can remember," I say shaking my head and taking another big gulp of coffee, scared to tell him more.

"Do you remember anything else about it?" He probes.

"It was white. And I think it might have been my..." I gulp, swallowing my next words, cursing myself for even thinking of telling him that.

I can feel the tears starting to drip down my cheeks, Quentin's gaze locking on mine.

"Might have been who Emilie?"

"I can't tell you. If he gets word that I'm alive and I told the cops he'll come after me."

"Oh Emilie," Quentin muses, grabbing my waist and pulling me against his chest in a hug.

My tears turn to wretched sobs wetting the white fabric of his dress shirt. He doesn't flinch, just pulls me closer, pressing a kiss to my hair.

Pulling back from his hug, I look up at him, straight into his dark chocolatey eyes.

I'm a goner.

Why do I want him so damn much?
When I know I need to keep my distance from him.

(30) Quentin

Emilie's eyes are locked on mine, after she's pulled back from our hug. The tension between us is sizzling, and all I want to do is kiss her. But I know it isn't the right time. The look in her eyes is showing me she possibly wants the same as me but also shows a hint of trepidation as well.

Still with my eyes locked on hers I brush a stray hair from her cheek. "Emilie, you're beautiful."

Hearing my words she shrinks back, pressing herself back into the corner of the couch, as though she wants to get as far away from me as possible.

"Don't say that," she grumbles, the tone sounding like hearing my words actually hurts her.

"I'm sorry...I..um...I got caught up in the moment," I apologise.

"Yeah, well I don't want to hear that from you."

Not knowing what to say I stand up from the couch, standing in front of her still sitting on the couch.

I'm about to walk away, but she stops me when she stands up, her body almost pressing against mine.

"I'm sorry Emilie, I don't think sometimes."

She just looks up at me, a puzzled look on her face.

"I've tried to keep my distance, but damn Emilie I don't want to."

A strange rush runs through me, like the tension between us is intensifying just by looking at each other.

"I don't want you to either and I'm sorry," she says softly, stretching up to kiss my cheek.

Touching my cheek, it feels like fire where her the smack of her kiss lingers. Pulling her close into my chest to hug her again, I rest my chin on her head.

"Please tell me Emilie, if you remember anything else ok? I want to help you move on from the past."

Pulling back she looks up at me again. "I will," she replies meekly.

Pressing a kiss to her forehead I say, "I know and we still need to talk about the past and what that means for both of us."

"I know," she replies again, this time grabbing my hand when I take a step back.

"I got to get back to the station, but I'm not staying away this time."

Still holding her hand I start walking towards the door. She follows, dropping my hand at the door. "I don't want you to stay away, and Quentin?"

"Yeah?" I respond, my hand on the doorknob when I turn to look at her standing next to me.

"Can you help me organise to say goodbye to Caleb?"

"Of course, I'll talk to you about it tonight."

"Thank you." She smiles at me, and I open the door to leave.

Walking to the car, I inwardly curse myself for the thoughts plaguing my mind of wanting to kiss her.

If I don't stay away, and spend more time with her, there's no way I'm going to keep my self control. The next time I see Emilie, I don't doubt that I will kiss her and if the tension sizzling between us with just a hug is anything to go by, kissing her will be nothing short of amazing.

Only the fact that I've been gone from the station a lot longer than my hour lunch break stops me from going straight back inside to kiss Emilie senseless in that very moment.

(31) Emilie

After Quentin left, I'd not left the couch all day, except to make Ember something to eat, before putting her to bed early.

Clutching a coffee in my palms I'd sat on the couch, crying thinking about the question I'd asked Quentin earlier about saying goodbye to Caleb. It's true I never actually loved him, but he's Ember's father and he was there for me when no one else was. And thinking about him still makes my heart hurt a bit.

Quentin knocks on the door again—at six pm—still in the same clothes from earlier. He makes navy dress pants and a white button down shirt look like the most sexiest outfit known to man. As soon as I open the door, he takes one lingering look at me before pulling me against his chest, wrapping his arms around me in a tight hug.

For a moment or so, we just stand there, not saying a word, the tension between us sending a rush of warmth between us.

Pulling back he asks, concerned, "What's wrong?"

"I've been thinking since you left earlier and I need to tell you about Caleb."

"Why?" he asks.

"You know why Quentin," I reply when he steps inside following me to sit back on the couch.

Just as Vlad mentioned a few weeks earlier, if the stranger ever set foot in the club again and requested me, we wouldn't be alone. I found myself in a double VIP room.

In one corner another girl, a new blonde girl was involved in a pleasure scenario with a guy I swore I'd seen before too. He had deep chocolate eyes I couldn't help but look into, even though his focus wasn't on me.

Unlawful Attachment

The mysterious stranger had me straddling him again, whispering in my ear, "Emilie, I want to fuck you tonight."

"Thats against the rules sir," I said, trying to be assertive.

"You know I don't give a shit about the rules Emilie," he jeered, reaching into his pocket, pulling out a shiny foil packet.

"No sir, we can't," I warn, his hand at my crotch, undoing the buttons of my lacy bodysuit. Freeing himself from his pants he rips the packet opening, sliding the condom onto his length.

Grabbing me by the waist, he lifts me up slightly, pressing my body back down onto his.

"Ride me, Emilie," he demands into my ear.

Leaning against his chest, I bounce up and down on his length, not able to look him in the eyes, as I know what I'm doing is wrong. Having sex with a client is breaking all the rules, but something about him makes me scared to not do what he asks.

As I continue to ride him, cursing myself for actually enjoying feeling having him inside me, I can't help but stare at the other guy in the room, his chocolatey brown eyes draw me in.

The stranger pushes me back from his chest, looking straight up at me, filling the condom with his climax.

"Fuck, Emilie," he screams out, his tone scaring me and sending my mind spinning at what I've just done.

Climbing off his lap, I don't look back, picking up my silk robe and shrugging my arms into the sleeves as I run out.

The other guy is behind me, running up to me and grabbing my arm.

"Are you ok?" he asks, sounding genuinely concerned.

My heart was racing in my chest when I replied, "No...I...I.."

"You can tell me," he muses at me, making me feel at ease but still I reply, "No I can't...you just saw what happened."

Without thinking, wanting to just get away, wanting to push him away, I touch a hand to his bare chest and feel a spark of attraction rush down my arm. I brush the thought aside, about to walk away when he asks, "Did he force you?"

"No, no," I reply, shaking my head.

Pulling up his pants the stranger I'd just broken all the rules with comes over, standing a little to close for comfort.

"Get your hands off my girl," he yells.

He fists his palms about to punch the other guy but swerving to the side skilfully he dodges the incoming fist and instead his fist smashes hard into the wall nearby.

Tension had gone up a notch, footsteps and a domineering presence approaching.

It was Vlad and he was beyond angry.

"What the fuck is going on?" he seethes, not directly at any of us.

"You both get the fuck out of my club," he yells, pointing at both of the men standing in front of me.

After they both leave, not even glancing to look back at me, Vlad asks me, "Did you use protection Vixen?"

"Yes, boss," I reply.

"Do you have feelings for him Vixen? It's not the first time he's been in and requested you."

"No, I don't boss."

"You've kissed him though Emilie and now it seems as though you've fucked him because he requested that, is that correct?"

"Yes, boss, I don't love him boss but he told me I was beautiful and he kissed me. I had to play along. And then he wouldn't take no for an answer. I was scared."

"You know the rules Vixen," he chastised, not caring that I was concerned for my own safety.

"No boss please don't punish me," I begged.

"You're lucky I'm not going to punish you right here! You will meet me at the playroom door in 15 minutes but go wash that cunt off first," he growls.

I cringe at his words, hating that word so much. Watching him walking away I can't help but feel a little worried for the stranger if he ever sets foot in the club again.

❧

"Emilie, please, tell me what's got you so upset?"

"Well, you know I never loved Caleb."

"You've mentioned that yes, but that doesn't explain why thinking about him has you in tears."

"Well, um...."

"What Emilie?"

"Have you ever been to Bloom Burlesque in the city?" I ask, my heart pounding .

"Yes, Emilie, you know I have."

"And when you said we needed to talk about the past, you meant..." I pause, wanting to hear him say it, that he remembers that night too.

"The night Caleb nearly punched me, after he forced you to fuck him."

"Yes," I reply, feeling the same attraction to him I'd felt then.

"But what happened after that Emilie?"

"I married him," I confess.

"Um yeah, but why? You didn't love him?"

"No, I didn't but he promised me that if I was his girl he'd save me from the club gig."

"So what's that got to with marrying him?"

"At first he was sweet. He tricked me into thinking he had money and then I found out I was pregnant."

"Ok," he soothes, moving closer towards me on the couch.

"He was so excited, and asked me to marry him right there and then."

"Was the baby Ember?"

"No, I...I...um actually lost that baby...because um..." I stutter, the emotions flooding me.

"Oh, Emilie I'm so sorry."

"Its ok, it's just that after losing the baby he made me feel loved but I couldn't let myself love him, as that hurt to much, you know?"

"Yeah I get you," he replies softly, touching my cheek.

"And now saying goodbye I want it simple."

"How so?"

"I just want you there beside me with Ember."

"Why Emilie?"

"I don't know. I feel safe with you...protected from my demons."

"Hmmm, yeah, I know what you mean."
He pulls me against his chest in a tight hug, pressing a soft kiss against my cheek. We sit there in each others arms for a few moments, the tension between us increasing.
Pulling back his beautiful chocolate eyes lock on mine. "Emilie I…"
"I know…"
"I don't want to hurt you, take too much from you."
"You won't…I need to feel something other than pain."
"Oh fuck Emilie," he growls, before smashing his lips against mine in a hard, consuming kiss.
His kiss is demanding at first—carnal—sending a rush of warmth through me, making a moan escape my mouth.
Slowing the kiss down he licks my lips, gaining entrance to my mouth, melting into me.
Kissing Quentin is like nothing I've ever felt before, the attraction between us makes his kisses set my body ablaze.
Pulling back from the kiss both completely breathless, he looks straight at me. "Emilie I'm so sorry I…"
Putting a finger against his lips I say softly, "Don't say that…"
"But Emilie I shouldn't have kissed you, I'm investigating your car accident. We can't get involved with each other."
"Yes, that's true, but you know…" I sigh, about to mention our past connection, but instead I say slightly meaner than I intend, "Forget it… just go home."
A look of hurt crosses his face, like I've stabbed him in the heart.
He stands up, not saying a word when he stomps towards the door to leave. He doesn't even turn back to look at me, and my heart aches from pushing him away when I need him.

(32) Quentin

Kissing Emilie was wrong—I know that in my head—but since she'd kicked me out a few days ago, our kiss has been on constant replay in my mind. Also I've been fantasying about so much more than kissing her.

My feelings towards her are scaring me, so deep, real and like nothing I've felt towards anyone before.

For work I know I should keep my distance, but I don't want to and I need answers, more answers about her past.

Honestly, when I'd realised our connection I felt guilty. I should have gotten her out of that hell hole, taken the whole place down as I'm sure there's a hell of a lot more going on than just a burlesque club.

I've started to research Bloom Burlesque, but nothing has come up that's out of the ordinary.

It's a registered business with an Australian Business Number, has phone numbers that are connected and a website that's updated frequently. The only thing that shocked me is the ABN being registered to MFI Pty Ltd.

Starting to research that company name, brings up a name I've heard before and my heart sinks when my work phone rings.

Hesitantly I answer, "Ridgehope Police, Constable Mackenney speaking."

"Hello, Constable Mackenney, just the man I was hoping to speak to."

"Ok, and who am I speaking to?"

"Sorry Constable, I'm Constable Mathers from Belair Police station."

"What can I do for you?"

"I'm calling about a lead on the accident that happened near Ridgehope."

"Oh?"

"Yes, we have recovered a vehicle down a ravine in the nearby hills, that fitted the description you entered in the APB database."

"That's great news. Do you have any registration details or anything else?"

"It had no rego plates, but we traced the VIN back to a registered business, MFI Pty Ltd."

"What?" I spit into the phone, the shock hitting me hard.

"You know of this business?"

"Um kinda, I was actually doing some research into them for the survivor of the accident."

"Ok, well you'll be happy to know that the owner of that business name is well known around here."

"How do you know that?"

"I can't go into details as yet, as we are currently investigating him for another case here, but MFI stands for Manning Family Industries."

"And the head of the Manning family, would his name happen to be Vladimir?"

"Yes, that is correct. He is currently under investigation here for another matter, so I will leave you to follow up on this accident."

"No problems,Mathers. I appreciate the call."

"Anytime, Mackenney. Drop me a call if you need anything else. Have a good day."

"You too, catch ya."

Constable Mathers hangs up, and my heart lurches. Emilie had been right, and I need to drop any worry about seeing her away.

I need to save her this time.

Quickly shuffling some papers on my desk, I grab my phone, racing out the door to go to Emilie's. It's time to get to the bottom of why she really left Adelaide and how Vladimir Manning is connected.

❧

My heart is pounding hard in my chest knocking on Emilie's door. Opening it to me, she looks a little dishevelled but so beautiful, it damn near breaks my heart.

"Hey, Quentin," she says looking at me with a pained look in her eyes. "I'm sorry about the other day."

"Hey Emilie, I'm not sorry, but I um...need to talk to you about something urgently."

"Ok," she says cautiously, ushering me inside. "Coffee?"

"Yeah, that would be great," I respond, following her inside to the kitchen.

Whilst I lean against the island bench, she makes the coffee's in silence, not turning back to even look at me.

All I want to do is hug her, take away the pain she's so obviously still feeling, but I'm not sure what she really wants from me.

Handing me a coffee, she walks over to sit on the couch and I follow, taking a sip of my coffee before I sit beside her.

"So, what do you need to talk about it?" she asks, so innocently, like the tension between us isn't the elephant in the room.

"I got a phone call about your accident."

"Oh," she gulps.

I quickly fill her in on the details of the truck being found, and finish by asking her, "Do you know the Manning family, Emilie?"

"I can't tell you, Quentin."

"Why Emilie? I can help you if you're in danger."

"If he finds out I told the cops, finds out where I am he'll come after me."

"Who will Emilie? Tell me please," I beg.

"I can't, he's evil, he'll come after me, don't you understand?" she questions me, fear lacing her voice.

"Emilie, I care about you. I want to keep you safe."

"You can't Quentin," she spits at me, giving me a feeling like she's slapped me.

I know I shouldn't let my emotions get involved, but her words hurt a little and I find myself asking, "Why Emilie? Are you telling me our kiss the other day meant nothing to you?"

"Oh god no I...I," she mutters, not able to get the words out and breaking my heart more.

"Emilie please tell me you don't regret it. I'm putting my job on the line to be with you."

My heart is pounding, waiting for her response.

She shakes her head slowly. "No, I don't regret kissing you, but its just Caleb couldn't protect me from him and neither will you be able to."

I don't respond, instead pull her closer to me hugging her tightly and pressing a kiss on her hair.

Resting my chin on her head I speak softly, "I have ways Emilie. Tell me who he is and I will do everything I can to keep you safe from him."

She lets out a muffled sigh against my chest, before she pulls back from my embrace and looks straight up into my eyes.

My insides stir with the fluttery feeling I get when her eyes lock on mine and even though I know what that look in her eyes means I'm a little taken aback when she stretches up to softly press her lips to mine.

Her kiss is sweet, and sends a warm rush coursing through my body. I do not kiss anyone like this, gentle and longing aren't in my vocabulary, especially when it comes to kissing someone, but with Emilie, having her kiss me no matter how is nothing short of amazing. Pulling back, I brush her cheek with the back of my hand.

"God, Emilie, you're so beautiful, please tell me who has hurt you?"

"You know who Quentin. Don't act like you don't."

"I don't know what you mean, are you talking about the club owner?"

"Don't please, you know that's exactly what I'm talking about...you know I remembered some of my past."

"Well, yes, and I know about Caleb, but isn't remembering our past a good thing?"

"Depends," she replies, a hint of hesitancy in her tone.

"On what?" I quiz her, knowing that we've only talked about Caleb and not our connection.

"If you remember anything else?" she states, in a questioning tone.

"Yes, Emilie, I do...you know I remembered Caleb being there, but I also knew something else was going on and I regret the choices I made back then."

"What do you mean?"

"It um...led me down a dark path and well after that night I saw you with Caleb, I um..."

"What Quentin? Please tell me," she begs, touching my thigh.

"I didn't leave straight away...I watched you talking with the club owner and Emilie...the way he looked at you made me feel physically ill."

Tears are running down her cheeks, and brushing them away with my thumb I continue softly, "If I'd done my job, and told an officer at the academy about what was going on I could have saved you from that place."

"But Caleb saved me," she suddenly replies through sobs.

I let out a low chuckle. "Really Emilie? Would you be in Ridgehope with me now if Caleb truly saved you?"

She shakes her head in response.

"So please Emilie, who will come after you?"

"Vladimir Manning," she replies cringing.

"He's the owner yeah? The one that I was just referring to?" I ask, connecting the dots in my head from my earlier conversation and the past.

"Yes, and he used to hit me....and..."

"And what Emilie, what else did he do to you?"

Sobbing again, her words are muffled, "I...he...would...punish...me."

"Oh God, Emilie, I'm sorry, I should have known."

"It's ok, I've blocked it out and I don't want to talk about it."

I don't respond, instead pull her close to hug her again, trying to quell the guilt that's completely overwhelming me.

After a few moments she lifts her head up from my chest, her face so close to mine, and she whispers against my lips, "Can you stay with me tonight?"

"Emilie, is that really a good idea?"

"Please? I just want to feel safe."

"I don't know Emilie, I don't trust myself around you."

Again she kisses me in response, the same longing evident as our earlier kiss. It leaves me wanting more, like I'm starving for her. When she pulls back, I feel hungry for her and her words make my heart pound. "Me either, but I feel safe in your arms and tonight I need you to hold me close and tell me it's going to be ok."

Before I have a chance to even think, to respond and say, *'no'* she grabs my hand when she stands up from the couch. My head is telling me to say no, to let go of her hand and not follow her down the hallway to her bedroom, but my pounding heart is winning, telling me to take the chance and not worry about the consequences.

Reaching her bedroom, I watch her getting out her pyjamas. I kick off my shoes and fumble with my belt buckle. My eyes are fixated on her, watching as she turns her back to me, lifting her dress over her shoulders when she takes it off. Her lacy black underwear clings to the curve of her arse, riding up a little when she steps into her pyjama pants.

Swallowing hard, I try not to make a sound when she reaches around her back to unclasp her bra, letting it fall down her arms to the floor in front of her. She turns her head to look back at me, a slight smile on her lips. I have to fight the urge to not cross the room and step up behind her, to not cup her perfect breasts in my hands whilst pressing my body against her delicious arse.

I swallow a moan when she slips her pyjama top on, giggling sweetly. Pulling back the covers of her bed she asks, "What do you normally sleep in?"

"Um...boxers or nothing," I reply laughing.

"Oh, well, um maybe clothes stay on tonight, but if you..." she pauses, smiling deviantly.

"What?" I jeer at her, not able to stop myself from grinning back at her.

"You can take your pants off if you want," she suggests, a hint of lust in her tone.

Not responding I fumble with the button of my work pants, sliding them down my legs whilst I watch Emilie dive under the covers.

Climbing in next to her, I pull her close, her back against me. Feeling her arse pressing against my groin sends the desire rising in my boxers. "Quentin, I...um.."

"Don't speak Emi, please," I soothe.

"Say it again," she demands sweetly.

"What?" I ask, hoping that I hadn't said what I'm actually thinking.

"Emi. I like how it sounds from your lips."

"Emi."

She sighs deeply, shifting a little in my embrace to face me.

Again she doesn't give me a moment to think before kissing me, this time with a little more urgency. Her lips on mine send the desire coursing through me and I can't help but deepen the kiss, licking along her lips to gain entrance to her mouth. Her tongue dances with mine, and I slip a hand underneath her pyjama top, feeling her skin heat at my touch.

Reaching her breasts I cup one in my palm, massaging it whilst I continue kissing her, taking all I can from her.

Pulling back breathless, I gulp. "Oh god, Emi, you have no idea what you do to me."

"I have some idea." She laughs.

"Yeah that obvious huh?"

"Just a little, but not yet." She laughs again, but there's promise in her voice.

"I know, let's get some sleep and see what tomorrow brings."

Again she sighs, so deeply, it's as though she's calming herself when she closes her eyes.

Pulling her close again, she nestles back against me and I lay my arm over her stomach, sneakily underneath the pyjama top to have it against her bare skin.

Laying there I listen to her steady breathing, not able to slip into sleep myself. After what seems like barely a few minutes her steady breathing changes to a quiet, slightly muffled snore.

Pressing a soft kiss against her hair, I whisper, "Emi, I think I'm falling in love with you."

(33) Emilie

The sun is shining through the gap in my curtains when I wake up still wrapped in Quentin's arms. Having a man in my bed could feel strange, considering it isn't Caleb. He's the only other person I've ever slept with, but Quentin looks so peaceful and so damn sexy in just his white dress shirt and boxers my heart is pounding just looking at him.
He stirs, murmuring deeply when his eyes flutter open and focus on me lying next to him.
"Good morning Emi," he teases huskily, before pressing a kiss to my lips.
"I could get used to this," he says, a seductive tone in his voice.
"Me too," I reply rolling onto my side to face him with my whole body. For a moment we lay there looking at each other, not saying a word, just feeling the tension building between us.
Again he kisses me, a little deeper, licking my lips like he usually does to gain entrance to take my mouth with his.
He moans into my mouth, his hands on the hem of pyjama top about to lift it over my head, when I pull back, hearing the pitter patter of tiny feet running up the hallway, a little voice yelling, "Mummy, mummy, wake up!"
Ember is at the bedroom door, diving onto the bed for a morning cuddle, but instead of even looking at me her sweet hazel eyes lock on Quentin, leaning on his elbow next to me.
"Kent, why oo in Mummy's bed?" she asks him. He looks at me, his eyes questioning me for what he should say in this very awkward situation.
"Sweetie, look at me," I suggest to her, watching her eyes dart between us.
Kneeling between our legs in the middle of the bed, her excitement peaks when she asks, "Is Kent oing to be my new Daddy?"

Laughing I look at Quentin, and he joins in before he speaks, "Oh sweetie, I could never replace your daddy."
"Then why oo in bed with Mummy?"
He turns to look at me, sending me a help me look.
"Ember, we are friends and last night Mummy was sad," I tell her, hoping it came out calmer than I feel.
"And Kent made oo ot sad?"
"Yes, sweetie, I was missing Daddy and Quentin made me feel better," I say looking at my daughter but also at Quentin at the corner of my eye. He has a slight smirk on his face, as though he's thinking about how he'd made me feel better by our hot consuming kisses.
"Does it mean Kent is oing oo be ere with us more?"
This time I don't have any words to say, a little unsure about what Quentin is feeling. I'm grateful when he responds to Ember's question.
"I hope so sweet girl. I care about your mummy a lot."
"You care bout me oo Kent?"
"Of course sweetie, come here," he suggests holding out his arms towards her.
Crawling up towards him, she falls into his outstretched arms for a hug. He kisses her forehead and she giggles.
Smiling at them, I climb out of bed. "How about I make pancakes for breakfast?"
Ember jumps up excitedly, standing on the bed and almost dancing on the spot. "Yes, please mummy," she squeals.
Grabbing her by the waist, I hold her against my hip when I walk out to the kitchen, winking at Quentin before leaving the bedroom.

I put Ember down on the barstool, and she props her elbows up on the bench, watching me as I get out the pancake ingredients.
A few minutes later, when I'm starting to mix the pancakes, Quentin comes sauntering into the kitchen, still wearing his white dress shirt untucked from his navy dress pants, with bare feet.
Looking at him, I gasp feeling my breath hitch in my throat. He looks so damn hot, I feel the desire pooling in my lower body.

Looking at him and kissing him is enough to send me so close to the edge I don't dare think about what actually sleeping with him would do to me.

Licking my lips, I have to put the bowl down for fear of dropping it when he asks, "How can I help?" His voice is still husky from sleep, and he leans against the bench, so comfortable in my kitchen and his own skin.

"Um, maybe help Ember get out some plates and juice," I suggest, pouring the first round of batter into the pan.

"No worries," he replies, grabbing Ember by her tiny waist and spinning her around in a hug, her legs out. Her delightful giggle reverberates around the kitchen and it makes my heart melt a little. Putting her down he kisses her forehead, and she totters towards the fridge to get out the juice.

Looking at Quentin, a smirk crosses my face, a knowing smirk thanking him for the way he'd reacted to the situation.

He seems so comfortable in my kitchen, like he belongs in my home with me and I have never felt more at home than I do in that moment. The feeling is amazing, I love how safe and happy it makes me feel, but also I'm scared about my feelings, because I'm worried about falling for him.

Worried that I'm going to fall in love with him, and he'll not return my feelings.

(34) Quentin

It has been a few weeks since I'd first spent the night at Emilie's and I've only spent a few nights at home in that time, checking on Tiberius and getting some clothes to wear.

We've spent nights together sitting on the couch, when Ember had gone to bed, talking about everything except the past. We'd made out like teenagers, both on the couch and wrapped in each other's arms in bed.

No doubt, I want more from her, want to taste her, tease her and make her mine completely, but I'm not sure she's ready to completely let me in. Her past has no doubt left scars, both physical and mental, and I'm afraid my darker side is going to make her run like it had with Sam.

My heart is involved now, I know every time I kiss her that I'm falling harder for her and if she runs from me and my darker side it will be the end of me. My heart would be shattered, even more so than by Addison's rejection.

I'm in the kitchen now, about to start making a coffee when I feel my phone buzzing in my pocket. Pulling it out, I glance at it to see Hunter's picture flashing on the screen.

Answering it I feel a pang of guilt for not taking the time to speak to him much lately.

"Hi Hunter," I say happily, hiding my guilt in my tone.

"Hey little bro, are you home?" he asks with a fatherly tone, further cementing my guilt in my chest.

"No, I'm at Emilie's, why?"

"No reason. I just miss you," he confesses, sounding sad.

"Um, yeah, I miss you to Hunter but um..." I confess but swallow my last words, not wanting to upset him by getting defensive about him calling me.

"I'm worried about you Quentin," he states, his tone laced with concern.

"Don't be Hunter, I'm good. Better than good actually," I declare, my heart pounding harder in my chest.

"Are you sure?" he questions me, patronisingly.

"Yes, Hunter, and I got to go read Ember a story, ok?"

"Ok, but please be careful Quentin," he warns sounding like a father again.

"I will Hunter," I promise, about to hang up when he cuts in.

"Ok, don't be a stranger little brother, bye," he laughs before hanging up before I can say goodbye.

Pushing my phone back into my pocket, abandoning the thought of making coffee I head down the hallway to Ember's room.

Emilie is kneeling by the bed, tucking Ember into the single bed that makes her look like a dwarf. It tugs at my heart seeing how sweet she looks, and I feel a sudden urge to want to make this room fit for a little princess.

Ember looks at me standing in the doorway, her eyes lighting up when she asks, "Kent, read me a stoi?"

"Of course, sweetie," I reply, entering the room and grabbing one of the only books on the small shelf near the bed. Sighing I look at the title, 'Green eggs and ham',remembering my grandpa reading it to me as a child. It was one of my favourites, that I'd ask for constantly, always giggling at the way he so gruffly said, *'I do not like green eggs and ham,'*.

Sitting on the edge of Ember's bed, opening the book I sniff back a few tears as I start to read, trying to put on the voices like my grandpa had. Ember giggles delightfully as I read, and my heart melts.

Emilie has walked out, stopping in the door jamb a moment to look back at me smiling. I'm definitely pushing myself deeper into their lives and even though I know it's wrong. I'm breaking so many rules but there's no place I want to be more.

The feelings I get being with Emilie are something I'm craving so desperately in my life, even more so than the darker side craving.

Unlawful Attachment

There's still a number of pages to go, but Ember's giggles have subsided as she'd slipped into sleep, clutching her pink teddy bear to her chest like life depends on how tightly she holds it.

Pressing a soft kiss to her forehead, I stand up to put the book away, walking quietly out of her room to find Emilie.

She's snuggled up on the couch, the fluffy throw rug across her legs, watching something on the television that's making her smile.

When I sit down next to her, she snuggles against my chest, and a contended sigh leaves my mouth, loving how comfortable it is just being together.

"Are you ready for tomorrow Emi?" I ask softly, during an advertisement.

"Yeah, it's time to say goodbye. Thanks for helping me organise it all."

"No worries, I know it must be really difficult."

She looks up at me, her hazel eyes locking onto mine. "Yeah it is but..." she pauses, as though she isn't sure of her words, or if she can continue.

"But what Emi?" I prompt, brushing my fingers against her cheek.

"I um...just um...having you in my life has helped so much."

"I'm glad, You've helped me to Emilie," I reply, sensing a shift in her body that she's a little shocked.

"How? I haven't done anything."

"But you will Emilie, you're changing me."

"I don't get you Quentin," she replies confused.

"You know I have a dark fucked up past Emilie."

"Yes but..."

"And I want to share that with you, but at the same time I've never wanted to just lay in bed with someone without it leading to sex," I confess, hoping I'm not going to send her running with my brazen honesty.

"Oh," she replies, a shocked tone in her voice that has my heart constricting in my chest.

"Um, ok yeah its been awhile since I've slept with anyone," she confesses biting down on her lip.

"You and Caleb weren't sleeping together?" I ask, hoping she doesn't think I'm prying.

"No, not really. Every so often but I never enjoyed being with him."

"Oh ok," I stammer, completely shocked by her declaration, but at the same time understanding.

"I just always associated being with him, like that, with the past, even though he loved me."

"Yeah, but I've been in your past too Emilie."

"Yes, I know, but things are different with you. I think I'm..." she starts to say the words but I cut her off, pressing a finger to her lips.

"Not yet Emi, please don't say that yet. Let me show you my darker side before you tell me how you feel."

Her reply isn't words, instead she stretches up to kiss me hard, passionately, showing me without words how she feels and I melt into her kiss, taking her mouth as though I'll never kiss her again.

Breathless, I pull back. "God Emi, do you know how wild your kisses make me feel?"

"Likewise Quentin," she replies, grabbing my hand and slipping it under her skirt beneath the throw rug draped over her lap.

"God, Emi," I hiss.

"Touch me please Quentin," she begs in a raspy tone that has the desire threatening to rise in my pants.

Again I take her mouth to mine, kissing her urgently, my hand grazing against her hot body.

Desperately I want to touch her, to make her scream out in pleasure when she comes, but I break the kiss. "I can't Emi, I won't be able to control myself if we take that step now, and we both need some sleep before tomorrow."

She pouts but nods, standing up when I pull my hand away.

Grabbing my hand, as usual I follow her to the bedroom to hold her close as we fall asleep. There's no doubt in my mind now that she feels the same way as me, and soon kissing her will not be enough. Soon I'm going to make Emilie mine completely.

(35) Emilie

When my eyes flutter open, I feel a rush of panic course through my body.

Turning to lay on my side, it leaves, relief rushing over me seeing Quentin laying beside me propped up on his elbow.

He'd been watching me sleep, and has a deliciously sexy smirk on his face.

"Good morning Emi," he coos, sending my heart rate soaring.

"Good morning Quentin," I reply, a teasing tone in my voice.

Pressing a kiss to my forehead, he softly whispers, "I love hearing my name on your lips."

"Hmm..." I murmur, watching his eyes. "I think you need a nickname."

"Really? What kind of nickname?" he asks in a teasing tone.

"I don't know, let me think about it." I laugh.

"Ok, so are you ready for this morning?" he asks, brushing a hand across my cheek.

Pouting I reply, "Yeah I guess...are you ever really ready to say goodbye to someone?"

"I know Emi, I know."

Sighing, I speak softly, pouring my heart out, "I'm worried about Ember, that she won't understand that her daddy is really gone."

Quentin lets out a lighthearted chuckle. "Emilie, your little girl understands a lot more than you think. Yes, she's only three but what she saw on the day of the accident is sadly in her mind and now her daddy not being here in a physical sense she knows he's not coming back."

Taking a deep breath in I reply, "That's what I'm worried about Quentin, what my little girl saw that day."

"I know Emilie, but having seen my fair share of trauma you need to give her time to share it with you..." he says, pain crossing his face as though he's remembering something. "And that may not be for years," he finishes, sighing deeply.

Nodding my head, I reply, "I know. Anyway we better get ready, don't want to keep the Reverend waiting."

Climbing out of my bed, I can feel his eyes on me. Turning back to look at him, the same pained expression is still on his face, his eyes almost glazed over.

"Are you okay Quentin?" I ask, stepping a little closer back towards the bed.

"Um, yeah, it's just um...last time I went to the cemetery was when Dad was buried and it just hits me hard."

My heart lurches in my chest when he gets out of the bed, standing next to it like he's lost.

Crossing the room I envelope him in a hug, hoping that he can feel how much I care for him and how sorry I am for asking him to do something that's causing him pain.

"I'm sorry, I didn't even think about anything like that when I asked you to help me."

"It's not your fault, Emilie. You didn't know about my past."

"But..." I stammer, not sure if I should push it more to ask him about his past.

"There's nothing to be sorry for. I said I'd be there with you and I will be. I care about you Emilie."

"I know and I care about you too," I reply, before he murmurs, pressing a soft, tender kiss to my lips.

It's so emotion filled, I feel as though my knees are going to give way. Pulling back from the kiss, to steady myself I ask, "Will you tell me more about your past too?"

"Yes, Emi, but not today."

Smiling, I kiss him with the same tenderness as he'd kissed me moments earlier. He moans, pressing his body against mine, the desire between us increasing. I can feel myself melting into him, breaking the kiss when a little voice behind us shocks me, "Mummy why oo kiss Kent?"

I bite down on my lip, not sure what to say to my little girl.

Looking at Quentin, and back to Ember I mutter, "Um sweetie, I um..."

Quentin smiles slightly at me, as he bends down to pick up Ember from the floor, placing her onto the bed so she's standing on the covers and eye level with him.

"Ember, sweetie," he says, in a caring tone, "you know how we told you that your Mummy and I are friends?"

"Yes, Kent, but fiends on't kiss," Ember declares, seeming too wise.

"No not usually sweetie, but your Mummy and I are special friends."

"Ecial fiends?" Ember asks, cocking her head to one side.

"Yes, sweetie and kissing is how special friends show they care about each other."

Ember jumps up and down on the bed. "But Mummy used oo kiss Daddy. Was he Mummy's ecial fiend oo?"

"Yes, sweetie he was, but you know that your daddy isn't here with us now yes?"

She puts her head down, ceasing her excited jumping.

"Yes, Daddy goed to heaven, agels ook im the car."

Quentin turns to look at me, seeing the tears that are now stinging my eyes. He has no idea how his sweet words have affected me, and how much they mean. I mouth, *'thank you'* to him and he nods turning back to look at Ember again.

"Yes, that's right sweetheart and this morning we're going to the cemetery to say goodbye to your Daddy."

"Ok Kent," she replies, as though she completely trusts him.

"Let's leave Mummy to get ready huh?" he says, picking Ember up by the waist.

As he carries her out to get her ready, he presses a kiss to my forehead.

"What did I tell you?"

"I know, it's going to be ok."

(36) Quentin

My heart is pounding hard in my chest, standing in the cemetery next to the graveside that has a makeshift wooden coffin for Caleb strapped over it.

I'm holding Ember against my hip, with Emilie standing beside me, a hand around her waist.

Reverend Peterson is on the other side, an open prayer book in his hands. He starts to speak, in a calm tone, "We have gathered here this morning to praise God and to witness to our faith as we celebrate the life of Caleb Mark Buccianti. We come together in grief, acknowledging our human loss. May God grant us grace, that in pain we may find comfort, in sorrow hope, in death resurrection."

The tears start stinging my eyes, watching Reverend Peterson make a sign of the cross over the casket, before he continues by saying the Lord's prayer, asking us to repeat it with him.

He makes his final blessing over the casket, committing Caleb to eternal life, before he looks up to Emilie and I stating, "Go in peace."

Glancing at Emilie, I notice she hasn't shed a tear, her cheeks dry. It seems odd—even though she'd told me she didn't love him—not shedding a single tear at his funeral seems callous. He's Ember's father and they have a past together, so surely she feels something for him and would be upset at having to say goodbye to him.

I try to piece together what I know about their relationship in my head from the past, but it still makes no sense to me. It's clear I need to ask her more about the past.

Pressing a kiss to her cheek, as the Reverend signals for us to say our last goodbyes I ask, "Emi are you ok? You haven't even cried?"

Sniffing she replies, "Yeah I'm ok. He was a great father, but there's no love lost for me."

"I don't get you," I reply, intrigued and confused.

"You know I never loved him and before we left the city I..." she starts to reply, stopping abruptly when a slight sob comes out.

"Don't tell me now Emi, later ok?" I soothe.

"Ok...um Quentin, thanks for being here with me."

"No worries," I reply when she stretches up to press a tender kiss to my lips.

"Emi, I need to tell you more about my past too, but um...."

"What? Are you ok?" she asks with a tone of concern.

"Yeah I just need a few moments alone to visit my Dad and Grandfather's graves. Is that ok?"

"Yeah take your time."

Putting Ember down on the ground, I kiss her forehead. "You ok sweetie?"

"Es Kent, I ok."

Smiling at her, taking a deep breath I walk to the other side of the cemetery where my family grave plots are.

At the graves I brush a finger over the lettering, reading the words I can still make out, focusing on the names firstly on my Grandfathers grave. The dates aren't visible but I know them anyway, as they will forever be etched in my memory.

Not much is visible on his grave, but his name *'Alexander Pierre Mackenney' is* still clear.

Seeing it makes my heartache, my own middle name the same as his and my nephew now having his first name as a middle name. It's almost too much to bare.

Looking at the gravestone through my tear stained eyes I notice something I've not looked at before.

Underneath where the dates are not visible anymore the other words written are,

'Beloved husband to Alice, Father to Isaak, Grandfather to R, Hunter & Quentin'

The 'r' name isn't completely visible as though someone has tried to erase it from the stone like I suspect has happened with the dates. Wondering I look over to my fathers grave, everything still clear to read on it.

Isaak Thomas Mackenney
Taken suddenly after illness
Born 23rd September 1943
Died 17th January 2015
Beloved husband to Grace, father to Hunter and Quentin

It seems strange there's no mention of the mysterious 'r' name on Dad's grave. My mind is trying to focus on the past, to find an explanation when Emilie walks up to stand beside me.
"Hey, are you ok, babe?" She asks.
I look at her, knowing a puzzled look is written all over my face.
"Um, yeah but I just seen something odd I've never noticed before,"I inform her, pointing at the two gravestones and showing her the absence of the r name on Dad's. She bends down, brushing a finger over the where the 'r' name is.
"I think it says Rudy," she declares, before asking, "did your Mum have a baby before?"
Shaking my head I reply, "Not that I know of, but it's not like I've ever asked her, or had a reason to ask her."
"Maybe it's time to talk to her about the past Quentin."
"I don't know Emi, it just hurts so much. Even just standing here brings it all rushing back."
She doesn't reply, instead envelops me in a warm hug. Ember squeezes in between our legs, giggling sweetly.
"I don't know what happened, but I can see how much its hurt you and I'm here for you Quentin. I'm here for you because I care about you."
"I know Emi, and I need you."

Unlawful Attachment

Again she kisses me tenderly, melting into me, her kiss so sweet I can't help but let out a moan, loving the feel of Emilie's sweet kiss on my lips.

I also can't help but think about how much I love kissing her like this as well, as opposed to when I'd kiss Samantha softly and all I wanted was more.

For me it only means one thing, and that is both scary and exciting.

Loving Emilie's sweet tender kisses means I'm falling in love with her.

Pulling back from the sweet kiss, I instead kiss her hair, trailing kisses over her ear before whispering, "Emi, I'm falling for you."

She looks up at me, her lips just a whisper away from mine. "Quentin I've..." I cut her words off with a soft kiss.

"Don't Emi, please, you don't have to tell me you feel the same if you don't."

She doesn't reply, kissing me again, a little harder than before but still so tenderly it makes my heart ache for her.

A thought crashes into my mind, a thought that even though I've said I'm falling for her, I'm actually already in love with her.

Pulling away from the kiss, I bend down grabbing Ember from between our legs and sliding her up my body to hold her against my hips. Emilie and I press a kiss to a cheek of hers each and she giggles when I declare, "Ember, sweet girl, I love you."

An adorable smile appears on her face before she replies, "I luv oo too Kent."

Emilie smiles wide, as do I at Ember's sweet declaration.

Putting her back down between us, we each take a hand, lifting her up off the ground as we walk back to the car. She swings her legs out in front of her, whooshing and squealing in delight.

It makes my heart ache more for a family of my own, and now more than anything I want that with Emilie.

I want her and Ember to be my family, but I'm still afraid that loving her won't be enough when she finds out more about my darker side and our past connection. Plus I'm also afraid of my own family's past, as she'll probably not want to be a part of my life when she actually finds out about the demons of that past that still haunt me.

The only thing I can hope for now is that love will be enough.

(37) Vladimir

Usually I'm not one to keep my office door open, it's a sanctuary from the rest of my club Bloom burlesque and prying eyes are never welcome.

Thankfully though today I've kept it open and Constable Alec Mathers is ushered inside with a flirtatious wave from my receptionist who knows better than and will need a good talking to and punishment later.

There's only one reason Alec has come into my office to talk, and I'm deviously excited to hear the news he has for me.

Phone calls are too risky, too easy to trace coming from the police station. He'd had to make one already for me and he'd been smart enough to use a burner phone.

As he struts up to my desk, sitting casually in the large tub chair in front, he puts one leg on his opposite knee and leans back, his arms together waiting for me to speak.

"Alec, did all go according to plan?"

"Yes, Vlad, Mackenney the fucking idiot gave it all up. Told me point blank there was a survivor."

"Great and he bought the story about investigating me for another matter?"

"Hook, line and sinker mate."

"Great, so phase two begins," I bellow, seeing Alec squirm in his chair at my menacing tone.

"You'll get your money Vlad, but do you really need to kill them?"

Scoffing I reply, "They wronged me Alec and you damn well know I'm not getting a cent from them unless they're dead!"

"I guess Vlad, but you know I might be corrupt, I still don't condone killing anyone."

"Fuck Alec, I'm not asking you to kill her!" I scream at him, a terrified look crossing his face. "I'm doing it myself!"

"I'll forget you said that Vlad."

"You fucking better Alec!"

He stands up, appearing a little scared of me. "Alright, I got to get back to the station, keep me posted and holler if you need anything."

"Will do," I spit back, hoping he'll make a hasty exit.

Thankfully he knows me well enough to shut the door behind him.

Immediately I fire up the computer, clicking the keyboard to search up the shit hole town of Ridgehope, hoping to find somewhere nearby I can lure Emilie to.

She has no chance anymore, she's going to die or she'll be back on stage performing as Vixen again.

Scrolling through the search results my mind wanders back to when I knew she was falling victim to the charm of the outside world.

The mystery man who had been constantly requesting Vixen had once again decided to grace my club with his presence.

He appeared to be heading down the hallways towards her dressing room, directly passing my office as he casually walked in like he owned the place.

Racing after him, I pulled him back into my office with a fistful of his jacket.

"What the fuck are you doing here?" I jeered menacingly at him, after kicking the door shut behind us.

"Coming to see my wife," he declared, as if I was supposed to know what he was talking about.

"Excuse me, your wife?"

"Yes, Emilie, my wife or you probably call her Vixen."

My anger was at boiling point, about to spill over.

"How dare you? You break all my rules, kiss her, fuck her, get her pregnant and marry her!" I seethed at him, balling my hands into fists, about to punch him when he responds.

"What are you talking about man? She's not pregnant!"

"Oh you poor thing, she didn't even tell you first. Some wife she is then," I taunted him.

"She probably wanted to surprise me."

"Yeah keep telling yourself that, but you aren't worth her time."

"God man, you're a fucking tool!"

"Don't cross me squirt! You'll regret taking my best girl away from me."

"Yeah we'll see about that mate," he spat at me, before turning towards the door in a hurry to get away from me.

The anger had risen even more at his utter insolence. I was seething; full of rage. There was only one thing to do and that was to punish Vixen, make the baby cease to exist, to make her feel the unbearable pain and in the meantime find a way to make her new husband wish he'd never met me. I was going to drag him through the hell of the Adelaide underworld, whilst the precious Emilie watched.

Slamming a fist against the keyboard, I curse thinking about how to get into contact with Emilie, knowing she most likely won't still have a mobile phone and all I know is that she's most definitely in Ridgehope. It's a small country town, so evidently people will talk and would know who she is.

There's really only one way forward, just like I'd said to Alec.

I have to do this myself.

It's devious, but it's perfect.

Rubbing my hands together, I laugh manically thinking about how wicked my plan is and I'm hoping like hell it will work in my favour.

It's time for the Buccianti's to pay with blood.

(38) Hunter

Things have been a little hectic in our lives, making me feel as though I'm running on empty. Savannah is barely able to move, her belly enormous with the twins growing furiously.

I've spent barely a night at home—out droving—bringing the cattle closer towards the main farm paddocks near the barn. The prospect of having to bring in feed is plaguing my mind, as we've barely had a drop of rain in the last few years and the long range forecast doesn't give a reprieve to the drought on the horizon either.

Not only am I worrying about that, but also about Quentin.

He's barely spoken to me in the last couple of months since Addison's wedding and his shock confession to me about being involved in some darker desires. Feeling a little naive I'd googled 'BDSM' and nearly fell off my chair at what graced my screen. I can't believe anyone would want to do that kind of thing, let alone my younger brother.

So with worry plaguing my mind, I don't even want to answer my phone when it rings multiple times with an unknown number.

The unknown caller doesn't leave a voicemail so when they try calling a fourth time I pickup.

"Hello, Hunter speaking."

"Oh, thank god you answered Hunter."

"I'm sorry, who is this?"

"Sorry Hunter, it's Martha from the rest home."

My heart sinks, hoping something bad hasn't happened to Mum, as with everything going on I've not taken the time out to visit her.

"Is Mum ok?" I ask.

"Well, um yes and no Hunter."

"Is she ill?"

"No, she's not ill but has taken a turn in her mental health that has us worried."

I don't need anymore worry. "I'm sorry, what do you mean exactly?"
"She has been sobbing uncontrollably, constantly saying, 'home home'."
"Thats worrying and not like Mum at all. Is there anything you can do to help her?"
"We were hoping she could stay with you for awhile?"
"I'm not sure, I have a lot on my plate at the moment."
"Hunter, I really think your Mum needs to be with family. She was so much better when she had those few days with you all before River was born."
"Ok, Martha, I'll speak to Quentin and we will sort something out."
"Thanks Hunter, I really think it's for the best."
"Yeah, I'll be in touch."
Hanging up I think for a moment about Martha's words, about how Mum was better when she was at Savannah's baby shower and even how she was at our wedding. She'd never seemed happier and I know Martha is right.
Fear is plaguing me though, as Mum wanting to come home only means one thing. It's time to face the past.

Dialling Quentin's number I don't even wait for his hello or say hello myself, instead I blurt out, "Brother, it's time."
"Time for what, Hunter?" he enquires, probably thinking the twins are on their way.
"To go back into the old farmhouse."
"Why? You know the memories of that day still haunt me Hunter," he utters, fear in his voice.
"I know little brother but Mum has had a turn and the rest home thinks it's best if she comes back here for awhile."
"But can't she stay in the main house? With you?" he asks, like it's the most obvious answer.
"I'd love that but with the twins practically here, River will need another room. We just don't have the space."
"I guess but fuck Hunter I don't know if I can step foot in there."

"I know but we have to face the past sometime."

"I guess...so what's the plan?"

"Can you come over on Sunday for dinner, maybe early arvo?"

"Yeah ok I guess...um Hunter can I..."

"What?"

"Can I invite Emilie and Ember?"

"Of course...is there something going on between you?"

"To be honest I don't know...kind of....but I'll um...I'll tell you on Sunday."

"Ok, little brother. See you on Sunday," I reply, hanging up.

I feel like the worst big brother ever, knowing what I'm asking of him. He knows more about that day than I do, and the thought of it brings me to tears. I can't even begin to imagine how it effected my younger brother. I can only hope that going into the old farmhouse will possibly bring him some closure, some peace that he couldn't have done anything to save our grandfathers life.

It was surely a tragic accident, one that we need to find the truth out about for our family's sake moving forward.

(39) Emilie

Knocking on Quentin's door I feel a little nervous. In the last months that I've been in Ridgehope the only time I've been to his house was when I'd turned up on his doorstep unannounced, clutching a thank you bottle of whiskey.

I laugh thinking back, wondering why I'd brought whiskey, not even knowing if he even drank it. This time, hoping it's a better option I've brought a cheap bottle of white wine.

The good thing about Ridgehope is not needing a car, as most of the houses are within a twenty minute walk from the town main street and it's flat land, with no hills to be found.

Opening the door to Ember and I, he looks as always, deliciously handsome.

His bare feet poking out of his black, three striped adidas trackies that sit low across his hips, with a black t-shirt that rises up his torso when he leans against the door, exposing the inviting 'v' leading to below the waistband of his trackies.

He'd as always not shaved for a few days, and he's sporting a dark beard, a little more than his usual five o'clock shadow. If it's even possible it makes him look even more handsome, and I swallow hard taking him in slowly. I still can't work out why he gets to me so much, but he does and I'm a goner.

"Hey Emi," he muses, looking me up and down with a devilish smirk like he's undressing me with his dreamy chocolate eyes.

"Hey babe," I tease.

"Babe is it?" He laughs.

I smile in response when he says, 'hello' to Ember.

"Kent, I play with cat," she states, brushing past my legs towards Quentin.

He bends down to her level. "Yes, Ember, you can play with Tiberius, if you can find him."

"Is cat lost?"

"No sweetie, he's probably just found a comfy place to sleep."

"Ok I ind im," she tells him, running into the house, calling out , *'cat, cat'.*

Quentin stands up, grabbing me around the waist and smashing a kiss to my lips.

"Fuck Emi, I've missed you."

"I've missed you to babe," I tease him again, stepping inside and pushing the door closed behind me.

"Go make yourself comfy in the lounge, I'll be in the kitchen finishing up the food," he instructs me, taking the bottle of wine from my fist.

"Ok, babe, " I reply, kissing his cheek.

From the couch I can see him at the stove in the kitchen.

For a moment he seems happier than ever, until his phone appears to ring and he answers it. I can't make out what he's saying and have no inclination of who he's talking to.

The smile he'd had on his face when I arrived disappears, a frown replacing it.

Putting his phone down, his body constricts, pain evident, and it looks like he's about to collapse to the floor in agony.

Without thinking I rush over, pulling him against my body in a tight hug. I think I hear him sobbing, but when I pull back a moment later he doesn't feel as tense and his cheeks are dry.

"What's going on? Is everything ok?" I ask, not sure if my question even registers in his mind, because he looks like he's a world away.

"Yeah, yeah everything's fine but..."

"But what Quentin? Something about that phone call has shaken you."

Sighing he replies, "My Mum is...is coming home."

"That's great isn't it?" I ask, completely confused, but trying to hopefully sound supportive.

"No, because Hunter wants me..." He gulps, swallowing his words.

"What? He wants you to what?"

"Go. Back. Into. The old...farmhouse."

"Why is that a bad thing?" I ask, even more confused.

"Because that's..." he stammers, tears now breaking free. "That's where it happened," he whimpers, emphasising, *'it'*.

"What Quentin? What happened?" I plead.

"Where I saw my grandfather..." He pauses, taking in a deep breath, struggling to continue his reply, "shot...right...in...front of me."

My heart lurches in my chest, hoping I hadn't actually heard the words right.

"Oh my God, Quentin!" I cry out, heartbroken for him. "I...I...I'm so sorry."

Time stops, he doesn't respond, instead just looks at me, the obvious pain and heartbreak in his eyes.

Without warning, he kisses me, fiercely. His kiss is hard, demanding and forceful, parting my lips by biting down on my bottom lip and taking my tongue with his, making our mouths one.

Moaning into my mouth, he suddenly pulls back from the kiss that has me shaken, but seriously turned on.

"I'm sorry Emi, I shouldn't have kissed you like that," he apologises.

"Why?"

"When I think about it, that day...I don't know...I can't explain it."

"You don't need to," I say comforting him.

"I'm going to hurt you Emilie. You should just leave and stay away from me."

His words stab at my heart, but I don't respond, waiting for him to continue speaking.

"There's no reason for you to stay in Ridgehope," he informs me.

But he's wrong, because there's a reason to stay in Ridgehope.

A six foot two reason standing right in front of me.

"Yes, there is, I'm staying in Ridgehope for you Quentin. I'm falling in love with you and nothing you do or say will change the way I feel."

A small smile dimples the corner of his mouth. "Oh Emi, you're amazing!"

Again he kisses me, more tenderly than before, as though my declaration has softened his heart a little and helped him block out the horror of his past.

Pulling away he asks, "Will you come out to Hunter's farm with me on Sunday?"

"Is that where the other house is?"

"Yes...and he wants me to go in to face the past."

"Are you going to be okay doing that?"

"I don't know, but he's right. It's time to face the past," he replies unconvincingly.

"Well, of course I'll be there," I say, replying to his earlier question, "and I'm sure Ember won't mind seeing River again."

"Yeah, she'll love that, and you'll get to meet them too."

"I hope they'll like me."

"Emi, they'll love you, especially when they see how much I care about you both."

"Thanks, so is it possible to order a pizza here?"

"Yeah, sounds good. I'll call the general store. Burnt spaghetti isn't very appetising."

"No, and it's getting late."

"Yeah, I think we need an early night."

"Are you going to be ok?" I ask him smiling.

"Yeah...but I might need you to hold me close again. Can you guys stay the night here?"

"Yeah, of course."

He presses a soft tender kiss to my lips, before grabbing his phone off the bench to order the pizza.

Wandering down the hallway I find Ember asleep on Quentin's bed, looking so sweet on the black satin sheets in disarray.

Standing in the door, I smile at her, gazing around the room, rubbing my eyes, hoping I'm seeing things when they focus on the hooks hanging down from the ceiling.

Also at the corners of each post of his rather inviting looking four poster bed are rings with black ropes.

Unlawful Attachment

My heart pounds and constricts, when I curiously enter the room, drawn to the cupboard in the corner.

Opening it, my eyes boggle and Quentin's words about hurting me crash back into my mind.

Closing it, my head snaps back to the doorway to find Quentin standing in the door jamb.

"Emi, say something please."

"Is...is this...what you meant by you'll hurt me?"

He enters the room, his presence seeming more dominating than before.

"Yes Emilie, and it's why..."

"Don't please, Quentin."

"But Emilie, I...I can't do this...with you...but..."

"You want to?"

"More than anything Emi, but at the same time if I had to give this up to be with you, I would."

Stepping closer to him I reply, "You don't have to. I meant what I said earlier."

"Really? But your past?"

"Was horrible yes...and involved some of the very things in this room, but that was never about pleasure."

"Oh Emi," he muses, brushing his palm across my cheek.

"I trust you, and..."

"What Emi?"

"Promise me that if..." I pause.

Am I really going to say this? Suggest that we have sex? Emilie, what's gotten into you girl.

"If what Emi?"

"That our first time together won't be like this."

"Oh Emilie, if I bring you into this bedroom you'll only experience pleasure, and the first time we're together definitely won't be in here I promise."

His eyes lock on mine, begging me almost for more, and my heart is pounding hard in my chest. Even with the thought of Quentin possessing the same dark desires I'd experienced in my past I've never felt more comfortable. I know there are only three words I can say to him in that moment.

"I love you, Quentin."
He gapes at me. "What? Emi, did you just say...?"
"Yes, Quentin, I love you."
"Oh Emi, god...I..." he says, not able to say the words back, instead he presses a tender kiss to my lips, a kiss that tells me he feels the same, but can't say the words just yet.

(40) Quentin

"Quentin, darling, you need to stay inside," my Mum's voice called out from the laundry.

"I am, Mum!" I called back, rounding the corner of the hallway pushing my toy car along the floorboards.

'Vroom, Vroom'

At the entrance to the kitchen I stopped in my tracks, an unfamiliar figure was standing in the kitchen pointing a gun towards my grandfather's head.

Opening my mouth to scream out to my mum, the words were muted, only a whisper escaping.

"Isaak," the unfamiliar person taunted, the rest of his words not making sense in my mind.

He edged closer to my grandfather. I wanted to scream out that he wasn't Isaak, but the man had a gun. I wanted to scream out to my Mum again, but my feet where glued to the floor and my mouth dry, only raspy gasps escaping.

Time had stopped, there was no sound in the room.

Until the sound of the shot rang out.

"No, No, don't...." I scream out, reaching out to get closer to the unfamiliar figure.

Feeling a world away, my eyes will not open, as though they're glued together, not able to face the horror I can see.

A sweet voice is filling my head. "Babe, wake up."

My body is being shaken lightly, warm, soft hands resting on my torso.

"Quentin, open your eyes, you're safe," the sweet voice coos.

Slowly, I force my eyes to open, blinking furiously to focus on the figure next to me.

"Hey, are you ok, babe?"

I look at her, my eyes locking onto her, feeling a sense of calm rush over me.

"Oh god, Emi, I...I.."

"What babe? A nightmare?"

"I...I...should have done something..."

"What do you mean?"

"That day...I was right there...I should have..."

"Stop Quentin, stop, you can't change the past."

"But Emi...I was there..."

"I know...but you were a little boy, there's nothing you could have done."

"I guess..."

"There wasn't Quentin, please don't ever think that."

"It was different this time Emi."

"I don't understand."

"The nightmare...it was different."

"How so?"

"I haven't had one for a long time...but usually I don't recall anything the man said..."

"And you did this time?"

"Yes...he said, 'Isaak'."

"Your father's name yeah?"

Unlawful Attachment

"Yeah, but it wasn't my father who got shot. It was my grandfather Alexander."

"Hmm...that's interesting. Do you think he didn't mean to shoot your grandfather?"

"I honestly don't know...but Emi, I really don't want to go back in that house on Sunday."

"I know, but if thinking about it has brought on a nightmare and you've remembered something that you hadn't before, maybe it's good timing and it might bring you some closure."

"I hope so. Emi, I'm really glad you're coming there with me."

"I told you Quentin, I love you and I'm here for you."

"I know, thank you, now come here, I need to forget and just feel."

She edges closer to me, running her hands up and down my bare chest, warming my skin and making my desire begin to peak.

"Kiss me Emi," I groan.

Her kiss against my lips is tender, loving and consuming. Entangling my legs with hers, wrapping my arms around her waist I pull her as close as possible against my body, so she can feel the desire in my pants.

"God, Emi, I seriously want to fuck you right now."

"I...I..."

"Emi, I know...but please can you touch me?"

She pouts, before a devious smirk appears on her face when she plunges a hand beneath the waistband of my trackies, grabbing my arousal in her hand. I silently thank myself for going commando.

"You like that?" she teases.

I moan, her hand running up and down my length. Her fingers splay across my sensitive skin, tickling me and driving me higher.

"God, Emi, you're going to be my undoing," I taunt.

"I'm only touching you, babe," she teases, smacking a hard kiss to my lips, whilst she continues her delicious torture in my pants.

Biting down on my lips, she grips my dick harder, spurring my hot climax.

Breaking the kiss, she pulls her hand out of my pants.

"I guess you liked that," she states, questionably.

"No Emi, I loved it....I Ill..." I affirm, before stuttering on verbalising my feelings.

Instead, I kiss her, taking her mouth as mine in thanks.

"I can't wait to watch you come for me, Emi," I admit, smiling.

"Not yet...I can't yet," she divulges.

"Emi, don't apologise. I want to be with you more than anything."

"I know, I love you," she responds, sending my heart pounding.

I open my mouth to reply, but only a whimper comes out.

I feel horrible that I can't say the words she wants to hear back, even though I feel exactly the same way.

Pressing a kiss to her forehead, I reply, "I know Emi, I'm just going to get cleaned up. Go back to sleep."

Climbing out of bed to head into the ensuite for a quick shower, I watch her roll over, stretching her luscious legs out. She moans, closing her eyes when I shut the bathroom door behind me.

Even though she'd just brought me to release my dick is straining, happy to be free of my pants that I drop to the floor.

Standing under the water, I bring myself to climax again, thinking about making Emilie mine completely and telling her I love her too.

(41) Emilie

Panicking I wake up, realising I'm in Quentin's bed and not my own.
My thoughts wander back to the night before, thinking about his other
bedroom.
Gazing around this bedroom as the light pours in through the crack in
the blind is such a contrast to that room.
I'm glad he doesn't actually sleep in that room all the time, as my body
and mind wouldn't be able to handle how that would make me feel,
like I'd always have to be ready for pleasure at any moment.

He's still asleep beside me, thankfully after his earlier nightmare and
my comforting presence he'd slept through. He looks so peaceful, and
not wanting to wake him I push back the cotton sheets, climbing out
and sneaking down the hallway to the guest room, where I wake
Ember.
She clutches my hand, not questioning why I'm abruptly waking her
and follows me down the hallway to the kitchen.
There's a discarded, open envelope on the bench, so grabbing a pen
from the collection at the end of the island bench I write Quentin a
note.
Pondering what to write I look around his house more, taking in the
neatness of it, but also loving how random things like pens and glasses
seem to be scattered everywhere as though they have no place to be.
Quickly, I jot down some words.

'Hope you're ok. See you on Sunday. I love you, Quentin.'

Putting the pen down, I pick Ember up, holding her against my hip.
She snuggles into my chest when we walk out.

For some reason, the thought of wanting to have a phone pops into my mind. I really want to send Quentin a naughty selfie of me, because Sunday seems so far away.

Closing the door behind me, the warm morning sun hits my face and wakes me up more. Ember yawns, and appears to wake up a little more than she was when the sun hits her too.

I put her down and we start to walk towards town. I'm not quite ready to go home yet, especially as it seems like it's going to be a nice day.

"Did you find Tiberius last night?" I ask Ember, as she happily walks beside me.

"No Mummy, he play hidey."

"That's no good sweetie."

"Mummy where we oing?"

"Mummy needs to get a phone sweetie."

We walk in silence for the next fifteen minutes, and once in town the main strip of shops doesn't appear to have any place that sells phones. My heart sinks a little, because I'm really feeling lost without one. Reaching the end of the main street, I sigh, about to go home when a police car drives past, triggering a thought in my mind.

The police station is a little bit longer walk and not far from my house. I feel kind of stupid for not thinking of it earlier.

Pushing the double glass doors open, I sit Ember down on the chairs inside the door and thankfully I can see her when I step up to the desk.

"Hi I'm Emilie Buccianti," I state, politely.

"Hi Ms, how can I help you?"

"I was um...involved in that car accident...and I was hoping they got some of my personal effects from the wreckage."

"I believe Constable Mackenney was in charge of that investigation. Has he been in touch with you?" she asks.

I feel a blush rise up my cheeks, her words, *'has he been in touch with you'* meaning something different to me.

Unlawful Attachment

"Um, no he hasn't," I lie, hoping she hadn't seen my obvious blush at her mention of Quentin.

"Well, um, he's not in today but I can check with the Sergeant if you'd like?"

"Yes, thanks that would be great."

She walks off somewhere in the station, before returning a few moments later with an unsealed cardboard box.

"This was in the main part of the car. It's all I have access to at the moment. Would you like Constable Mackenney to give you a call on Monday?"

Shaking my head, I take the box from her and reply, "No thanks, I'm sure he'll contact me if he needs to."

"Ok Miss, have a good day."

Nodding a reply, I shift the box to hold it under my arm and take Ember's hand with my other hand when she jumps off the seat.

Again we walk home in silence, my thoughts racing with what might pop up on my phone when I turn it on, if it's in the box.

Reaching my house, I let myself in, dumping the box on the bench. Ember runs to her room without a word. I'm thankful she's independent most of the time, because now I definitely need some space to deal with all the thoughts in my head.

Sitting in the middle of the box, open so its contents are spilling over the edge is my 'Guess' handbag; the black one I loved that Caleb had brought me for my last birthday. Right on top of it is my phone, and lying next to the bag is my charge cable. I have to fish through my bag for the duck head to plug it in.

When I find it and plug it into the wall my nervousness begins to rise. There's surely going to be messages and missed calls from my family. I'm not sure if I want to face them.

It buzzes when it turns on, searching for signal a few moments later, and then the notifications start popping up on the screen like crazy. The first one that catches my eye is from my older brother.

Bro: Em! Where are you? We're beside ourselves! Call me!
Bro: Em, call me! Are you ok?
Bro: Em! Wtf! Pls call me!
Bro: EM!

Closing the messages I click into the call log to find a hundred missed calls from my brother. Not really wanting to talk, or have him try to trace the signal if I do I send him a text.

Emilie: Sorry Alec. I'm ok. I'm safe, but Caleb isn't.
Bro: Oh my god Em! Seriously!

I'm about to reply again, when his picture flashes up on my screen. Hesitantly I answer.

"Hey Alec."
"Em, oh my god, we thought you were dead."
"I'm sorry Al, I should have called."
"Damn right you should have Em. It's been like four months."
"I know, but I just got my phone back."
He laughs. "Trust you to not have my number memorised."
"Sorry Al, but I'm ok."
"What about Ember and Caleb?"
I sniff, before replying, "Ember's fine but Caleb, um...he died at the scene."
"What Emilie? You had an accident? Are you ok? Where are you?"
I think for a moment, trying to process a coherent answer to his multitude of questions.
"Yeah we did and yeah I'm ok...better than ok actually but I can't tell you where I am."
"I just want to make sure you're safe."
"I am Al. The local cop is..." He cut me off.

"Em, don't get me started. I can't protect you if I don't know where you are."

"Just stop Al, I'm ok. I'll call again soon. Bye."

I hang up before he can get another word in, hoping he won't call back and push the issue of finding out where I am.

Something doesn't seem right in his tone, because he'd known part of the reason why I left the city. It seems strange that he's so intent on knowing where I am but hasn't come looking for me.

A loud pounding breaks my thoughts, and Quentin knocks on the door barging in like an angry elephant when I don't respond.

As soon as he sees me he calms a little.

"Oh my god Emi, when I woke up and you weren't beside me I thought something bad happened to you."

"Sorry, I left you a note on the bench."

"I didn't see it."

"That's ok, no need to worry, I'm ok."

"You don't look ok. Has something happened?"

Nodding I reply, "I um...went to the police station and got my phone back."

"And?"

"My brother just called."

Handing my phone to him, I point to the messages from my brother.

As he scrolls through them, seeing my reply his eyes darken in shock.

"What's your brothers last name? Your maiden name?"

Confused I reply, "Mathers, why?"

"Is he a cop?"

"Yeah, why?" I ask, confused and worried about his probing questions.

"He called me about your accident."

"You expect me to believe that? He knew nothing about it until I just told him."

"Are you sure about that?"

"Yes, Quentin, it's my brother we're talking about!" I snap at him angrily.

"Well, I'm not so sure, but believe me Emilie I don't think Ridgehope is the safest place for you right now."

"I'm not going anywhere. I'm staying here with you."

He doesn't reply, instead hugs me for a moment, his body melting against mine, as though he's never going to hold me again.

Pulling back from the hug, his words confuse me more. "I need to go to the station for something but I'll pick you up on Sunday at three."

"Ok, are we ok? Isn't it your day off?"

"We're better than ok Emi and yes it is but I just want to speak to Sarge about something in person."

"Ok should I give you my number?"

He shakes his head at me. "No, take out the sim and I'll bring you a new one on Sunday."

"Why? That seems a bit extreme."

"Trust me Emilie."

"I do...I love you."

Softly he presses a kiss to my forehead. "Good, so trust me on this."

As he turns to leave, I sigh, feeling a deep ache in my heart.

Before putting my phone down I turn it off.

His distrust of my older brother seems peculiar and I can't help but wonder if they are both hiding something from me.

(42) Quentin

Tooting the horn of the car, I wait for Emilie and Ember to come outside. My nerves are already on edge just thinking about seeing the house, let alone actually setting foot on the doorstep of the house and going inside.
The fact I'd had a nightmare about it again, remembering some of his words had really shaken me. Emilie's behaviour and her talking to her brother hasn't helped the situation and my uneasy feeling that our world is about to be shattered.

Putting Ember in the backseat—buckling her in—Emilie then slides into the front passenger seat, sighing loudly when she looks over at me.
"Hey, are you ok?" she asks, touching my hand.
"Yeah, kinda, just um...just nervous."
"I know, but it will be ok."

Starting the engine again, I reach into my pocket to hand her the new sim card.
"Here, put this in your phone. The number's on the back of the card."
"Thanks, but I really don't think it's necessary."
"Please Emi, just trust me."
"I do trust you, but if I change my number my brother and Mum won't be able to contact me."
"Exactly, something is off about your brother."
"How can you say that? Alec's always been there for me."
"You're not making much sense Emi."
She huffs, crossing her arms and turning away from me to stare out the window.
"Emi, I'm sorry. I might be jumping to conclusions, but I just feel uneasy."

"I know, I'm sorry too."

She smiles at me then, melting my heart a little. I can't say I'm not worried, but I have to keep my panic about her brother in check and focus on facing the past.

❧

Arriving at the farm, the Kingswood's engine rumbles like it's saying, 'hello' to the house. I feel guilty because I rarely drove out to the farm anymore, and at times feel like I'm drifting away from my older brother. Part of me knows that I should make more effort, especially now River is in our lives.

When we pull up in front of the new farmhouse, Hunter is waiting on the verandah. He waves at me, but looks nervous as well.

Getting out I don't say a word to Emilie, my heart pounding in my chest at what I'm about to face.

Stepping up to Hunter, he pulls me into a hug, sensing my unease.

I can feel Emilie and Ember stepping up behind me.

"Hey, Quentin."

"Hi Hunter, this is Emilie and Ember," I politely say, even though I just want to get everything over with.

Hunter reaches out to hug Emilie. "Hi Emilie, nice to meet you."

"You to Hunter," she replies, excepting his hug.

Hunter bends down to Ember. "Hi Ember, would you like to see River?"

"Es please."

"Do you want me to go with you inside the house Quentin?" Hunter asks.

"No, I need to go myself first."

"Ok, are you sure?"

"Yes, I just need a few minutes," I respond, trying to not sound like I'm terrified.

"Ok, I'll take Emilie and Ember inside. Come in when you're ready, but dinner won't be long."

Unlawful Attachment

Watching them walk away I take a deep breath, telling my feet to just move, to get it over with and face the past.

It's only about five hundred metres to the old house, but the walk seems forever, each step I take slower than the last.

Reaching the front door, I push it hard. It's unlocked, but weather worn and creaks hard, the wood cracking a little.

Once inside the musty smell is overwhelming, having been locked up for years with no ventilation. It feels like we've never left as the same furniture is still around the kitchen, extremely dusty from years of neglect.

Again taking a deep breath, I head down the hallway towards my old bedroom, tripping over my toy car on the way. Picking it up, the memories hit hard, the tears breaking through and cascading down my cheeks.

Hearing the gun shot, my feet finally cooperated, lurching me forward as I screamed out a bizarre combination of 'No' and an actual scream.

The unfamiliar man turned to look at me, a strange evil in his eyes, before he quickly left without saying another word.

Mum came rushing into the room, not looking at him, screaming out 'Alexander'.

My grandfather had fallen back on the chair, crashing to the ground as the bullet hit his forehead. Blood had spattered towards me, splattering over the front of my shirt.

I shake the thoughts from my head, hearing Emilie calling my name, "Quentin, Quentin, where are you?"

In the hallway near the kitchen, she stops dead when she looks at me —my cheeks tear stained—leaning against the wall.

"Are you ok Quentin?"

"No, it's just..." I sob, feeling the emotion overwhelm me looking at her. "It's just..fuck it, it hurts Emi."

"What, what hurts?"

"Being in here. Seeing it all again like it was yesterday. It hurts my heart."

"What else happened Quentin? Did you get hurt that day to? You can tell me."

"No, I didn't, and no I can't tell you, because I don't honestly remember."

She steps closer to me, nearer to the arch into the kitchen, pulling me into a tight hug that I find myself melting into; her body so close to mine. "I'm here Quentin, for you, please tell me."

"Oh fuck, Emilie I can't..."

She gives me a lustful look, as though she can tell my sense of control is waning.

"Please Quentin...do what you need to do," she drawls at me, a slight smirk on her lips.

Growling I push her against the wall kissing her hard, hungrily and lustfully. Turning the kiss carnal by biting her lips to urge her to open her mouth. She moans furthering the kiss, taking full control of the most passionate kiss we've shared by biting my tongue, fighting for dominance.

Completely breathless, and satisfied I break the kiss.

"Oh fuck Emilie that was...fuck..."

A sneaky smile appears on her face and I fist my hands together, not knowing what to do with them.

"God Emilie I want to..."

"What Quentin?" she taunts.

"Fuck you so bad right now..."

"Hmmm really?" she muses, teasing me.

"Please Emilie don't tempt me," I drawl at her, gasping when she grabs my dick in her palm.

"Why not?"

"Because you have no idea what I want to do to you."

"If that kiss was just a tease, after seeing your black room the other day, then I have some idea."

Unlawful Attachment

"Not here...not yet but damn Emilie I'm gonna have you begging soon," I taunt her, my voice cracking as desire courses through my body.

"Hmmm sounds wicked," she teases.

"Oh fuck yeah," I reply in a teasing tone.

Grabbing her cheeks in my palms I kiss her hard again, taking control of the kiss until she pulls back to whisper in my ear, "You can touch me anywhere."

Without letting me process her words, she wraps an arm around my neck to pull my lips to hers again.

I run my hand over her hips, up across the sensitive skin of her stomach that makes her gasp at the callousness of my touch.

My hands then continue moving up to her breasts, delighting in the fact she's not wearing a bra under her t-shirt.

As we continue kissing, not wanting to move apart, I tease the sensitive buds, making them rise to attention. Her moans increase, making my desire rise as I slowly grind against her, our kiss hungry and consuming.

I hear Hunter coming in, calling out, "Hey guys dinners ready."

Reluctantly we pull apart, and I chuckle a little whispering in Emilie's ear, "I hope he didn't see us dry humping, just then."

Emilie laughs, blushing when Hunter appears in the hallway.

"You ok Quentin?" he asks in an odd tone that makes me not sure about what he's implying.

"Yeah, I'm fine...was just, um about to head back over for dinner when Emilie came in."

"Hmmm yeah ok," he replies like he doesn't believe me. "Well, it's getting cold."

He gives me a knowing smirk, as though he knows what Emilie and I were really up to.

Looking at Emilie myself I see her lips are red from kissing me and she blushes crimson when we follow Hunter back to the new farmhouse.

My hand brushes against hers and I lace our fingers together, holding her hand tight for a moment before lifting it to my lips to kiss the back. Leaning into her side I whisper in her ear, "Thank you for that back there. I needed that so bad."
She smiles at me when we step onto the porch and again I whisper into her ear, "I need you Emilie."
Pressing a kiss to my cheek, she replies, "You don't have to thank me for needing me, Quentin. I love you."
"I...I..."

Why can't I just tell her how I fucking feel?

She cuts me off, pressing a soft kiss to my lips.
Being with her is going to be my undoing, as without a doubt I'm in love with her.
I'm just afraid to tell her, because something is not right about her past and I feel as though once I tell her how I feel, our relationship will come crashing down when I lose control.

(43) Savannah

Pottering around the kitchen with my large belly in the way is a challenge. Being seven months pregnant with twins is making me feel like an elephant.

Quentin walks in, his hand laced with Emilie's.

I let out a squeal of delight. "I'm guessing you two are together then?"

"Yes, Savannah, we are," he replies, smiling wide.

"I'm really happy for you Quentin, you seem like a sweetie Emilie."

"Thanks, Savannah. I was so nervous about meeting you," she admits, smiling at me.

"Aww, Emilie," I reply, feeling a blush rise up my cheeks.

"Can I help you with anything?" she asks sweetly, letting go of Quentin's hand to walk further into the kitchen past the dining table.

"Yeah, that would be great. Hunter's getting some drinks from the shed, and I could do with some help serving up the food."

"No problems," she replies, elbowing Quentin in the side when he moves to stand beside her. "You didn't tell me she was pregnant, babe."

"Didn't come up, I guess," he replies sheepishly and I stifle a laugh at her calling him babe.

"Fair enough, go help your brother," she instructs him.

"Yes, boss." He winks at her, walking out and leaving us both in the kitchen.

At the bench, she looks me up and down, a little unsure of what to say. Slicing the roast meat, I break the silence, "I'm really glad he's found you, Emilie."

"Yeah?" she responds questionably.

"He's a great guy and Addison broke his heart big time."

"Addison?" she asks, confused. "I thought he was with a girl called Sam before?"

"He was for a bit, but he'd been in love with Addison since they were kids. And her marrying Zane really got to him."

"Yeah I get that. I don't plan on breaking his heart."

"I know, but just tread carefully."

"I will," she replies, blushing deep crimson.

"You're already in love with him aren't you?"

"Yes, absolutely," she confesses, her blush deepening when she smiles.

"Have you told him?"

"Yes, but he hasn't said it back."

"Trust me Emilie, the fact that he's brought you here and shared some of his past with you, he's definitely got it bad for you. Just give him time."

"Yeah I will. Thanks Savannah...so when are you due?"

"Two months."

"What? Two months?"

"Yeah I'm having twins."

"Oh my god, thats amazing!"

"Yeah, we can't wait. Speaking of kids, Ember is a cutie."

"Yeah, she definitely is." She laughs.

"I'll go get her and River for dinner if you don't mind putting the plates on the table?"

"Sure," she replies, grabbing a couple plates in her hands when I waddle down the hallway to River's room.

Stopping in the doorway I smile at them, playing cars on his racetrack rug.

"River, sweetie, it's time for dinner. Can you help Ember wash up please?"

"Yes, Mummy, I elp her," he replies sweetly.

"Good boy," I praise him, laughing when he stands up taking Ember's hand to lead her to the bathroom.

He starts skipping down the hallway, Ember mimicking him, eagerly following him and giggling.

In my stomach, the babies kick hard, making my breath hitch and a chuckle escapes my lips when I head back to the kitchen. It makes me so happy seeing River with Ember, knowing in my heart that he's going to be the sweetest big brother.

(44) Hunter

Quentin walks into the shed, a spring in his step that I've not seen him exhibit for a long time. Standing up from grabbing the drinks out of the spare fridge I look up at him when he asks, "Need some help Hunter?"
"Yeah thanks Quentin," I reply, handing him some lemonade to put into the milk crate at his feet.
"Are you ok little brother?" I ask him, a little confused by his happiness but silence.
"Yeah, nah, I don't know Hunt," he replies confirming his confusion.
He runs a hand through his hair in an effort to calm himself.
"I shouldn't have asked you to go in there."
"I needed to Hunter, its actually helped me remember some details."
"Yeah like what?"
"That he said, 'Isaak' and was yelling at him accusingly."
"So you think he was after Dad instead?"
"I don't know, seems like it. Do you know who he was?"
"Yeah, Addison's grandfather," I divulge.
"What the fuck Hunter? How did I not know this?"
"Mum and Dad kinda shielded you from everything after what you saw."
He curses under his breath, again running a hand through his hair.
"Why do you think the Yorke's moved away," I reason, realising it sounds like a question after I've said it.
"Fuck, I can't believe it! Does Addison know?"
"As much as I do yeah, but none of us, not even Mum knows the real reason he killed him."
"Yeah, god, I can't believe it," he muses, shaking his head.
"Me either and with Dad gone, after what you've just told me; maybe we'll never know."
"Yeah so um..." he says, biting his lip nervously.

"What little brother?"

"What do you think of Emilie?"

"She's gorgeous Quentin and obviously smitten with you."

"Yeah, she told me she loves me," he confesses.

"Have you said it back?"

"No, I can't," he snaps.

"Why? Is this a repeat of the Sam drama again?"

"Fuck no brother, I'm in love with Emilie, bad, but I just can't bring myself to tell her."

"Why? I don't understand Quentin."

"I'm scared, that when I share the darker desires of my past with her, she'll go running just like Sam did."

"Quentin, I don't think that will happen this time."

"Why? How do you know that?"

"She seems a lot more mature for one thing and..." I stop mid sentence, feeling the blush rise up my cheeks.

"You saw us before yeah?"

"Yeah little brother, I'm scarred for life." I laugh.

"Sorry about that. How do you know she still won't leave?"

"I don't, but the fact that you've clearly fallen for her too has to mean something Quentin."

"Yeah true...um Hunter?"

"Yeah?"

"I've met her before, back in Adelaide when I was at the academy."

"Really? Are you sure?"

"Yeah, definitely. She worked in the...um...the um...gentleman's club I went to and her boss used to..." He stops, the words he wants to say caught on his tongue.

I nod. "I get you...so that's why you're afraid to show her your darker side?"

"Yeah I don't want her to go through that," he admits, hanging his head low.

My heart aches for him. It's clear he loves her. I reach out to hug him for a moment.

"Little brother, when your heart is on the line, you have to take the risk."

"But I can't lose her a second time; I should have gone after her then."

"Maybe, but you've been given a second chance, so take it. You deserve to be happy and I think this time it might be your turn."

"I really hope so. Thanks Hunter. I love you so fucking much, big brother."

He reaches out to bro hug me, pulling me into his side and patting me on the back. Patting his back as well, I exclaim, "Right back at ya, little brother. Let's get these drinks inside huh?"

He nods, picking up the crate of lemonade when I pick up the crate of beer and wine.

Walking back into the farmhouse a few minutes later, we find the girls and kids sitting at the table with their plates in front of them.

"We thought you got lost," Savannah jokes.

"Nah, just having a man to man chat," I reply, winking at Emilie.

"Ok well, dig in! I didn't slave away in the kitchen all day for all this food to waste," Savannah says with a laugh whilst I grab drinks out for everyone.

Pouring them into the glasses on the table I sit down, smiling.

Taking a few bites of food, I lift my glass up to make a toast.

"To love and family," I toast, clinking our glasses together and winking at Savannah when I utter the word family.

She smiles at me, and my insides stir. *'I love you, my wife'* I mouth to her, before lifting another forkful of food into my mouth.

She makes my life complete.

(45) Emilie

After helping Savannah with the dishes, I head towards the lounge room where Ember is playing on the floor with River.

Her giggling is so sweet, it makes me smile. Quentin and Hunter are sitting on the couch, watching a movie that's on the tv.

"Are you ready to go Quentin?"

"Yeah if you are?"

"Yeah Ember, darling say goodbye to River."

Quentin stands up, grabbing Ember up by the waist.

She kicks her legs against him. "No! Want to play with iver."

"Sweetie it's time to go home," he says to her.

"No! I ot!"

Walking up behind me, having heard Embers protest, Savannah asks, "Ember, would you like to stay with River and us tonight?"

Ember nods, and Savannah looks to me. "If that's ok with Mummy?"

"Yes, that sounds like a great idea."

"Great, Hunter will bring her home tomorrow when he's in town."

Quentin puts her down, back next to River and she jumps up and down excitedly.

Walking out Quentin quietly says to Savannah, "You're sneaky sis-in-law."

Taking my hand we walk out, with Hunter following.

"See you tomorrow Hunter, not to early bro yeah?" Quentin says at the door, winking at his older brother.

I love how close they are, not just brothers but friends.

ea

Once in the car, I glance at Quentin giggling.

"Why do I get the feeling we've been set up?"

"Because, we have Emi," he says laughing, driving out the farm gate, stopping outside it to jump out and close it behind him.

Getting back in the car he teases,"And I intend to take full advantage of our night." He leans over to kiss me sweetly.
Driving off, he rests a hand on my thigh, the contact on the thin fabric of my leggings sending shivers towards my core.
Leaving it there, he speeds towards town, smiling devilishly.

Rounding the final corner into town, he asks, "Your house or mine?"
"Yours, just in case you know..." I suggest.
"Oh God Emi, really?" He almost groans at what I'm suggesting.
"Yes, I want to..." I say, my words cut off when we pull up in front of his house and he's out the car before I can finish the sentence.
Rushing around to my side, he opens the door, extending a hand to help me out. Without another word, I shut the door behind me, closing it with my butt and he pushes me against the car, kissing me hard.
His kiss is firm, passionate and he moans an 'Mmmm' against my mouth deepening the kiss, before he pulls back.
"You know what I was thinking about all night?"
I shake my head no, but don't speak.
"The fact you didn't wear a bra."
Giggling, I tease, "Take me inside now, babe."
He lifts me up by the waist, and I wrap my legs around his body.
With our lips locked, we stumble to the door.

Reluctantly he puts me down, fumbling to open the front door with his pile of keys. The smile on my face is eager, a literal 'fuck me now' smile and he laughs, pushing me against the door the moment we are inside.
His lips are on mine again, kissing me softly, before he brushes my hair aside kissing my neck. He whispers seductively in my ear, "Emi, I want to lick you, taste you..." He stops when his kiss reaches my lips. "And fuck you."
"Hmm," I moan, kissing him zealously, reaching down to the hem of his sweater to pull it over his head, our lips only parting for a moment when his face is covered.

Running my hands over his chest, he gasps. "Emi, I love it when you touch me."

Shrugging off my jacket, I murmur, stretching up to whisper in his ear, "I'm not wearing any underwear."

He groans, swiftly lifting my thin t-shirt over my head.

"Fuck Emi, you're so fucking beautiful," he drawls, looking me up and down longingly.

"Follow me, I can't wait any longer to make you mine, Emi."

Leading me down the hallway we pass the black room, and I pull him back for a kiss. As I kiss him, I try to pull him back into the black room, but breaking the kiss he murmurs, "No Emi, I'm keeping my promise to you."

Smiling at him I nod, and he pulls us towards his main bedroom. Pushing me down on the bed, he climbs over me, kissing my neck when he whispers in my ear, "So I'm going to kiss you here." He murmurs, trailing kisses over my collarbone. "And here."

He then kisses over my breasts. "And lick these," he teases taking a nipple into his mouth, teasing it with his tongue.

He delivers the sweet torture to one breast and then the other, his lips not leaving my skin for a moment. "And then I'm going to kiss you here," he teases again, trailing kisses to my belly button.

Growling he grabs the elastic of my leggings, pulling them down my legs, following the fabric with kisses on my thighs. Yanking them off at my ankles, he stretches back over my naked body to kiss me deeply.

"God Emi, your body is fucking perfect," he utters running his hands over my bare skin, causing heat to rise all through my body.

As he touches the flat skin of my stomach my hips buck towards him, asking for more. Again he kisses me, plunging a finger inside me. Breaking the kiss, his words make my desire increase.

"And now I'm going to taste you, Emi."

Slowly he pulls his finger out, licking it clean with his eyes locked on mine. He doesn't let me speak instead kisses me, before trailing kisses down my body until he spreads my legs, diving between them.

His mouth finds my entrance, his tongue teasing my clit, and he licks furiously, lapping up all I'm giving him.

I've never felt so turned on before, and almost cry out when he lifts his head a moment.

"Fuck Emi, you taste like heaven."

My eyes dart to the front of his jeans, his erection clearly begging for release. Sitting up on the edge of the bed, I reach out to undo his jeans, pushing them to the floor.

"Emi." He groans. "I want to make you come first."

I don't respond, instead grab the elastic at the top of his boxers, pushing them down his legs to the floor as well. A gasp escapes my mouth looking at how hard he is.

"Mmmm," I moan, taking his hard length into my mouth, teasing him with the tip of my tongue.

"Fuck, Emi, so good..." He groans, reluctantly pulling my mouth from his body with a fist full of my hair.

"Emi, I need to fuck you right now," he declares pushing me back down on the bed.

Leaning over my body to kiss me, he slides inside my waiting core.

"Oh," I gasp, "so good..."

"Mmm, Emi, god you feel so nice around my cock." He grunts, as he pushes in and out of my body, increasing the pace.

Slamming into me harder, my pleasure is rising, sending me to the brink when he presses a sensual kiss against my lips.

He slows his thrusts, slowing the pace when I break the kiss.

"Babe, I'm coming...oh fuck..."

My body clasps around him, my release unrestrained when he pushes deep into me again, crying out my name in pleasure, "Emi, fuck Emmmiii!"

His release into me is hot and he sighs, collapsing against my chest.

(46) Quentin

After a soul shattering climax I withdraw myself from Emilie's body crawling onto the bed to lay down beside her.
Pulling her against my side I sigh. "Emi, that was..."
I don't know what word to use to describe how she'd just made me feel, what being with her made me feel.
It was so much more than I'd shared with anyone.
"Amazing..." She says finishing my sentence before continuing meekly, "I've never come like that before."
"What? You've never come before?" I spit, shocked at her confession.
"No, no, I've come before just not from sex," she admits, blushing.
"Well, don't plan on it being the only time."
"Hmm, I look forward to it," she taunts before turning onto her side to face me.
My eyes lock on hers, thoughts filling my mind of how incredibly beautiful she is, especially after sex with an adorable flushed glow to her porcelain skin.
The look in her eyes is the one she has when she wants to kiss me, looking straight through me this time, as though now she can see how I feel about her.
She murmurs before smashing her lips to mine, entangling her legs with mine to roll my hips to meet hers again.
Her kiss is passionate and eager for control, that has me longing to give her whatever she wants and not take the control like I usually would.
"Ready for round two huh?" I tease, after breaking our breathless kiss.
"No, I just want to kiss you and be in your arms naked."
"Mmm, sounds fun but I'd like to see you come again so..." I tease, sliding a finger inside her again.
Her hips buck, and I glide the finger in and out, caressing the sweet spot that makes her gasp in pleasure.

"Watching you in pleasure Emi, is so fucking hot," I drawl, licking my lips.

She moans at the pleasant torture. "So hot Emi," I tease.

Her moans increase, her body climbing higher as she reaches her peak, onto my hand.

A smile crosses her face when I lick my finger clean, taunting her, "I'll never get tired of how you taste Emi."

"Really?" she laughs.

"Really Emi I..."

"Don't Quentin, please don't say you..."

I cut her off, pressing a tender kiss to her lips.

"Please don't say what?" I ask, smiling.

"That you..." she starts, this time her words cut short by my finger against her lips.

"That I love you."

A gasp escapes her mouth. "Did I just hear that right? Or was it in my head?"

Chuckling softly I reply, "You heard me Emi, I love you."

"I love you too Quentin," she replies, the words never sounding so soothing and I pull her closer.

"Can I make love to you now Emi?" I whisper in her ear.

She moans, rolling over to kiss me, showing me with fervour how much she loves me. I can't help but think of how incredible it feels to have finally told her how I feel.

It seems like some strange coincidence that we found our way to each other again, like we were meant to be but the timing wasn't right all those years ago.

Breaking the kiss, she murmurs against my lips. "Take me to the black room."

"Not yet Emi, but soon."

"Ok can you say it again?" she asks smiling.

"Say what again?" I tease her.

"You know what."

"What?" I taunt, smiling at her when I continue, "That I love you."

Unlawful Attachment

"Yeah that," she replies with a sweet laugh, before I kiss her again, a soft kiss brushing our lips together.

With our lips just touching I whisper, "I love you," against them, before rolling to be on top, deepening the kiss, ready to make love to her over and over again.

(47) Emilie

The sun is peering through the blinds when I finally open my eyes, bleary from sleep. It's incredible to wake up still in Quentin's arms. We barely slept a wink, making love a few more times late until the early hours of the morning.

Being with Quentin, actually giving myself to him fully, and being in love with him made sex so much more than it ever was with Caleb.

"Morning Emi," he purrs, pulling my still naked body close. "Did you sleep well?"

"Hmm , I don't remember much sleeping happening." I giggle.

"Yeah , me either, but sleeps overrated when I can make love to you."

About to reply, the words I'm about to say are stifled when a pounding knock comes from the front door.

"'Fuck, what time is it?" Quentin moans, looking across the clock that reads ten am.

"It must be Hunter. Can you answer the door Emi? I just need a minute to um deal with...well you know." He nods towards his crotch.

"Ok, babe," I reply with a laugh, getting out of bed and pulling my leggings on, that thankfully are on the floor at my feet.

"Babe, a shirt?" I ask looking around the room, not afraid of my nakedness in front of him.

"Yeah, top drawer, grab any one."

I grab a black t-shirt out, slipping it on, and laugh at Quentin's words.

"Damn Emi , my shirt looks good on you."

Quickly, I dash to the door, prepared to greet Hunter.

Opening the door, it's not Hunter standing on his brother's doorstep but my brother Alec.

"Em?" he asks, looking at me perplexed.

"Hi Alec," I greet him.

"What are you doing at the constable's house Em?"

"Um, how did you know this was Quen... um constable Mackenney's house." I stumble on my words, about to tell him more than I'm ready to share.

"I asked at the police station Em."

"Fair enough, but that doesn't explain why you're here Al."

"I was...I am here to talk to Constable Mackenney about the accident that happened here."

"I don't think he'll be able to talk about that with you."

I hear the shuffle of Quentin's feet coming from behind me and turn to find him wearing only his jeans, shirtless. I gulp taking in the gorgeous sight of the man I love, but my heart lurches when his eyes focus on Alec standing on his doorstep.

"Um, Quentin, this is my brother Alec."

"Oh right , what brings you to Ridgehope , Constable Mathers?" Quentin asks in a friendly but patronising tone.

"Just wanted to see my sister and thought I'd drop into see you as well about the accident. I didn't expect to find my sister at your house though."

I feel a blush rise up my cheeks. "Um...Al, I'm um..."

"What Em?" he questions.

"Al is it?" Quentin asks.

"Yeah?" Alec replies, looking between us.

"Emilie and I are together."

I take Quentin's hand in mine, squeezing it , awaiting my brother's response.

"God, Em it's been like four months...no wait hang on..." He thinks out loud, before he rakes a hand through his hair.

"What Al? You look confused."

"Well, um...I am. Was your accident the same one with the white truck?"

I look towards Quentin, not sure if I should respond to my brother's question.

"Are you asking as Emilie's brother or as a cop?" Quentin enquires.

"To be honest both, because I um..."

"Al, what's wrong? I feel like your hiding something."

"Um, Em, I um... can I talk to you alone for a minute?"

"Yeah ok," I reply stepping outside with him when Quentin heads down the hallway, nodding at me.

"Em, I need to tell you something."

"What? Is Mum ok?"

"Yes, Em, Mum is fine. But I am..."

"Al , what? Your scaring me."

"I'm not the one you should be scared of Em."

"What? Are you telling me to be scared of Quentin?" I laugh at his statement, even though I'm a little worried about what he's implying.

"For one yes Em, I'm sure I've seen him before."

"You probably have, in the past yes, but there's nothing to worry about."

"Oh Em, how can you say that? Caleb fucked up for you. How can you drag someone else from your past in?"

The blush rises up my cheeks again and I can't find the words to reply, knowing that my blush will tell my big brother what my mouth can't.

"Really Em?"

"Yes, I'm in love with him."

After my confession, Alec glares at me, shocked and annoyed.

"God Em, really? After everything with Caleb."

"I never loved him,Al, you know that."

"Um, actually Em, I didn't. You married him for fucks sake."

I laugh at my brothers words. "Yeah to get away from Vlad and that hell hole I worked in Alec."

"So, um , the accident Em, was it the same one?" he asks, a fearful tone in his voice.

"Yes, but what has it got to do with you being here and with Quentin?" I ask confused and still getting the sense he's hiding something.

"Because... God Em, I can't believe I'm telling you this..." he says, suddenly stopping as though he's not sure he should continue.

Fear is rising in my chest, images of the past flashing in my head.
"What Alec?"

"I've been working with Vlad, and I know all about the accident, partly thanks to your new boyfriend and Em..." He pauses, waiting for me to speak.

I can't bring myself to say anything, hating how he said, 'new boyfriend' and scared that I'm right that they're both hiding something from me.

Tears well up in my eyes, the emotions overwhelming my already confused mind.

"How long Alec?" I mumble through sobs.

"Um... I um...organised Caleb to get with you...to make him trick you out because I knew Vlad's past and I knew there was no other way to get you out...the stupid bastard wasn't supposed to fall in love with you though."

"But...I...don't...I..." I mumble, not able to think let alone speak a coherent thought.

"He basically stole a lot of money from Vlad , and to pay it back he became a drug mule , but I intercepted the deal..."

"How did I not know this?" I question.

"Because I... because Vlad paid me to kill him, but I couldn't Em. I told him to go home and take you both away from the city."

The tears are streaming down my cheeks, my heart aching when I reach out to hug my brother.

"And?...Our accident?"

"After the drug intercept I told Vlad I'd killed Caleb but he wanted evidence I couldn't give him."

My heart is pounding, so afraid of what my brother's answer to the next question is going to be. "So...um were you driving the truck?"

"God, Em no... how could you think that?"

"I don't know, I'm just a little...no a lot shocked."

"I'm sorry Em, I'm so sorry. I hate myself."

"Don't say that Al. You're still my brother."

"I know Emilie. I love you so much and I um..."

"What? Do you know who was driving the truck? Is that what you came to tell Quentin?"

"Yes, Em, and I know you love him, so this is gonna be hard to say, but you need to leave Ridgehope."

"Why? I don't want to," I sob defiantly .

"Em, Vlad was driving the truck and I'm not proud to say it but after my conversation with Quentin I told him you were alive."

"Alec, I don't know what to say."

"I know Em. All I can tell you is to get away from here."

"I can't Al...I won't break Quentin's heart."

"There's no choice Em. If you stay here and Vlad comes to town, he will kill you."

I don't reply, instead I pull him close into a hug, hoping a little that it won't be the last time I hug my older brother who obviously went off the tracks a little when Dad was killed for his involvement in the Adelaide underworld.

Pulling back, I softly speak, "Please Alec, don't go back to the city. My house is in the next street over."

"Ok, little sis, I'm really sorry."

"I know, I'm going to stay here, say goodbye to Quentin and I'll um...let you know what I'm going to do, but Alec?"

"Yeah Em?"

"I don't know it I can forgive you for this."

"I know Em, I'll never forgive myself," he muses, looking down at his feet.

"Even it I survive, losing Quentin...leaving Quentin makes me feel like I'd rather be dead."

He reaches out to try and hug me but I refuse, shaking my head, not wanting to make this goodbye any harder.

As I turn to go inside I slam the door in his face and find Quentin standing in the kitchen, rubbing his wet hair with a towel.

He looks absolutely tempting wearing black trackies, low on his hips, exposing the 'v' of his muscles. The tears are still flowing down my cheeks and he asks with a caring tone, "Emi, what's wrong?"

I don't reply, instead I run over to him, kissing him hard, demandingly. He drops the towel to the floor, lifting me onto the edge of the island bench, his mouth still on mine, kissing me furiously like he can't get enough.

Breathless, he pulls back, moaning. "God, Emi, I love you so much."

"Take me Quentin," I drawl, locking my eyes on his.

"I have, Emi, I'm yours," he teases.

"No, take me to the black room," I suggest seductively.

He doesn't reply for a moment , kissing me instead, a little more tenderly. He kisses my tear stained cheeks before whispering in my ear, "Go in, and find something you like. I'll be there in ten minutes."

Jumping down from the bench, my body presses into his. I smash a kiss to his lips—a carnal kiss—biting his lips to show him how much I'm ready for his darker side.

Heading down the hallway, I look back to see him watching me, leaning against the bench. I'm more than ready to give him everything— anything he wants from me—but my heart is aching at the thought of leaving him.

(48) Quentin

Watching Emilie walk down my hallway towards the Black room makes my heart pound and my desire rise in the front of my track-pants.
Hoping he isn't already on his way over I send Hunter a message.

Quentin: hey bro...do you think you could drop Ember off a little later?

His reply is almost immediate.

Hunter: Yeah ok little bro...things going well huh? Lol
Quentin: I don't kiss and tell big brother
Hunter: I don't need to know Quent...how about I drop her off tomorrow instead?
Quentin: Really? I don't want to put you guys out
Hunter: its fine...I kinda like having her here...its like having a daughter
Quentin: thanks Hunter...it means the world
Hunter: no worries...I'll text you when I'm heading into town

Leaving my phone on the bench, I adjust myself in the front of my track-pants heading towards the black room.
The door is ajar, and I find Emilie standing against the bed wearing only a black leather jacket and black hipster knickers.
I lick my lips, stepping into the room and kicking the door closed behind me.
"Fuck Emi, you're gorgeous."
She moans, grabbing my waist to pull me close, kissing me so intensely she takes my breath away.
Pulling back I ask, "Tell me what you want Emi?"

Unlawful Attachment

She nods towards the hooks on the ceiling, reaching behind her to grab some cuffs. Licking her lips, she holds them up to me, and replies, "Hook me up there, tease me however you want and take me hard."

"Fuck Emi, really?"

"Yes, Quentin, I'm yours."

"Take off the jacket Emi," I demand, lustfully.

She obeys, her quick submission driving me wild. Handing me the cuffs I put them on her wrists, doing up the clasps as tight as she can handle without whimpering.

"Ok Emi?"

"Yes," she drawls, looking down at her knickers.

"Leave them on."

She nods, smiling deliciously when I grab her by the waist to take her over to the spot under the ceiling hooks.

Without my asking she lifts her arms up ready and I clip the cuffs onto the hooks, smashing a kiss to her lips that is hot and drives my already peaking desire higher when she moans in pleasure.

"Do you want a safe word Emi?"

She shakes her head. "Emi, you need to use words."

"No, I don't."

"Emi, please...I..."

"Ok...fire then."

"Hmm...I hope you don't say fire, Emi."

"I won't...take me now please Quentin."

I chuckle a little, walking to the drawers to take out a feathered crop. Running it along my fingers, I gasp from the way she looks at it, licking her lips like she's anticipating the pleasure to come.

"Are you ready Emi?"

She nods. "Words Emi," I demand.

"Yes, Quentin, I'm ready."

Standing in front of her, firstly I run the feather along her lips.

A melodious hiss escapes them, and I continue moving the feather down her body, over her neck and across her collarbone. She shifts, straining against the cuffs when I run the feather between her lush breasts. Her gasps of pleasure drive me wild, the feather passing over her erect nipples.

Continuing to pass the feather down her torso towards her stomach, I taunt, "Did you like that Emi?"

She mutters an 'mmm' biting down on her lip.

"Words Emi," I demand again.

"Yes," she hisses, the feather splaying across the sensitive skin of her hips and stomach.

Dropping the feather crop on the floor, I grab her by the waist, pulling her down a little engaging the drop frame the hooks are attached to in the ceiling.

Smashing a kiss to her lips, my desire strains against her stomach and against my mouth she begs, "Take me now babe, please."

"Not yet Emi," I taunt her, sliding my fingers down the side of her body and yanking her knickers down, ripping them so they fall off her body. Leaning into her ear I murmur, "Your exquisite body is mine, Emi."

"Yours," she whispers back in my ear.

To tease her I kiss and lick down her body—reaching her hips I stop— and look up at her.

"Emi, I'm going to put your legs on my shoulders. Are you ready?"

"Yes," she replies, lifting her hips up when I grab her arse and hoist her legs over my shoulders. Her core is now a whisper away from my lips, and I inhale her honeyed scent.

Without any warning I bury myself between her legs, ravaging her sweet folds with my tongue. Her moans are wild and she pushes her pelvis against my face. "Quentin! Oh god....I..." she screams out in pleasure.

Stopping my pleasant torture I look up at her, taunting in my demand, "Don't you dare come, Emi."

She pouts. "Mmm, I..." she mutters, gasping when I grab her waist and pull her down more, towards my aching groin.

Instinctively she wraps her legs around my back, gripping me tightly so I'm able to push my track-pants and boxers to the floor.

The tip of my hardness is at her entrance, ready to impale her.

Unlawful Attachment

"Are you ready Emi?" I drawl, locking my eyes on hers, eager for her response and loving how she's giving me full control over her pleasure.

"Yes, I'm..." she hisses, biting her lip when I embed myself in her before she can finish her response.

Slowly, I glide a little in and out, not letting her take the control away. Her moans are carnal, wild and stop for a moment when I run my hands over her body.

"Come for me Emi," I demand slowly, looking straight into her desire filled eyes.

Her legs press into my back, thrusting me deeper inside her folds. Around my dick I can feel her contract, knowing I've hit her g-spot when she twitches, her whole body shaking with her climax ripping through her.

Without saying a word I reach up to unclip her from the hooks.

Falling against my chest, she wraps her arms around my neck, before she looks up at me.

"I love you Quentin."

"I love you too Emilie," I reply, kissing her and stepping back towards the bed.

Turning around I drop her onto the black satin sheets.

"Fuck Emi, you're so beautiful," I drawl, leaning over to kiss her passionately, lifting her arms above her head.

"Mmm, can you fuck me again? Hard?" She taunts, licking her plump lips.

"Oh god Emi, I'm going to fuck you so hard you're going to scream my name."

Her smile is wide, and I demand, "On your knees, babe, hands behind your back."

Quickly she obeys, looking back at me smiling with her fuck me now look. Still painfully hard I enter her from behind and she hisses in pleasure as I rock in and out.

My pelvis smacks into her curvaceous arse which I run a hand along but stop when she whimpers slightly and looks back at me shaking her head at me.

Not ready for release just yet, not wanting her to call out 'fire' I know not to push her too far. It's clear that slapping her arse is painful for her.

"Touch yourself, Emi," I demand and again she quickly obeys.

Again I slam into her, feeling her climax building, as I'm rising towards my own.

"Emilie, come for me babe," I growl, pounding into her slick arousal. Stopping for a moment holding myself inside her, she shudders bringing herself to an explosive climax, screaming out, "Quentin, fuck, oh my god, fuck."

Her words spur me on to push deep inside her, her body still coming down from her orgasm when my own release fills her.

She flops down on the bed, lying on her stomach and I lay down beside her for a moment.

"Are you ok Emi?" I whisper into her ear.

"Am I ok?"

"Yeah?"

"I'm better than ok Quentin, that was incredible."

"You're incredible Emilie and I'm so glad you didn't say fire."

She chuckles softly, rolling over and looking up at me.

"You know I nearly did?"

"Yeah, but Emi, I'll never do anything to you to cause you pain...whenever you enter this room it will be about pleasure."

"I know babe, I trust you."

"I love you Emilie, so much," I drawl kissing her lips tenderly.

"I really should get to my house, now that Alec is here," she announces sadly.

"Yeah, but how about a shower first," I suggest.

Sitting up she replies winking, "A hot shower together?"

"Of course sexy, I wouldn't want to waste water."

"Hmmm...sexy huh?"

"Sexy doesn't even begin to describe you, Emi," I tease with a smirk, standing up and grabbing her hands to pull her up with me.

Unlawful Attachment

Still holding her hand, I open the black room door and lead her down the hallway to the bathroom.

The look on her face is a little forlorn and I can't help but wonder what's going through her mind, just for a moment.

My dirty mind takes over any melancholic thoughts, when we step into the bathroom and thoughts of making love to her in the shower take over.

Without a doubt I'm completely, whole heartedly, head over heels in love with her.

(49) Vladimir

The engine of my blue Maserati Grand Turismo purrs when I roll into the town of Ridgehope.

I can't help thinking about how out of place I feel in this backwards town. It's a shithole for sure and it's evident that something or someone is keeping Emilie here.

I pull the Maserati up in the Main Street, cutting the hum of the engine and suddenly feeling deafened by the silence.

Getting out of the car, I click it locked before going into the supermarket.

Waltzing up to the counter, I'm greeted by a young girl. "Hi Sir , can I help you?" She asks politely.

"Yes, I'm looking for my granddaughter Emilie."

The checkout girl smiles at me, replying innocently, "Oh yes sir, she lives around the corner."

"Do you know the address?" I ask trying not to sound like I have no idea where I am.

"Sorry sir no, but it's one street over from here. It's a small cottage."

"Ok, so which way?" I enquire, hoping she gives me some direction to head because my brain has lost all sense of direction.

She points towards the back of the store. "That way, you won't miss it. There's a big gumtree in the front yard."

"Thanks miss, it will be lovely to surprise her," I respond lacing my voice with fake sincerity.

"Yes, I'm sure she'll love to see you."

This time I don't reply, walking out quickly and getting back into the car.

Gunning it I skid around the corner, seeing her house straight away when I correct the steering to pull up in front of it.

Unlawful Attachment

At the door I knock hard—chuckling to myself—going over my plan in my head.

The door opens, and I don't find Emilie greeting me, but Alec Mathers.

"Oh, Alec, what are you doing here?" I ask, even though I already have an idea running through my head.

"I could ask you the same question, Vlad."

"I'm here to see Emilie. I was told this was her house."

"Um...sorry I don't know who you're talking about," he replies, his eyes telling me a completely different story.

"Alec, you think I'm a fool boy," I jeer menacingly.

"No, Vlad, I don't know an Emilie."

"Don't lie to me boy," I jeer at him again, raising my voice.

"I'm not!" He shouts, taking a step back into the house.

"Alec, I'm no fool! I've checked my records at the club and you can't lie to me."

He steps further inside, and following I slam the door behind me.

"If you didn't have a reason to be here related to Emilie you wouldn't be here Alec."

"Fine, she's my sister," he confesses, confirming what I already knew but wanted to hear from his traitorous mouth.

I laugh evilly. "And you came here to warn her after our convo?"

"I...I had to Vlad," he stammers, unconvinced.

With a hand against his chest I push him into the kitchen.

"You didn't have to do anything Alec. I had it all under control."

"You were going to kill her Vlad and leave her daughter an orphan."

"What? What daughter?"

"Oh shit," he curses, backing further into the kitchen with me invading his personal space.

He stops, crashing into the bench.

"So Alec, you will tell me where she is or your next words will be your last," I threaten grabbing a knife from the block on the bench behind him.

He gasps, the only other sound in the room the scrape of the knife against the wooden block.

"Where is she Alec?" I demand, holding the knife up in my racing gloved hand.

"I don't know..." he hisses, clearly lying.

"I told you to not lie to me boy!" I shout, raising the knife higher, the blood pumping through my veins at what I'm contemplating.

"I'm not...I just came here to speak to her but she's not home."

"Boy I told you not to lie," I snarl, reminding him of my earlier words, hoping he will reveal what he knows.

"Even if I did know, why would I tell you? We are done Vlad!" he bellows, puffing his chest out.

"We are done when I fucking say we are done Alec!"

He has the gall to laugh at my threat, the rage rising in me at his non compliance. His eyes lock on the knife I'm still clutching.

Adrenaline is coursing through my veins.

"What? You got nothing to say now boy?"

I raise the knife.

"Don't, please don't hurt my sister."

"Oh dear boy, if she plays nice I won't, but as for you...well you had your chance."

Looking straight at him, I stab the knife into his chest, the sound of the fabric ripping as the sharp cleaver slices it is strangely thrilling.

He gasps before screaming in agony when I pull the knife back out.

"Fuck Vlad!" he screams, clutching the wound on his left side to try and curb the blood.

"Say another word and I'll drive it back in," I taunt with a menacing laugh.

His eyes are glazed from the pain, and he slides down the bench to his arse, still clutching his chest but not stopping the blood loss.

Stepping over him, I rinse the knife in the sink, making sure the blood all runs down the plug hole before returning the knife to the wooden block on the bench.

Unlawful Attachment

Bending down to his level, I hiss in his face, "You knew not to cross me, Alec Mathers."

"I...I..."

"Fuck up Mathers, you always were weak. You wouldn't be in this situation if you'd knocked off your sister's husband like I'd asked."

Spitting on him, I stand up and walk over to the lounge room to sit on the couch.

I'm sure it won't be long until Emilie arrives home, and my Vixen is in for a few surprises.

(50) Emilie

After making love to Quentin again in the shower, we barely make it back to his bedroom before we're making out again.

Stumbling into his bedroom, we fall against the bed, entangling ourselves in the covers as we kiss. His body is over mine when he pulls back a moment, breathless and groaning. "You're insatiable Emi."

"Mmm...so are you," I tease, lifting my hips up against his.

Kissing me zealously he slides inside my body, pulling in and out.

"Insatiable Emi," he muses when we come apart together mere moments later.

When he lies next to me, looking down at me, a thought crosses my mind.

"Babe, we um..."

"What Emi?"

"Haven't used protection."

He curses under his breath, then asks, "Would having a baby together be a bad thing?"

"No, I guess not." I smile. "Ember would love a sibling."

"Yeah, she would and I bet you look beautiful pregnant, Emi."

I laugh. "No, I look like a beached whale actually."

"You'd still be beautiful to me Emi. I love you so much and if it's all good with you I don't plan on ever using protection when we're together."

"Fine by me," I declare, feeling a flutter in my belly, at the prospect of being pregnant again and with Quentin's baby.

At least if I did, I'd always have a part of him to remember him by.

I shake the thought away, because it's only making the thought of leaving him even harder.

"What's wrong Emi?"

"I really need to get going, back to my house to see Alec."

Unlawful Attachment

"Ok babe, I love you," he says softly when I climb out of the comfort of his bed.

"I love you too," I reply leaning forward to give him a soft, tender goodbye kiss. "Let me know when Hunter drops Ember off tomorrow."

"Of course, I'll bring her home when he drops her off."

Quickly, I get dressed, pulling on my leggings without knickers.

I grab one of Quentin's t-shirts out of the drawer and inhale the smell of him on it as I pull it on, loving how it smells like a mixture of him and washing detergent.

Walking out I blow him a kiss, and he pretends to catch it and presses it against his lips.

Passing the black room, I pick up my jacket shrugging it on and I run into the kitchen.

Quietly I rummage through the drawers of the island bench, knowing that he keeps his gun and holster belt in one of them.

Of course it's in the last one I look in. I'm afraid he's going to come out to see why I haven't left so I quickly pocket the gun, leaving the drawer open.

❧

Sprinting back to my house takes me about fifteen minutes. Opening the door I call out, "Alec, are you here?" I'm worried that the house seems eerily quiet.

As soon as I step inside, my jaw falls to the floor and I gasp in shock finding my brother slumped in a sitting position against the kitchen cabinets. He's surrounded by a pool of blood, with his head cocked to one side.

Rushing over to him I kneel in front of him, running my hand over the gaping hole in his chest. Touching his cheek I ask softly, "Alec are you ok? What happened?"

"Em...he...s...s...stab..." he drawls out between laboured breaths.

"Who Alec? Who did this to you?"

He tries to reply, taking in a shaky breath, but struggling to speak at the same time.

My own breath catches in my chest when I hear a voice behind me, a voice so chilling my heart starts to pound harder.

"Hello Vixen."

Turning towards his chilling voice I see Vlad sitting on the couch, a wicked smile at the corner of his mouth. Anger bubbles inside my guts, and I launch myself across the room towards him, beating my fists against his chest when he's within reach.

"How could you stab him? My brother Vlad!" I seethe at him.

"You're mine Vixen and it was either your brothers life or your precious daughters."

"I don't have a child," I spit a him, clenching my teeth.

"Oh, Vixen, your brother dearest confessed everything to me," he taunts and chuckles evilly.

"Still Vlad, you didn't need to stab him. He could die!" I protest, my heart constricting when the words leave my mouth.

I turn to look back at Alec, hoping he can hold on just a little longer until I can get help.

Vlad is laughing manically. "Looks like he has already Vixen."

It takes my mind a moment to process what he's saying, before I rush back to Alec's side.

I can't hear his laboured breaths anymore and even though I know he's gone I still beg, "Alec, please wake up! Please don't leave me, please Alec."

But when he doesn't move, doesn't take another breath I know he's gone and I collapse against his chest sobbing wretchedly.

Barely a minute passes when I feel the presence of Vlad standing behind me. He grabs me by the hair, pulling me up with my back to him.

"You're mine Vixen, now look at me," he demands in an menacing tone.

I turn to face him, scowling.

"No Vlad, I'm not! You killed my brother and my husband!" I scream at the top of my lungs.

"I did what I had to, to right the wrongs Emilie."

I cringe at hearing him say my name, utterly confused by his words.

"How is this right?" I ask shaking my head and pointing back towards my brother.

"Because it is Vixen!" He yells at me. "And you're going to come back to the city with me or you'll suffer the same fate as your dear brother here."

"No Vlad I won't! I don't obey you anymore," I protest defiantly.

His hands are suddenly around my neck, his fingers pressing into my flesh as he chokes me.

My breath catches and I feel the blood draining from my cheeks.

"You'll do as I fucking say or you'll die after watching your precious daughter die in front of your eyes!"

Trying to take a breath in without suffocating, I hiss a loud, "No!"

And with as much strength as I can muster I stomp my foot down on his.

Cursing he unclasps his fingers from around my neck, jumping up and down a little to soothe his throbbing foot.

I take that as my chance to muster up some more strength, balling my hand into a fist and punching it straight into the front of his pants.

He screeches in pain, stumbling backwards.

Not hesitating for a moment I know I have to run. Feeling the adrenaline coursing through me I rush past him, patting my pockets to check I still have my phone and Quentin's gun.

After slamming the door I run out onto the road, heading towards Quentin's house. That's when I notice Vlad's Maserati parked up the street a little, and looking at it and not where I'm going I stumble on a tree root.

Failing to put my hands out to break my fall, I feel my body crash to the ground, the side of my face hitting the hard red dirt.

Taking a deep breath I tell myself to get up, but I can't get my body to cooperate, seeing blackness take over my senses.

(51) Vladimir

After a few moments, when the pain in my groin has subsided I rush out of the cottage to find Emilie.

Shaking my head, I look around hoping that she hadn't thought to jump into the Maserati because the keyless entry and start would have worked with me being only a hundred metres away in the house.

It's one of those stupid new fangled technology things some genius had come up with, that really isn't that genius at all, especially on a hundred grand car.

I needn't have worried, as just nearby where the Maserati is parked—a little to the left of her house—her body is lying face down in the red dirt by a large gumtree.

Calmly, I walk up to her, bending down to brush her luscious brown locks away from her face. It's clear she has passed out from hitting the ground.

I should feel happy about this and how I can use her unconsciousness to my advantage but the guilt having offed Alec is already getting to me. He'd told Emilie that it was me who stabbed him, so I have to tread carefully if I want to keep her around and not have her go snitching to the cops.

With my hands on her waist, I lift her body up to cradle her in my arms, bridal style. She flops in my arms, dangling her arms by her sides and her head falling back, nestles in the crook of my elbow.

Slowly I walk back to the Maserati, putting her down to stand up against the back wheel. Her feet don't keep her up and she slides down to land on her backside, her legs out in front.

Her jacket falls to her sides and her phone falls out of one pocket and a hand gun falls out of the other.

Picking up her phone, I glance at the screen to see a message from, 'Q' has just popped up.

Unlawful Attachment

Q: I love you Emi. You're mine sexy.

I scoff reading the strangers words to her, because my Vixen doesn't belong to anyone but me.

Laughing, I throw the phone towards the back of the car, knowing that I'll likely drive over it.

Picking up the gun I pocket it, before opening the car door.

Again with my hands around her tiny waist I pick Emilie up, hoisting her into the seat. When I buckle her in she stirs a little, and I softly mimic 'Q's words to calm her, "Emi, I love you sexy."

"Mmm, I love you to babe" she replies dazed, not registering who said the words to her.

Shutting the door I sprint to the driver's side, sliding in as soon as I open the door.

Putting the gun in the centre console I glance at her beside me before reversing away.

Even over the hum of the engine I can hear the crunch of the back tyres crushing her phone. It's a rather pleasant sound, knowing that I'm limiting her chance of being able to contact anyone.

Speeding out of the shithole town, I again look towards her.

My heart pounds a little in my chest because she looks so incredibly beautiful and more like her mother everyday.

Most people who think they know me, think that the callous Vladimir Manning isn't capable of feeling any emotion, let alone love, but it isn't true. I'm desperately in love with the beautiful woman sitting beside me, as I was with her mother so many years ago.

Driving is always soothing, and my thoughts wander back to the day I met Emilie.

A soft knock rapped on my office door. I really wasn't in the mood to speak to anyone, surrounded by a mountain of work, but when a sweet voice asked, "Boss, can I come in?" I found myself replying, "Yes Elodie."

When Elodie entered the office, she looked gorgeous with her dark chocolate locks free, her midriff showing beneath her ripped t-shirt and her thighs barely covered by the mini skirt that skimmed them.

Tears were in her eyes, and her face had a forlorn look.

"What's wrong? Who is this?" I asked looking at the teenage girl standing beside her, who had the same luscious chocolate hair, a childlike but developing body not hidden beneath the floor length dress she was wearing.

"Um...boss this is my daughter Emilie and..."

"And what Elodie?"

"I'm offering her to you...to work here."

The girl whimpered at her mother's suggestion.

"Whatever for Elodie? Your my best dancer, and I love you...I'm not letting you go baby."

"I know Vlad...but I can't dance for you anymore."

"Why not baby?"

"Because things are shit at home...her Dad is in prison and my son is doing really shit at school. I just...I just..."

My heart lurched in my chest at my Elodie's words, she was hurting but she was breaking my heart.

Leaving the comfort of my desk behind, I raced to her side embracing her tightly.

"Shhh...baby...it's ok. I'll work it out," I cooed into her hair.

"How Vlad?"

Taking a step back, I took her hand in mine, taking another glance at her daughter beside her.

"I'll accept your offer, but firstly Emilie here will only work at cleaning the rooms, until she's a little older."

"Ok, I think that's good...she's only fifteen Vlad so you know..."

"Yes baby, I know..."

"I'm sorry Vlad...I'm really sorry."

"Don't be baby...I get it that you need to step away to look after your family."

"Will you look after my girl?"

"Of course...but will I see you again?"
"No...I can't Vlad...her Dad is already suspicious and now he's in prison I just can't...I need some space."
"Oh god Elodie," I moan, smashing a kiss to her lips, saying goodbye to the only person I've ever loved without words.

We've been driving back towards the city close to an hour when Emilie opens her eyes, looking across at me.

Her facial expression is emotionless and she doesn't move an inch, just glares daggers at me with her eyes.

"Hi Vixen, ready to go home?" I ask, touching a hand to her thigh and grinning. —

(52) Quentin

Sometime after Emilie left, I'd drifted to sleep, panic rising in my chest when I woke up without her beside me. How she'd left has me a little shaken, as it feels a little like she's not just leaving but saying goodbye forever.

Grabbing my phone from the beside table, there's no response to my earlier text I'd sent her after she'd left.

Sitting up in bed, I dial her number. It doesn't ring, instead an automated message cuts in, *'the number you are calling is not available. Please try again later.'*

Cursing, I throw the phone on the bed beside me, feeling my heart constrict in my chest. I try to take deep breaths in, to quell the panic that something is wrong, but it doesn't help.

My heart is hurting thinking one, that Emilie has left me and two that something has happened to her. If she's just left I'll be able to find her, to make her come back to me.

Climbing out of bed, not wanting to waste another minute dwelling on the what if's, I grab a pair of jeans from the clothes basket, pulling them on hastily, before shrugging on a t-shirt from the open drawer.

I grab my phone off the bed, shoving it in my pocket to rush out to the car.

Passing through the kitchen I stop a moment wondering why the drawer I keep my gun and holster belt in is open.

Glancing into the open drawer, the holster is there, but my gun is gone. It makes my heart constrict more, the panic increasing as it can only mean one thing. Emilie has taken my gun, and if she thought she'd need my gun then she's definitely in trouble.

Once in the car, I speed straight around the back streets to her house.

Unlawful Attachment

Racing out of the car, I ran up onto the porch, calling out her name, but no response comes.

Walking inside—because the door is unlocked—my eyes boggle at the sight in front of me. I'm completely shocked to see Alec slumped in a pool of blood in Emilie's kitchen. Running over to check if he's alive, a crazy thought runs through my mind.

Did Emilie shoot her own brother?

Bending over his body, it's a no brainer that he's clearly dead, and has been for maybe a couple hours.

Glancing around the room, I try to find the murder weapon, thinking that maybe my gun is nearby. I can't see anything that seems like it could have been used to cause the injury to the chest that Alec has though. If it had been a gunshot wound, there would have been blood spatter. And there isn't.

Confused, I lean against the bench, grabbing my phone from my pocket to call Sarge.

He picks up straight away after the first ring. "Sarge, it's Quentin."

"Hi Quentin, doesn't sound like you're enjoying your RDO?"

"Um...yes...no...I'm at Emilie's," I stammer, worried about what his response is going to be.

"Who's?" he questions, waiting a moment for a response from me that I don't provide.

It dawns on him and he bellows, "The accident survivor!"

"Yes...and um..." I say, not really sure if confessing to Sarge is a good idea.

"Quentin, I don't need to tell you the rules do I," he says, not as a question.

"Um, Sarge...I..." I stammer, words catching in my throat.

"Quentin Mackenney, you didn't pursue her did you?" he demands, a father like anger in his voice.

"Sarge I...I need to..."

"Quentin, if the board finds out you got involved with someone that an investigation is being carried out on, they'll ask you to step down."
I sigh deeply taking a deep breath before I try to speak. "I know Sarge , but..."
"But what Quentin, you're a good cop...but you know better."
"Yes, Sarge I do, but there's more to it than that."
"There better be or your job is as good as gone Quentin."
Again taking a deep breath, I somehow pluck up the courage to tell him what he doesn't want to hear.
"Well, Sarge, for one thing, I'm in love with her and two you need to get here now, with Detective Masterson and the Coroner."
"What? Wait? Why? You love her?"
"Yes, I do, but did you not hear the rest of what I just said?"
"I heard you alright, I'll be there in fifteen," he informs hanging up.

As I wait for them to arrive, I take another look around the house, trying not to touch anything.
It's strange that nothing appears out of place or any different and it doesn't sit well in the pit of my stomach.
Sarge arrives, as he said fifteen minutes later. He looks around the scene with a questionable look on his face, like he is somehow blaming me.
Detective Masterson taps me on the shoulder.
"You good to answer some questions Constable Mackenney?"
"Yeah, no problems Detective."
He taps his iPad screen, and then looks up at me.
"OK great, so do you know the deceased?"
"Yes, and no...I met him earlier today briefly. His name is Alec Mathers. He was Emilie Buccianti's older brother."
"OK and was their any contact today from family or friends?"
"Yes, Emilie was at my house today and Alec came to speak to me about the accident under investigation because he was a cop in Adelaide."
"Who's house is this?"

"It's the emergency house, but Emilie has been staying here since her accident about five months ago."

"OK, great and do you have any idea who might have killed Mr Mathers here?"

"No, not at all. You're not implying that I did anything?"

"No Constable, not at all, just want to get as many facts as we can."

"Good, cause I was just coming over to see Emilie and I found him…I…"

Sarge comes up to stand next to me, seeing my obvious unease.

"That will be all Detective Masterson. I'll have a word to Constable Mackenney here now if you don't mind."

"No problems Sarge, we'll take a look around and get things sorted with removing the deceased. I'll catch you back at the station."

Sarge rests his hands on my shoulders.

"I'm sorry about that Quentin, are you doing OK?" he asks looking into my eyes, his words sounding fatherly.

"Um…no," I reply, wanting to just hug him.

"Come on, step outside with me. We need to have a chat."

I follow Sarge out, my heart pounding thinking about what he's going to say.

I love Emilie desperately, even though I knew all along that falling for her was going to be detrimental for my career. Maybe her leaving is for the best and I have to let her go, even though this time I know I'll never love anyone again.

My heart is shattered.

(53) Tobias

Seeing Quentin upset tugs at my heart. He's done the wrong thing by falling for the woman, but it's a big deal for him, that I know from what his father told me about the family's past.

Isaak instructed me to look out for his boys no matter the cost, and I might have been harsh on Quentin from a boss' perspective, but I love him like a son.

Leading him outside, I close the door behind us the moment he breaks down into tears.

"Quentin, son, please talk to me," I say soothingly.

Through sobs, he mutters, "I'm...s...s...s...sorry Sarge."

"What for? Falling for a beautiful woman?"

He looks up at me, confused by my change of approach. "But you said my job..."

"Yes, I did say that...but Quentin, seeing you this way breaks my heart. Your Dad told me to look out for you boys."

"But I...I've fucked up...I shouldn't have gotten involved with her Sarge."

"That's true Quentin, but you can't help who you fall in love with, and yes I'm angry at you for getting involved with her whilst you were supposed to be investigating her case, however I suspect it may have helped you get some details?"

"Yes, kinda, but I actually can't share some of those with you...it's ahh...kinda personal."

"I'm not going to push you to tell me Quentin, but you're now officially off this case, and I think in the current circumstances it might be best if you take a leave of absence."

He sniffs, looking at me confused. "Sorry what? Are you going to report me to the board?"

"Technically I should, yes, but despite this and your previous indiscretion with Constable Prattman, you're a good cop and this force needs you."

"So why the leave then?"

"Because as I said before, your Dad asked me to look out for you. Right now it seems as though you need a break."

"I don't know about that Sarge...it's not like Emilie is here anymore."

It's my turn to look confused. "What do you mean? She left you?"

"Well, I'm not sure to be honest. Her phone isn't ringing and I think she took my gun."

"I'll look into it, but the leave of absence stands. Maybe spend some time with your family. I heard your Mum is coming out of the rest home?"

He nods, smiling. "Yeah, they think it's best she's with family, but I'm worried there's something they're not telling us about her MS."

"That's possible, just spend time with her and try to enjoy the time off."

"Yeah, I will try Sarge." He sniffs again, trying to hold back more tears. Reaching out I pull him close to hug him, rubbing his hair softly when his tears break through.

"Don't cry son, it'll all work out."

Pulling back from my hug he frowns. "I miss her Sarge. I finally let someone else in and she's left me too."

"Did she tell you she loved you?"

"Yeah, but she still left."

"Then son, let her go. Move on with other aspects of your life and if it's meant to be it will be."

"I hope you're right Sarge, because I can't stand feeling as though my heart has been ripped from my chest."

Even though his words are sad I let out a lighthearted chuckle.

"You've got it bad for this woman, son."

"Yeah, I can't tell you all the details, but I think I've been in love with her since I met her when I was nineteen."

"Sounds like she's the one. She'll come back to you."

"I hope so. Thanks for being so understanding Sarge, you're a good cop."

"Like I said, I think of you as my son."

"Thanks, you're like a father to me too," he says with a hint of gleefulness in his tone.

"I've got to head in and speak to Masterson, you'll be right to head home?"

"Yeah, might go catch up with Mark and Hugh first."

"Ok, come in tomorrow and we'll do the paperwork for your leave. Take it easy Quentin."

"I will, Tobias," he replies, walking to his car.

When I enter the house again, I hope I've made the right choice in giving him some space to sort his feelings out. He'd done the wrong thing definitely, but it's clear he loves her and nothing gets to me more than young love. Having met my wife Tiffany at around the same age, and then losing her to cancer only a few years after we got married, I totally understood both the love he's feeling but also the heartbreak of that person being gone without much warning.

Quentin is honestly like the son I never had, and I only have his best interests at heart. I can only hope I've made the right choice for him.

(54) Quentin

Stumbling into the pub, I don't even raise my eyes in greeting to Mike, just stammer when I walk past, "A beer and then a whiskey Mike."
My eyes dart straight to the corner booth that Mark and Hugh are sitting in next to each other. They look a little cosy—it's definitely odd for them to be sitting on the same side of the booth—but I shrug it off sliding into the other side, across from them.
Hugh greets me in his usual jovial tone, "Hey man, you good?"
"Nope, shit man," I reply when Mike comes over putting the beer on the table in front of me.
Without a second thought I gulp it down like water.
"Easy mate, what's going on?" Mark remarks, concern lacing his voice.
"I fucked up again, thought with my dick like I always do."
"What man? Who'd you get with? I thought Sam skipped town," Hugh says, his jovial tone sounding more patronising.
"She did."
"So who'd you get with then?"
"You know Hugh," I declare.
"I do? Come on man, give me a clue?"
"Sweet little girls mum."
"Oh shit, man...you didn't?"
"Yeah, full on."
"You slept with her?"
"Yeah." I blush. "But I'm in love with her."
"So why so glum then?"
"Well, it's a long arse story, so I'm not going to bore you but she left me."
"Come on man, did you tell her you love her?"
"What do you reckon?" I spit at him, signalling Mike for my previously ordered whiskey.

"And she loves you?" Hugh asks, a smile at the edge of his lips that irritates me.

"She said she did, but obviously not."

Mike appears again, barely able to put the whiskey down on the table before I grab it and scull it.

"Another Mike yeah? Keep them coming!"

Mike shoots me a warning glance, asking, "Are you sure Quentin?"

"What do you think Mike? Just get me another!"

He walks off, back to the bar a little taken aback by my abruptness.

"Mate, that was a bit harsh," Mark pipes up, finally opening his trap.

"Seriously, can you just lay off! You both haven't been the most supportive mates lately."

"Sorry man, its just um..." Hugh stammers.

"What? You finally gave into one of the girls after you Hugh?"

Before he answers Mike is back with a tray of four whiskeys.

"This is all I'm giving you tonight Quentin."

"Fine," I snap at him, giving him the finger behind his back when he walks away.

"Quentin, seriously you need to calm ya tits!" Mark chastises me.

"Whatever!" I snap back at him, downing two of the four glasses of whiskey successively.

"So, Hugh, did you finally get laid?"

"Um, yeah man I did but..."

"Well, who is she?" I taunt him.

"Not she mate," Mark replies, holding up his hand that Hugh is clutching.

Evidently they're secretly holding hands under the table as their fingers are laced together.

"What the fuck! You're shitting me yeah?"

"No, man, we're not," Hugh declares.

"So you're together?"

"Yeah, for about, um a couple months, since Addison's wedding."

"So you're seriously telling me both of my best mates are fucking pansies?"

"Come on Quentin...can't you be happy for us," Mark says softly.

"Why didn't you fucking tell me?"

"Because we knew you'd react this way."

Grabbing another of the whiskey's I gulp it down.

"How were you expecting me to react?" I spit furiously at them, running a hand through my hair. "God, fuck I don't need this shit, I'm out of here."

Downing the last whiskey, I seethe at them both, "You two can go to hell!"

Shakily I stand up, the alcohol suddenly hitting me hard. I start stumbling to the door. Hugh runs after me, grabbing my arm to try and pull me back.

"Wait Quentin please!"

"Don't touch me you pansy!" I spit at him, trying to sound harsh.

He lets go of my arm, shrinking back when I crash out the doors and continue stumbling down the footpath.

My feet have a mind of their own, leading me straight to Emilie's house. The front door is unlocked and walking in I'm happy to find that the coroner has done his job in cleaning up the horrific scene in the kitchen.

Still unsteady on my feet, I stumble down the hallway to Emilie's room. Falling into the bed, I clutch the sheets to my chest, inhaling the smell of her sweet floral perfume on the pillow.

It's then that the tears start to fall down my cheeks. I thought that by telling Emilie I loved her, and her acceptance of my darker side that we'd have forever together. But obviously that was just wishful thinking.

(55) Hunter

Putting my Akubra on the hat stand by the door, about to call out I'm home to Savannah I feel my phone vibrating in my pocket.
For some reason panic rises in my chest, and I grab it out, seeing unknown number flashing on my screen.
Hesitantly I answer, "Hello, this is Hunter."
"Hello Hunter, it's Martha from the rest home."
"Oh hi Martha, how's things?"
"Good Hunter, we're just wondering what's happening with taking your Mum home?"
"Um, to be honest we haven't really discussed it yet."
"Um ok, do you think it could be this week sometime? She's still doing well physically but not mentally."
"I know, look I'll talk to Quentin and get back to you, but the end of the week should be fine."
"Ok sounds good, let me know if anything changes."
"Will do, bye Martha," I reply hanging up.

Walking into the kitchen Savannah is sitting up at the table with a cup of tea.
"Hey baby, you look worried, what's up?"
"The rest home just called. They want us to have Mum out by the end of the week."
"That's really soon. I'll have to get a move on cleaning the place up then."
Stepping up the table next to her, I kiss her forehead. "Baby, you will do nothing of the sort. You need to take it easy, keep the twins baking for as long as possible."
She stands up, putting her cup on the table, hugging me.

"I know Hunter, but I feel so useless at the moment. I'm as big as an elephant and I'm so tired."

"You're not an elephant Savannah, you're the most beautiful woman in the whole fucking world. I love you!"

"Oh Hunter, I love you too," she replies, grabbing my cheeks to pull my lips to hers for a sweet tender kiss.

Pulling back I laugh. "In some ways, I can't wait for the twins to be born so I can have my wicked way with your body again, baby."

"Me too, Hunter." She giggles.

"Go get some rest baby, I need to head into town to take Ember home."

"Yeah, you'll have to wake her though. She's napping with River in our bed at the moment."

"Okay, maybe you should lie down with our little boy, and have some mummy and only son bonding time before the twins take you away from him."

Slapping my arm when we walk down the hallway she replies sweetly, "Not a chance of that happening, he'll always be my baby boy, even if both of these new bubbies are boys."

"I know Savannah," I muse stopping in our doorway and melting at the sight of my sweet baby boy sleeping next to Ember.

They look like angels.

Stepping up to the bed, I shake Ember slightly. She stirs, opening her sweet brown eyes, looking up at me.

"Are you ready to go home sweetie?" I ask when she sits up rubbing her eyes.

"Es, miss Mummy."

I pick her up, pulling her out of the bed when River sits up looking at me like I'm taking away his favourite teddy bear.

"Daddy, what doing?"

"I'm taking Ember home sweet boy."

"But I wa her ay here."

"I know you've had lots of fun together River, but she has to go home."

"Ok, but she pla oon."

"Yes, sweetie, she might be able to go to kindy with you soon."

"Eally Daddy?"

"Yes, sweetie, go back to sleep ok? Mummy is going to lay down with you," I reply when Savannah walks in sitting on the edge of the bed and pulling him into a hug.

When we walk out, Ember waves at him, with her hand opening and closing like a duck's mouth. He waves back, and sweetly blurts out, "Luv oo m."

She giggles, like she knows what River is actually saying to her, and I'm literally floored by my son's words. He is only three, but going on sixteen and I laugh, strapping Ember in the car seat.

What am I in for with my cheeky son?

After getting in the car, I quickly text Quentin.

Hunter: Heading into town now. bringing Ember. We need to talk about Mum.

His reply is immediate but has me a little worried, as it's just an, *'ok'*. For some reason, whilst I'm driving I feel as though I should turn around, worry plaguing me that something is wrong with my younger brother.

Reaching his house twenty minutes later, I get Ember out of the car, carrying her against my hip, putting her down at the front door when I knock loudly.

Calling out his name, after knocking a few times there is still no response. Ember appears restless, jumping up and down on the spot. Sighing I pluck my phone from my back pocket to text Quentin again. He doesn't reply, so I dial his number to call him instead.

He answers with a grunt.

"Hey little bro, you ok?"

"No, where are you?" he asks, sounding like he's been crying or asleep.

"Your house, with Ember. I text you before.

"I'm not there."

"I figured that, since you're not answering the door. What's going on Quentin?"

"She left me."

"Who? Emilie?"

"Yes, I can't tell you everything. Official police business, but I'm at her house."

"So hang on? What? You're there and she's not?"

"Yep bro and you can't bring Ember here. I don't want to see her."

"Quentin I..."

He cuts me off, rather abruptly.

"Don't Hunter, yeah. I fucked up ok? I need some space."

"Fine, I'll take her back to the farm," I snap, feeling angry but concerned. "But we still need to talk."

"What about? I'm not really up to talking at the moment."

"Well, I'm sorry little brother I honestly didn't see her leaving you, but we need to talk about Mum coming home."

He lets out a deep sigh. "Yeah I know."

"Could you come out to the farm later, maybe?"

"I don't know Hunter. I can't deal with all that right now."

"It's hard little brother, but we need to get the house sorted. The rest home want her out by the end of the week."

"You still want her to live in the old farmhouse?"

"That was the plan."

"Well, its a shit plan! She can stay with me, well at my house."

"Are you sure?"

"Yes, Hunter. I'm not letting Mum face the hell of going back into that house like I did."

"Ok I get you, I'll let the rest home know. Can you go there and organise things?"

"Yeah, tomorrow ok?"

"Ok, are you sure you'll be alright little bro?"

"Yep, broken hearts heal."

"Ok, let me know if you need anything, and when I can drop her off?" I ask, looking at Ember who is dancing around on Quentin's porch trying to catch a butterfly.

"Ok, just give me a day or so. Tell her Mummy and I had to go pick up a special surprise for her."

"Quentin, you can't lie to her!"

"Just let me deal with it Hunter. I love her like my own kid."

"Fine, how about you tell her now?" I snap.

Pressing loudspeaker, I hand Ember the phone and she half puts it up next to her ear, holding it awkwardly.

"It's Quentin sweetie, he wants to talk to you."

"Kent?" she asks the phone looking at it like, 'where is he?'

"Hey sweet girl, I miss you."

"Iss you oo Kent," she yells at the phone.

"Are you having fun with River?"

"Es, but iss oo and Mummy."

"I know sweetie but we had to go get a special surprise for you. I'll see you in a couple of days ok?"

"Ok Kent, Mummy alk now?"

"No sweetie, she's busy, but we'll see you soon. I love you sweet girl."

He makes a kissing sound into the phone and Ember replies, "Luv oo to Kent."

She holds the phone up to me and taking it off loudspeaker I try to hold my anger at my brother in.

"This plan of yours better work Quentin or you'll have a heartbroken little girl to deal with."

"I know, just trust me brother ok? I'll see you in a couple of days when Mum's at mine. I'm going back to sleep."

"Ok, little bro, I love you."

"I love you to Hunter," he replies before hanging up.

Taking Ember's hand in mine, I look down at her.

Unlawful Attachment

"Sorry sweetie, you'll have to come home with me again, is that ok?"

"Yes, Unci Hunt. I ike play wit iver."

My heart swells from her calling me Uncle. Picking her up I smile at her, walking to the car to buckle her back into the car seat.

Only one thought keeps playing on my mind and I'm hoping like hell that Quentin isn't going to make her life even worse than it already is. He said he loves her, but he can't let her lose both a father and a mother within months.

(56) Quentin

The moment Mum is brought out from her room, tentatively walking slowly with her walker my heart swells with love.

Her eyes light up, a wide smile spreading across her face when she sees me. I've not been the best son, barely making any effort to visit her like Hunter had and I feel horrible about it.

"Are you sure about this baby boy?" she asks, using her childhood nickname for me, when I hold the door open for her.

"Yes, Mum, I'll be happy to have you around."

"Yes, Hunter said your girl left you."

"Please, Mum, it hurts too much," I say when we reach the car.

Opening the door, I wait until she gets in the car, helping her slide into the seat before I fold her walker and put it in the boot.

About to start the car—once I've slid into the drivers seat—she looks across at me asking, "Baby boy, do you love her?"

"Yeah Mum, more than I've ever loved anyone before."

"Did you tell her?"

"Yes, I did and she still left," I say, turning the key in the ignition to start the car.

"Oh, Quentin, my baby boy, if you told her you love her she'll be back."

"How do you know that Mum?"

"Because a Mackenney man loves her and they never let go of those that they love."

"Yeah I've fallen hard for her Mum and I miss her so much."

"I know baby boy," she replies smiling when we pull up to my house.

Hunter is waiting on the doorstep with Ember by his side.

"Oh shit, I'm not ready for this," I curse, blushing because I'd just sworn in front of my Mum. She doesn't seem to mind, which is strange.

"Not ready to see your brother? Or?" she asks, eyeing Ember standing next to him.

"No, to face telling Emilie's sweet daughter her Mum isn't with me."

"Oh Quentin, you love her like she's your daughter. Tell her the truth."

"I can't Mum, she's already lost her father."

"That may be so, but she has you now."

Not replying, feeling as though there are no other words to say I get out of the car.

Hunter comes walking down the path to help Mum out of the car, and Ember rushes straight towards me. As soon as I'm out of the car, Ember wraps her tiny arms around my legs.

Scooping her up into my arms I hug her tight.

"Hey sweet girl, I missed you."

"I miss oo too Kent. Wher Mummy?"

"Oh sweetie. Mummy had to stay away a bit longer."

"But she coming ack?"

"Yeah, soon sweetie. Do you want to see Tiberius?"

"Yes, I miss im."

"He's missed you too sweetie," I reply, kissing her cheek, carrying her against my hip to the door.

Putting her down I unlock the front door, and she rushes inside the moment the door is open.

"You good, little brother?" Hunter asks, helping Mum inside. I follow, closing the door behind us.

"Yeah I'm ok. Mum always knows what to say and I'm glad she's here now."

"Me too baby boy," Mum replies, smiling at me.

"Cool, well I gotta go pick River up from kindy. Maybe we'll come in for dinner next week,"Hunter suggests, his eyes looking between Mum and I.

"That sounds wonderful son," Mum replies, and Hunter leans over to kiss her cheek.

"Look after each other." Hunter winks at both of us before he walks out.

Mum is smiling at me. "So, baby boy, let me meet my granddaughter."

"Mum, please don't say that."

"Baby boy, you're that little girls father at the moment, so she is my granddaughter and I'll treat her as one."

Kissing her cheek I reply, "Thanks Mum."

"Anything for you baby boy, I've missed you terribly."

"I know," I muse, laughing when Ember comes running in holding a very annoyed Tiberius in her arms.

"Ember, sweetie, can you put Tib down. I want you to meet someone."

Dropping Tib, she giggles when he runs off, probably glad to be free of her holding him for dear life.

"Ember, this is my Mummy Grace. She's going to help me look after you whilst your Mummy is still away. Is that ok?"

"Es, is she ike a gandma to me?" Ember asks, making my heart pound.

"Yes, sweetie, exactly."

"Ok she eem ice," she replies innocently, looking at Mum, before running straight to her.

Mum wraps her arms around her, hugging her. It melts my heart, and even though I'm still completely heartbroken my heart is pounding, swelling with love.

I know in that moment that no matter what happens, if Emilie comes back or not, I want to be Ember's father.

I love her like she's my daughter, and if Emilie never comes back I know I'll try my darnedest to love her enough for both of us.

(57) Hugh

Quentin had always been such a supportive mate, always willing to do anything for those he cared about, so I was definitely taken aback by his reaction to mine and Mark's coming out.

I completely understood he was hurting about his girl leaving, and much to Mark's objection I thought we needed to see him and be his friend like he'd been to us so many times in the past.

It had been just over a week since the day he stormed out of the pub, and Mark was still pissed with him. Me, not so much, as I tried to put myself in his shoes, wondering what it would feel like if Mark just left me without so much as a word.

We'd pulled up in front of Quentin's house in my red Monaro. Mark was in the passenger seat, behaving like a baby with his arms folded against his chest.

"I'm not going in, I don't want to talk to him," he huffs at me when I cut the engine.

"Aww, boo, don't be like that."

"I don't know why you want to make the effort to apologise Hugh."

He huffs at me even louder than before.

"Because he's our friend Mark, and he's hurting. I don't know if he would have reacted that way if his girl hadn't left."

"Yeah, whatever, Hugh. You go and find out that Quentin is not the friend we thought. I'm staying in the car," he replies—pressing the switch for his window to roll down—before I get out of the car.

Not saying another word to Mark, I confidently stride up to Quentin's front door, knocking a few times.

The door opens, and it isn't Quentin who greets me which is a little bit of a shock.

"Hello Mrs Mackenney, what are you doing here?"

She looks me up and down, as though she's trying to place how I know her and who I am.

"Well, hello, Hugh Witmer. It's been years dear. I could ask you the same question I guess?"

"Yes, it has. Are you well?"

"Not exactly dear. You know I have MS?"

"Yeah, Quentin told us. Horrible disease, but you're here out of the rest home, so are things better?"

"A little now I'm not in the wheelchair, but I missed my boys too much."

"So you're staying here with Quentin?"

"Yes, and at a good time too. His girl left him and he's heartbroken."

"Yeah, thats actually why I'm here."

"Oh, he told you already?"

"Yes, and I also shared something important with him and his reaction was out of character, so I wanted to come see how he's doing."

"Oh really dear? What was your news?" she asks, stepping aside to usher me inside.

"I'm gay, Mrs Mackenney and I'm seeing Mark Lidano."

"Oh dear, thats lovely you've found someone special."

"Thanks, so is Quentin home?"

"Yes, dear, he's down in Ember's room."

"Thanks," I reply smiling.

"Would you like a drink dear?"

"A coffee would be lovely."

"No problems, dear, I'll let you know when its ready."

I head down the hallway, listening for voices to find the right room.

I hear a sweet little girls voice protesting, "Kent oo ot play ight."

Stopping in the doorway of the bedroom that is decked out with everything a little girl could desire, I laugh watching Quentin kneeling on the floor with a Barbie doll in his hand.

Ember is standing in front of him, with her hands on her hips and a scowl on her face.

She looks up at me. "Who oo?" she asks.

Unlawful Attachment

Quentin turns to face me, standing up and dropping the doll.

"Hi Hugh," he mutters.

"Hey man, just popping in to see how you're doing?"

Brushing a hand against my arm he ushers me out of the doorway, turning back to speak to Ember, "Sweetie, I just need to speak to my friend Hugh here, ok?"

"Ok Kent," she replies going back to playing dolls without a care in the world.

"I'm doing better, thanks to Mum being here."

"Yeah, it's great she can be back with you."

Reaching the kitchen, Mrs Mackenney has a piping hot coffee on the bench. She winks at me when she heads down the hallway.

"So about the other night Hugh, I...I'm really sorry for how I reacted."

"It's ok, you were upset and drunk."

"It's not ok man, I honestly don't care if..."

"You don't have to apologise."

"Yes, I do...what I said was really hurtful. I'm honestly happy for you and Mark. Is he here too?"

"Yeah, he's in the car. He's super pissed at you still."

"I don't blame him, I was an arse. Do you know what though?"

"What?"

"I always kinda thought Mark was gay, but I didn't think you were. I was just shocked."

"Yeah, I was shocked when I found out Mark was and that he had a crush on me." I laugh.

"Yeah, I kinda can't believe I didn't twig onto that, but kinda makes sense now."

"Yeah, so are things good with us?"

"Always man, no matter what you guys are my best mates, but I don't want to know about your sex life ok?"

"Ok, and likewise," I reply laughing, sipping my coffee that is finally cool enough.

"So what happened between you and your girl?"

"If I knew I'd tell you, but pretty much after we slept together she said she loved me, took my gun and I haven't heard from her since."

"Oh man, that sucks big time. I don't even know what to say."

"Yeah it hurts so fucking bad man. I fucking love her so much."

"More than you loved Addison?"

"Way more man, way more and Ember too."

"The sweetie playing dolls down the hall?"

"Yeah, her daughter. It's like she had it planned all along and I feel like she lied to me about loving me."

"Aww man I don't think so, you're pretty loveable," I jeer at him, poking his arm.

"Don't get any ideas man, I'm not switching teams," he replies with laugh that makes me smile.

"I know man, but you know what I mean."

"Yeah, so when's Mark going to talk to me?"

"When he gets his head out of his arse. You know how stubborn he is."

"Yeah, tell him I'm happy for you guys and we'll catch up for a drink next week."

"Alright, I'll drag his arse out, unless you want to talk to him now?"

"Nah, I'll give him some space. But yeah just let him know no hard feelings. I love you guys."

"Oh really? So your going to switch teams then?" I tease him.

"Yeah, haha Hugh, you know what I mean."

"Yeah, I do. I better get going, thank ya Mum for the coffee. I'll catch ya for that drink soon. Shoot me a text."

"Will do," he replies when I stand up and he follows me towards the door.

He bro hugs me, an arm around my waist and gives me a pat on my back when I walk out.

"Catch ya, man," I announce walking away.

He waves at Mark in the front seat, who flips him the bird in response. It's going to be tough to get Mark to come around and realise that Quentin's reaction wasn't how he really feels. But I know he'll come around eventually, as he isn't one to hold a grudge, too caring to stay mad at anyone and it's one of the reasons I love him so much.

(58) Emilie

The days have become a blur. I'm barely able to think about what has happened in the last few days, let alone the past few weeks.
I know my surroundings, because I'd been in the back room of Bloom Burlesque more times than I ever want to remember, but now it feels like a new kind of torture because I'd not left the room and Vlad hasn't exactly been pleasant towards me.
He says he loves me, because I remind him of Mum, which I for one think is disgusting, and two he treats me like his play thing, not someone he loves.
My heart is literally shattered in my chest, the days blurring into one another and I can't help but wonder if I'll ever see Quentin again.
I've fallen so deep for him, that I honestly don't feel like I could ever love anyone else again.

Waking up I panic, hearing the click clack of Vlad's dress shoes on the floorboards. I don't want him to be coming into to the room, because he'll most likely slip me some type of drug again and I can't remember anything he does whilst I'm out of it.
When he opens the door, I let out a scream, hoping someone will hear and know I'm here.

"Keep it quiet Vixen!"
"No, Vlad, why are you keeping me here?"
"I told you! You're mine Vixen!"
"I'm not yours Vlad, I never was...what my Mum did was despicable! It doesn't make me yours."
"No, Vixen the contract you signed all those years ago made you mine."

"Fuck your contract Vlad!" I spit at him sitting up in the bed, taking a deep breath to try and ease my panic.

"Seriously Vixen your words don't hurt me." He laughs callously.

"I want to go home."

"You are home Vixen! You belong with me and if you play nice I'll let you out of this room."

"Excuse me, I'm not your fucking prisoner!" I scream at him.

"No Vixen, you're my slave." His words are callous and stab me in the chest at his brutality when he continues, "Sex slave."

"You're eehh...heinous Vladimir Manning!" I screech at him, hoping my words hurt.

"Only in bed Vixen, outside of the bedroom my love for you is endless."

"Love!" I spit. "You don't know what love is Vlad!"

"Oh I know love, my sweet Vixen! Kiss me and I'll show you how much I love you."

I try to protest, to not take the kiss he's about to give me when he stops by the edge of the bed but I still don't have the strength.

He's on the bed, about to grab me, so taking a deep breath I courageously say, "Only if you let me out of here."

"Fine, anything else?" He says, a promising tone in his voice like he actually does care.

"And let me contact Quentin."

"Not a chance, Vixen. He is no longer a part of your life."

"What about Ember?" I ask, my heart constricting at the thought of never seeing either of them again.

His eyes appear to soften a little when he looks into mine.

"Fine," he snaps again. "I'll try to work out a way for you to contact your daughter, but that's it, or you'll never leave this room again."

Against my better judgement I give in to the kiss he smacks against my lips. It's horrible and callous like all his kisses and my insides squirm in disgust.

As he kisses me a feeling of panic increasingly rises in my chest.

I shouldn't believe a single word that comes from his mouth. All he knows is lying and I know I can't believe Vlad's words.

The feeling rushing through me isn't just panic but that unmistakable feeling of bile rising up into your mouth, like you're going to vomit.

This isn't just from Vlad's kiss—that would make anyone vomit—but it feels as though it's coming from the depths of my stomach.

Abruptly pulling back from Vlad, I launch myself out of the bed, racing to the bathroom.

Reaching the toilet just in time, I vomit into the bowl, feeling like I've just lost everything I've eaten for the past few days.

Standing up wiping my face with my sleeve I turn to find Vlad standing in the doorway.

"Vixen, are you not telling me something?" He asks with a slightly wicked grin on his face that kind of makes me want to vomit again.

Instead I shrug, standing up to wash my hands and gulp down some water from the tap.

Pushing past him out the door I taunt, "Let me out of here and I'll go find out."

"Fine, but you come straight back here to take it right in front of me," he suggests worriedly.

"Of course, Vlad," I taunt, walking out to get dressed into something other than the underwear I have on.

I'm secretly hoping that I am indeed pregnant and that it's Quentin's. The timing makes sense and it makes my heart flutter.

In my head whilst Vlad watches me dress I think about a plan to go to the police station so they can put me in contact with Quentin, but the look in Vlad's eyes has changed.

It appears that he's thinking way too much, and I know there's probably no chance of leaving this room on my own ever again.

Quickly dressing I can feel Vlad's eyes on me, his gaze making the sick feeling rise again. Swallowing hard to push the bile back down my throat, I screech at him, "Vlad, please, I need some space."

"Not a chance Emilie," he responds in a harsh tone, confirming my feeling he's worried about letting me go out on my own, for fear I'll run.

"Why? I'm not leaving I promise," I reply sweetly, hoping my tone hides the fact that I'm clearly lying.

"I love you Emilie, but that doesn't mean I trust your words."

"Well, why don't you take me to a doctor instead?"

He scoffs at my question. "Yeah sure..."

He's looking at me like he's saying, *are you a fool Emilie?*

His next words just cement more in my mind that he is a heinous man, not capable of the love he says he feels.

"Not going to happen Vixen...I can't have people thinking I get my girls pregnant."

"Well, Vlad, for one I'm not your girl and two if I'm pregnant I'm hoping like hell that it's Quentin's."

"Why would you want it to be his?" he says oddly, pushing me against the wall.

"Because I love him! And he loves me!" I yell.

"He won't love you now, thinking you left him when he let you in about his past."

I feel my eyes go wide, shocked that Vlad is insinuating he knows something about Quentin's past.

"What do you know about his past?"

"I make it my business to know all my clientele, especially those who cause trouble."

"Since when did he cause trouble?"

Scoffing he replies, "He was just as bad as your pathetic excuse for a husband and your six foot under now brother. Mackenney wanted you more, but he was too much of a pussy, wimpy arsed cop to go up against me."

"You can't be serious Vlad?"

"Dead serious! Mackenney and your dead brother were never and never will be a match up against me."

"If you hurt Quentin, I'll..." I say, not able to find an insult that would hurt him.

"What? What are you going to do Vixen? You can't hurt me!" he jeers menacingly at me, grabbing me around the neck with a tight grip.

He's practically strangling me, when he smashes a hard kiss to my lips. My breathing is shallow and I gasp against his lips on mine, hoping that I'm not about to black out. When his lips pull from mine, I gasp, taking in the deepest breath I can.

"I can hurt you Vixen, remember that," he spits at me, before he steps back.

"Go get in the Mas...I'll be out in ten."

Reaching into his pocket, he hands me the key fob, lifting my hand to kiss it for a moment before I snatch it back scoffing at him.

"No Vladimir you don't get to do that."

"I can and will do whatever I want with and to you Vixen. Just go and get in the fucking car or all deals are off!"

He laughs, slapping my arse when I walk away.

Descending the steps two at a time, I quickly find myself in the basement and underground parking garage of Bloom. His blue Maserati is parked right at the base of the staircase, and I press the key fob to unlock it.

Opening the door, I slide into the seat, taking a deep breath and sighing as I sink into the seat.

Thoughts of the day I left flash in my mind, tears stinging my eyes and wiping them away I try to focus on what I had with me that day.

Frantically, I search the car, remembering I took Quentin's gun.

Firstly I check the glove box but it's not there, next I check the console, finding it loaded end pointing to the bottom. Thankfully the safety is on and I pull it out hastily.

Sitting forward I slip it into the waistband of my leggings, just as Vlad opens his door and slides into his seat, giving me an odd look like he knows I'm hiding something from him.

He doesn't say a word though, instead presses the start engine button, revving the engine and driving out of the parking garage.

He's driving with such force I can't get my seat-belt to cooperate and I'm scared my life is again going to be over. Vladimir Manning already has too much blood on his hands, but Karma is a bitch.

(59) Vladimir

Not saying a word to Emilie, I slide into the drivers side of the Maserati giving her a sideways glance. I run the car into gear to gun it out of the parking garage.

Revving the engine, pressing my foot hard on the accelerator I give the car my anger, loving how it hums ready for a gear change when I reach the road.

Turning left out of the parking garage to head towards the shopping centre, I gun the Mas to get there as quick as possible.

Barely a kilometre down the road, I see the flashing lights coming up fast behind me in the rear view mirror. Sliding the Mas over to the side of the road I roll the window down when the officer steps up to the car.

"Hi, drivers licence please?" He asks, looking at me incredulously.

"Don't have it on me, I'm urgently taking my wife to the hospital constable," I reply touching and squeezing Emilie's leg. The officer is looking at me oddly, like he knows who I am.

"Is that you Mr Manning? I didn't know you were married."

I laugh, smiling at him. "Yes, officer, just happened last week. So are we good?"

"Yeah, no worries Mr Manning. Have a good day."

"You to, Constable."

Rolling the window up, I look across at Emilie who's shaking her head at me.

"Really Vlad? Are you in with all the cops?"

"You could say that. Thanks to your brother, cops don't bother me, even for petty things like speeding."

"I can't believe you Vlad, speeding is not petty. My father nearly killed someone because he was driving drunk and speeding."

"Keyword there is drunk, Vixen, not speeding."

She scoffs at me as I the slide the Mas back onto the road, entering the traffic again. Having wasted enough time I again gun off towards the shopping centre, arriving a mere fifteen minutes later.

Effortlessly I glide the Mas into a carpark, not far from the entrance of Elizabeth shopping centre.

"Go in, get a test and come straight back," I instruct Emilie.

"And if I don't?" She taunts, her fingers brushing against the door handle.

"Every cop in Adelaide will be sent out to search for you," I seethe at her, cutting into her with my eyes. She huffs, unlatching her seatbelt and opening the door, a little too carefully sliding out.

I watch her when she walks inside, and I think that she is already waddling like a pregnant woman, which is a little odd.

My mind wanders a moment thinking about the prospect of being a father, of seeing Emilie pregnant with my child.

I can't help but feel mixed about it , as fear for my reputation as a club owner would be tainted but mainly it's a feeling of worry for the child being brought into the corrupt world of the Manning family.

My phone ringing breaks my thoughts, the sound cutting through the bluetooth speaker.

Glancing at the number flashing on the touchscreen I don't recognise the number, so answer hesitantly, "Hello, Vlad speaking."

"Vladimir Manning, what in the world are you doing at Elizabeth?"

"Personal business, Don," I snap recognising the voice of an old acquaintance.

"You scouting out girls?"

"No, and this personal business is of no interest to you."

"Right, so what's with the pretty as fuck brunette who just slid out of your Mas then?"

"Again, Don, none of your business," I snap annoyed at his questions, wanting to hang up but not doing so because he'll keep calling back.

"Have you got yourself a mistress, Vlad?"

"That would have to mean I have a wife for one and two if I did Don, that wouldn't concern you."

"Sorry Vlad man, feels like forever since we've had a man to man chat."

"Yes, Don but I don't have time for that type of shit. How did you know I'm at Elizabeth?"

"Look towards the entrance," he instructs, sounding like he's smiling when I turn my gaze to where he's suggesting. My eyes focus on Don waving to me but I also notice that Emilie is walking out behind him.

"Don, I need to go. Emilie is coming back."

"She's fine Vlad , take her back to the club to dance."

"She has before Don, and will again as soon as I deal with something," I promise hanging up when Emilie slides in the car holding a small plastic bag.

"Who was on the phone?" She asks softly.

"Just an old friend," I reply, hoping she hadn't heard my last words to Don.

"Oh ok, so what will happen if the tests are positive Vlad?" she taunts me whilst I drive out of the car park.

"We deal with it Emilie," I snap at her.

"Oh no Vlad! That will not be happening. I will not let you take my baby away a second time!"

"If you want to live you will do whatever I tell you Emilie. You're mine forever, only you. No baby or any other living person will take you away from me again."

She doesn't reply to my words and I feel a pang of guilt hit me. She shifts uncomfortably in her seat like there is something pressing into her back. I can't help but smile—a wicked evil smile at her—knowing she will do whatever I say like she always has.

She turns away to look out the window and I notice the tears on her cheeks. I curse myself for being so callous to her, even though I love her more than anything.

My callous nature once again rules out, it's the only way I know to get what I want and all I want is my Emilie.

(60) Emilie

The drive back to the club seems to fly by but it's also agonisingly slow. I can feel the cold metal of the gun pressing into my back and I shift uncomfortably in the seat itching to get out of the car.
My mind is racing with thoughts. Thoughts of how to get in contact with Quentin if the tests are positive, thoughts of what Vlad will do to me if the tests are positive and whether or not I can even bring myself to pull the trigger of the gun if things go pear-shaped.
The look Vlad is giving me as he drives is scaring me because it's an odd mix of lust and the evil I've only ever seen in his eyes.
It's difficult to play along with his demands, to let him use my body how he wants but I don't know what else I can do.
Staying alive amidst his torture sometimes doesn't seem worth it, but somehow I know that Quentin will find out what has happened and will rescue me from the hell this time, just like he promised.

Turning into the parking garage, Vlad slides the Maserati into his carpark and no sooner has he cut the engine, I'm out of the car racing to the elevator to beat him upstairs.
"Emilie, wait up! You're not to take the tests without me."
I laugh at him, watching as the elevator doors close despite his efforts to make them open. He looks pissed off, but I'm glad to have the moment to myself to stash the gun before heading to the bathroom to take the test.
Surprisingly he's left the back room open, a seemingly careless move because no one is allowed to enter the back room without his explicit permission.

Unlawful Attachment

Looking around the room when I walk in, I grab the gun from behind my back, wondering for a moment where to stash it. About to slide the drawer open by the bed, I hear and feel him step up behind me.

"What the fuck are you doing Emilie?" he taunts when I turn towards him.

Dropping the bag of tests on the floor, I grip the gun with two hands pointing it directly at him.

"Don't come any closer Vlad or I'll shoot you!"

"You wouldn't dare Vixen!" he seethes at me, stepping further into the room.

Closing my eyes, I take a deep breath in, flicking the safety off and depressing the trigger without a second thought.

The power of the gun firing makes me drop it to the floor. I'm almost too scared to open my eyes, because time stops for a moment before I hear Vlad curse, "Fuck Vixen! You fucking shot me!"

Opening one eye, I see him standing in the middle of the room clutching his thigh to try and curb the pain.

"I...I..." I stammer, not wanting to apologise but not sure what else there is to say. He steps forward towards me and my whole body tenses, paralysed with fear when he picks up the gun and he crashes into me.

Pushing my body against the wall, he presses the gun against my stomach, looking directly into my eyes when he snarls at me, "You will go take a test now Vixen and you better pray hard it's not positive or you'll feel this gun rip you in two."

Nodding I try to reply, but my mouth is dry and nothing comes out.

He steps back and I slide across the wall, before dashing quickly to pick up the bag with the tests in it.

In the bathroom I pee on the stick, knowing the moment I finish taking it that it's clearly positive. The pink lines come up immediately and super dark.

My heart leaps in my chest. I know such a dark test means for sure I'm pregnant with Quentin's baby.

"Vixen, have you taken it?" Vlad's voice calls out from behind the door. I can tell he's still in pain from the wound to the leg.

"Yes," I call back, "and it's Quentin's."

I hear him take in a breath, seething when he lets it out, "Open the fucking door, Vixen."

I hesitate, clutching the test in my fist, rubbing the other hand over my stomach before I open the door.

Snatching the test from my hand, he looks at it, anger crossing his face. My hands find my stomach, hoping to protect my baby, even though I know that nothing will save us if he follows through with his earlier threat.

I can't stand looking at him, so I close my eyes and await the impact of the bullet, hoping that it's not my last moments.

He scoffs loudly before his fists slam into my stomach, pushing my body against the tiled wall of the open shower. Hitting my head against the tiles, my body feels shaky, and I slide down to the floor.

"Please, please don't hurt the baby," I scream out feeling his presence over me and his blood dripping onto my leg.

Again he scoffs, before laughing wickedly and he places the gun in my hand.

"I'm not going to hurt anyone Emilie," he taunts.

My eyes feel glued shut and I don't even want to open them anyway. He walks out of the bathroom, and I hear him mutter, "You'll wish you were dead Vixen. Use the gun when you're ready."

Taking a deep breath in after I hear him leave the room, cursing from the pain of the bullet wound in his thigh I muster all the strength I can to stand up.

Slowly I open my eyes, shocked by how much blood trails across the floor, all the way into the bedroom and out the door into the hallway. It's even on the door handle, and I hope that he's collapsed and is slowly dying from losing too much blood.

Sitting down on the bed, I open the bedside drawer hoping he'd still left the mobile phone there. Thankfully my fingers brush against it and it has just enough battery for a phone call.

Unlawful Attachment

I dial triple zero asking for police, informing them of my location and the fact that he threatened to kill me and my unborn child. The operator asks a few more questions that I can't answer because Vlad enters the room with his leg bandaged tightly.

He limps towards me, seething from the pain.

"What? Who the fuck are you talking to?"

"No one. I was um just...um going to call Quentin," I reply ending the emergency call and racing back towards the bathroom.

Again I grab the gun, about to point it towards him again when he stops in the doorway grabbing me around the waist and pulling me against his body; trying to grab the gun from me.

I hear the gunshot go off again, but Vlad makes no sound this time, even when his body slides down mine to the floor.

I stand over his body, holding the gun in my hand still, completely paralysed with fear that I've killed him.

(61) Quentin

I'd barely slept a wink since Emilie left, tossing and turning with dreams plaguing me the moment I closed my eyes. I've had to sleep in the Black room and it tortures me because all I can think about is the time I spent in there with Emilie in my arms, our bodies entwined together when we came undone. Thankfully Mum hasn't asked questions and hasn't ventured into the room.
It has been easier in some ways having Mum staying with me, because she's cooked and cleaned up the house, just letting me be.
My days are filled with trying to make things seem normal for Ember, but it has been weeks since Emilie had left and I can't keep up the facade anymore.

Waking up, unsure of the time I grab my phone from next to me on the black satin sheets. Pressing the home button, the screen lights up to tell me it's six am. The room is inky, still so dark from the boarded-up windows even though outside the sun would have been making an appearance.
Throwing the sheets back I shoot out of bed, straight over to the window. Yanking hard at the edge of the boards over the windows I pull them down, not caring if I damage the wall behind.
The sun streams in—lighting up the room—warming my whole body.
Standing at the window for a moment, lost in thought I'm startled when Mum raps on the door.
"Baby boy, what's going on in there? Are you ok?"
"Yeah, fine Mum. Just give me a minute," I call out, crossing back to the bed and frantically stripping the sheets.
Balling them in a pile, I carry them to the door, opening it slightly to find Mum still standing in the hallway.

Squeezing past her I shut the door behind me to head down the hallway to the laundry.

"Baby boy, what happened?"

"I um...knocked something over when I fell out of bed."

"Are you ok? Can I help with anything?"

"No thanks, Mum. Just sorting some things out in my room."

"Ok, baby boy. Let me know if you need anything."

"I will Mum, but honestly you need to take care of yourself. I've let you do too much around here and I can see it's hurting you."

She follows me down the hallway to the laundry, standing in the doorway when I shove my sheets into the front of the washing machine. She lets out a sigh when I scoop powder into the slot.

"Baby boy, did I teach you nothing?"

"What do you mean Mum?"

"You should always wash black items with liquid detergent and those sheets should be washed in cold water."

"Oh, um yeah." I laugh, turning the dial to thirty degrees.

"Are you sure there's nothing I can help you with in your room baby boy?"

"No, it's fine Mum. Could you maybe get Ember up though?"

"Sure baby boy," she replies nodding and starting to hobble back down the hallway. "When are you going to tell her that her mother isn't coming back?"

"I don't know Mum. But I have to," I reply passing her when I head back to my room.

From the linen cupboard, I grab out some plain soft cotton sheets and once back in my room, I make the bed stepping back to admire how it looks so much better with the sun pouring in and dancing across the sky blue sheets.

The black walls still feel foreboding, so I grab my phone to write a list of supplies to pick up from the hardware store later.

On the screen, there is a missed call and a voicemail from an unknown number.

Hesitant to even listen to it, I sit on the edge of the bed, running my hands through my hair. I take in a deep breath and holding the phone up to my ear to listen to the voicemail, my heart pounds fiercely beating in my chest the entire time.

'Constable Mackenney, this is Constable Thompson from the Adelaide CBD station. There has been an incident here with a gun registered to you. The young woman involved is asking for you. Please call me back as soon as possible.'

I listen to the message again, letting the words sink in and connecting the dots in my head. Emilie took my gun, Emilie is alive and wants to see me.

Racing out of the bedroom, after pulling on some jeans and a t-shirt, I call out loudly to Mum, "I gotta go to Adelaide, like now."

I find her in Ember's room watching her play with her Barbies.

"Why baby boy? What's happened?"

Handing her my phone, I press play for the message to play through the speakerphone.

"Can you look after her? I'm going to call him back before I head off."

"Ok baby boy, but you'll need to drive extra careful. There's a storm coming."

"I know Mum," I reply kissing her forehead when she hands my phone back.

Scrolling through my contacts I find the Adelaide CBD number, and I'm shocked it only rings once before it's answered.

"Adelaide police station, Constable Thompson speaking."

"Constable Thompson, it's Constable Mackenney returning your call."

"Great, glad you got back to me so quick."

"I'm a little panicked actually."

"Understandable. Were you aware your gun had been stolen?"

Gulping I reply, "Yes, I was actually. It's a little complicated."

"I'm gathering that from what's happened here at Bloom Burlesque."

"Are you charging the young woman with anything?"

Unlawful Attachment

"She will be charged with unlawful possession of a firearm, but at this stage nothing else. We believe the multiple shootings to the victim were in self-defence as she was quite shaken up when we arrived at the scene."

"Um, so who was shot? Is the victim still alive?" I ask, trying to process his words.

"The victim was a Mr Vladimir Manning and yes he is alive but currently in custody due to some other outstanding matters."

"Oh, and the woman, is she in custody?"

"No, she's currently in the base hospital due to shock. She also had some unexplained pain and bleeding."

"So do you need me to head down?"

"Yes, we do. You realise that not reporting your gun as missing is a major breach of conduct?"

"Yes, I'm fully aware of the consequences of my actions." I sigh, hearing Sarge Ryan chastising me in my head.

"She has been asking for you as well. We can have a chat when you arrive."

"Okay, thanks, Constable Thompson. I'll be down by nightfall."

"Thanks for your time Constable Mackenney. See you later this evening," he replies before hanging up.

I find Mum in the kitchen, making a coffee in a thermos mug for me.
"You heard?"

"Yes, baby boy. It's your Emilie isn't it?"

"Yes, but I'm in big trouble Mum. I could lose my whole career over this."

Handing me the thermos, she shakes her head. "I'm sure it won't come to that baby boy. You're a good policeman. Ridgehope needs you."

"Yeah, let's hope it works out. I'll let you know when I arrive in the city."

Giving her a lingering hug, grabbing my keys I race out the door.

For a moment I contemplated going to the station and getting a cop car, but taking a car without permission whilst on suspension is likely to get me in more trouble that I can't risk.

Getting in the Kingswood, belting up after putting my coffee in my makeshift cup holder I crank the radio up and reverse down my driveway to head to the city.

It's only eight am, but the sky is dark with black foreboding clouds that as I head south to Adelaide I'm driving straight into.

I hope it won't hit until I get closer to Adelaide, because the roads out here are dead straight and scary to drive on at the best of times, let alone in a thunderstorm.

My heart is pounding, my head spinning with thoughts of what has happened with Emilie and Vladimir Manning. I know he was being investigated for some incidents concerning his club by Emilie's brother but we'd not looked into details in Ridgehope. The thought crosses my mind that maybe Vladimir had murdered Alec, but there's no evidence. No cop can put an innocent man in jail just because they have a feeling he has committed a crime.

After driving for about four hours I stop in Clare, grabbing a Farmers Union iced coffee and a Balfour's meat pie to munch on. I'd filled up the gas tank, surprised to actually have not needed much over twenty litres to fill it. My Kingswood might have been practically ancient in the world of cars but she still drove like she was new.

Driving out of Clare, heading towards the bend to turn towards Balaklava the clouds are practically on top of me. Taking a big sip of iced coffee I gulp hard, braking a little when the clouds erupt, pelting rain so hard it's almost deafening.

Flicking the wipers to high, they streak across the windscreen full pelt without even a chance to wipe away the rain.

I know that I shouldn't keep driving, but there's nowhere safe to pull over on these country roads. Slowing the car to sixty kilometres an hour, I drive on.

Moments later, I practically jump out of my seat when a massive clap of thunder follows a bolt of lightning that makes it seem like daylight. My foot involuntary collides with the accelerator lurching the car forward suddenly. With the roads excessively wet, I feel the tyres struggling to grip the road.

Gripping the steering wheel, the car begins to hydroplane and in trying to correct my path I only make it worse, sending the car spinning over to the other side of the road.

Closing my eyes, knowing I can't do anything when I see the trees come into view I feel the impact against the front of the car on the passenger side.

The windscreen cracks when my head hits it, the car colliding with the tree. I can feel the seatbelt cutting into my stomach, can smell my iced coffee mixed with blood that has spattered all over the inside of the car.

My eyes are glued shut, and I don't even want to open them to see what is causing the pain in my leg and stomach. Blood is trickling down my cheek into my mouth, making me breathe shallowly and sputter at the metallic taste.

There's a hiss coming from the engine, the rain still pelting down not blocking it out. My mind is racing, thinking about never seeing Emilie again.

I'm going to die out here—alone—and it feels like mere moments will pass until my heart stops beating. There's no way I'm going to survive this; the pain that is becoming unbearable.

My mind goes blank then, unconsciousness taking over.

(62) *Hunter*

The storm is looming on the horizon when I head into town to pick up River up from Kindy. The drive home with him in the car and a storm erupting around us is going to be twenty plus minutes of torture. River hates thunderstorms. For his three, nearly four years of life whenever a storm was around he'd cover his ears, screaming at the top of his lungs with high pitched wailing cries that make me want to take the storm away but also block my own ears to not have to listen to his pain.

It tears at my heart whenever my little boy is in pain. He doesn't handle any illness well, screaming as though he's dying from just a simple blocked nose. He'd not taken to Kindy well, not wanting to play with anyone but Ember. I know all the signs point to the fact that my little boy is autistic but living in Ridgehope it isn't exactly easy to get him tested.

Arriving into town, I pull up out the front of the local Prep to twelve school. It's always busy at this time of the day with local parents picking up their children.

Getting out of the ute, rolling up my sleeves I lean on the side of the ute sighing. The local kindy teacher Millie is standing at the nearby gate greeting parents when they walk in to pick up their children.

"Hi Hunter, you ok?"

"Hi Millie and yes, yes I'm fine. Just not looking forward to taking River home with this storm looming."

"Yes, he's been quite tense today."

"He hates thunderstorms. You're lucky you haven't seen him during a meltdown."

She bites her lip, looking at me apprehensively. "Um about that Hunter? Have you talked to Savannah about taking him to the city for a psychological assessment?"

"No, I haven't. Things have been super busy with Savannah being pregnant again with the twins and some other stuff at the farm."

"I understand that Hunter, but I believe things are going to get harder for River when the twins arrive and it would be in your family's best interest to rule anything out."

I'm about to reply when my eager son comes bounding down the footpath towards the gate. "Daddy, daddy, orm coming."

Nodding to Millie, I scoop River up into my arms, holding him against my hip.

"Yes, sweetie, there is a storm coming. We better get home before it starts raining."

"Don't want orm Daddy," he replies, squirming in my arms.

"I know, Riv. Say goodbye to Miss Millie ok? You'll see her next week."

He giggles, waving his tiny hand towards Millie. "Bye Miss Millie."

"Bye, River. Be a good boy for Daddy ok?"

Again my cheeky son giggles and I walk to the passenger side of the car, strapping him into his car seat. About to get into the driver's seat, my phone rings loudly in my pocket, making me jump out of my skin. Hesitantly seeing what appears to be an Adelaide number on the screen I answer, "Hello?"

"Hello. Am I speaking to Hunter Mackenney?"

"Yes, and who might you be?"

"Hi, Hunter. This is Sarah Bazta. I'm a nurse at Adelaide base hospital."

"Oh um ok," I reply, words tumbling in my head.

"I hate to make this type of call, but you're listed as an emergency contact for Quentin Mackenney."

"Um, yes. He is my younger brother."

"He has been admitted after a car accident near Clare. We're unsure of the extent of his injuries at this stage but he's currently in surgery."

My head is spinning.

Accident. Clare. Surgery.

"I'm sorry what? My brother is what? I....I..."
"I'm sorry Mr Mackenney. It may be best for you to come down here as soon as possible to be with your brother."
"Um ok. I...I will have to head down tomorrow as it's unsafe to drive now."
"That's understandable. After surgery, he may be placed in a medically induced coma to help him heal from any internal injuries."
"Ok, thank you." I sigh, still not sure if this conversation is even happening.
"No problems Mr Mackenney. Goodbye now," she replies, hanging up before I can even think of another word to say.
Getting in the ute, River is looking at me with an apprehensive look on his face like he knows something is up. Instead of heading home, I drive around the corner to Quentin's house, afraid and worried to tell Mum the horrible news I've just heard.

Rapping on Quentin's front door, my heart is pounding in my chest. River is standing next to me, clutching my hand, jumping up and down excitedly. He knows Ember is living with Quentin and always loves coming over to play with her and to also see his beloved uncle.
I'm petrified my little brother is going to die without getting a chance to meet his new nieces or nephews.
Mum opens the door, looking us up and down before stretching up to kiss my cheek.
"Hi, sweet boy, what brings you over with this storm coming?"
I usher her inside with a hand on her back. "I was just picking River up from Kindy and received a rather unpleasant phone call."
Mum looks me up and down, obviously noticing the panicked look on my face.
"Is everything ok with Savannah? The twins?"
"Yes, Savannah and the twins are fine, but Mum...Quentin isn't."

Her face falls—a knowing look—a horrified look painting her face like she knows something I don't. She looks to River, bending down a little to be closer to his level. "River dearest, can you go play with Ember in her room?"

He nods, dropping my hand and racing down the hallway without a backwards glance.

"Mum," I say, taking her hand with mine to lead her over to the couch to sit down. After following and sitting on the couch next to her I begin speaking again, barely able to get the words out. "Um…Quentin…he…um…had…a…"

I stop speaking, the words caught on my tongue.

"A car accident?" Mum asks, touching my hand comfortingly.

"Yes, how…how did you know?"

"He left early this morning to go to Adelaide. Something happened with his Emilie and a constable from the CBD called him and asked him to head down as soon as he could."

Anger hits me hard in the chest. "And you let him go with the storm coming?"

Mum hits me back with even more anger in her tone. "Don't you dare raise your voice at me, Hunter! Nothing would've stopped your headstrong younger brother from leaving the minute he got that phone call."

"True, but I didn't think he was that stupid."

"You daren't speak about your brother that way! You would've done exactly the same thing if something happened to Savannah," she chastises me, making me feel about four foot tall.

"I know Mum. I'm sorry, I just…I can't bear to think of saying goodbye to him."

"It won't come to that son."

"How do you know that Mum? He's in surgery and will be in a medically induced coma because they're unsure if he has any internal injuries."

Mum sighs, pulling me to her in a comforting hug, tears starting to stream down my face.

I feel her chest move when she takes a deep breath in, exhaling hard before she kisses my hair.

"Quentin will not die from this Hunter. It takes a lot more to bring a Mackenney man down."

I let out a lighthearted laugh at what Mum is implying, lifting my head up to look at her again, surprised she's not crying too.

"Yeah, I guess. I survived a bullet to the chest."

"Exactly, sweet boy. Have you spoken to Savannah yet?"

"No, I came straight here."

"Call her. You can leave River here whilst you head back to the farm to pick her up. We can head to the city first thing tomorrow morning whilst Savannah stays here with the kidlets."

"I guess that could work. I'll let Addison know, just incase anything happens with the twins."

"Ok sweet boy," she replies, kissing my cheek before slowly getting up to go see what River and Ember are up to.

The last twelve or so hours feel like a complete whirlwind. My body has run on some crazy amount of adrenaline.

I'd gone back to the farm, explaining everything to Savannah as we headed back into town to Quentin's house. We'd barely slept a wink thinking about Mum and I leaving for the city and what was going to happen when we got there.

The six-hour drive to the city passed relatively quickly, after our single stop in Clare to grab a coffee and some food.

On the side of the road just after the bend, I saw some debris from an accident and my heart lurched in my chest, bile rising in my throat as I passed knowing it was where Quentin had his accident.

I don't say a word to Mum, our only conversation being chit-chat that will distract us until we're amidst the city traffic and I have to take deep breaths in and out to focus in the hustle bustle that makes me glad I live in the country.

Unlawful Attachment

We reach the hospital, driving into the underground carpark,
thankfully able to park in a disability spot close to the elevators.
Leaving Mum in the car, I grab a ticket to display on the windscreen
before I help her out of the car.

Leaning against me, I can tell her pain level is higher than normal after
being in the car so long. I hand her the walking frame, but ask softly,
"Do you want a wheelchair Mum?"

"No, sweet boy I'll be fine," she affirms by nodding when I lock the car
and we head to the elevators.

The quick elevator ride takes us straight to the main hospital reception.
Helping Mum sit down in the chairs along the wall, I step up to the
desk.

"Hi, we're here to see Quentin Mackenney."

"Yes, you must be his brother Hunter," the nurse states, giving me a
slight smile before she frowns to inform me, "He's currently in
intensive care on level four. You will need to speak to the nurses in
charge to see him."

"Ok, thank you," I reply, sighing and turning back to Mum. She's
standing up clutching her walking frame with white fingers that show
the panic she's keeping inside.

We take the elevator up to the fourth floor. It's so eerily quiet and the
overwhelming smell of bleach assaults my nostrils every time I take in
a breath.

Stepping up to the nurses station, with Mum at my side this time, my
eyes immediately lock on the nurses name badge, *'Sarah'*. She knows
the moment she looks at me who I am.

"Hunter I'm presuming?"

"Yes, and this is our Mother Grace."

She nods at us both, before speaking softly, "He is in room five. As I
said to you yesterday he is in a medically induced coma but you're
welcome to sit with him. Let him know you're here."

"Thank you," I reply, running a hand through my hair sighing to prepare
myself at what condition I'm about to see my little brother in.

"Which way is his room?"

Sarah laughs light-heartedly, leaving the nurses station and appearing in front of us.

"I'll show you," she volunteers, leading us down the narrow white-walled hallways to rooms away from the elevators.

Opening the door of room five, she ushers us in without saying a word and looking at my baby brother in the bed in front of me, tears break free from my eyes.

His right leg is in a cast from thigh to ankle, held up off the bed in one of those contraptions. His face has tubes and an oxygen mask covering it, whilst the machine next to him beeps steadily.

The sheets are pulled up to his chin, his skin the same pale white.

Mum is frozen next to me and lets out a muffled yelp of pain before she falls to the floor.

(63) *Savannah*

The moment Hunter and Mum left for the city my loneliness and panic set in. Every part of my body aches and simple everyday tasks are so difficult with my belly sticking out in front of me.
I feel enormous, bigger than an elephant.
I've been extremely lucky that things with my pregnancy have been going so well, but being thirty-six weeks pregnant with twins I'm about ready to cut them out myself.
River and Ember had excitedly run around the house all day and thankfully being around Ember when the storm hit, had stopped River's usual thunderstorm screaming match from happening.

Sitting on the couch I sip my tea watching my son interacting with his best friend, giggling whilst she chases him around the room.
He stops abruptly when a large clap of thunder shakes the house, the look on his face like he's about to scream.

Ember giggles, pecking his lips cheekily, so obviously unaware of what she's doing. His eyes light up and he smiles back at her before running off continuing their game of chasee.
My heart pounds and I laugh, knowing already that my sweet boy is going to be a heartbreaker when he's older. The twins kick me hard in the belly as though they're fighting for space inside me. I know their days in my belly are coming to an end, but I hope that Hunter is going to be home for their birth.
I've not heard from him all day, so pick up my phone to text him.

Savannah: baby, did you get to the city ok? How's Quentin?

His reply is almost immediate and makes my heart fall.

Hunter: hey baby. made it fine...but Quentin is not in good shape and Mum had a fall
Savannah: oh my god baby...wish I could be there. Is mum ok?
Hunter: yeah she's just resting...seeing Quentin in a coma was a bit of a shock
Savannah: I bet...are you ok baby?
Hunter: yeah it's horrible baby...but I'm fine...miss you heaps
Savannah: miss you too Hunter...I love you
Hunter: love you to Savannah xxxx kiss Riv goodnight for me yeah?
Savannah: I will baby...if I can get my fat arse off the couch to give him a bath lol
Hunter: you're not fat baby...you're my gorgeous wife growing my twins
Savannah: thanks baby...I still feel like an elephant and I'm scared you won't be here when they are born
Hunter: I hope to be baby...but even if I'm not you'll be fine with Zane taking care of you
Savannah: I know baby...goodnight xoxo
Hunter: a thousand kisses to you my beautiful wife goodnight

Putting my phone down on the coffee table, I smile, pressing my palms into the couch to hoist myself up.
River comes skidding into the room, rushing straight over to me and stops looking up at me like he doesn't know what to do.
"Mummy, elp you?"
"No baby boy, mummy's fine but it's time for your bath."
"Don't want bath!" he protests defiantly stomping his foot.
"You don't have a choice in the matter, River. Go get ready in the bathroom with Ember please."

Naughtily he sticks his tongue out at me before running down the hallway, calling out, 'Em, bath!'

Unlawful Attachment

Waddling as quick as I can, I find them both standing in the bathroom buck naked with their clothes in piles at their feet.

They're looking each other up and down, obviously wondering why each other has different body parts.

River looks up at me with a sweet innocent look in his eyes, asking softly, "Mummy, why don't Em have a penie?"

Smiling, I gulp, wishing Hunter was here for this awkward conversation with his son.

"Because River, girls and boys are different. They have different special parts to their bodies."

Ember is shifting on her feet, making me feel even more awkward and not wanting to overstep my boundary because I'm not her mother.

Am I her Aunty though?

The thought confuses me, but I shake it away, trying to focus on the present situation of making her feel more comfortable.

"Ember, are you ok sweetie? Has your mummy spoken to you about this before?"

She shakes her head, bursting into tears at my mentioning of her Mother. I curse myself, kneeling down and pulling her against my side in a hug.

"I'm sorry sweetie, but Uncle Hunter has gone to the city to help bring your mummy home."

At my words, she sniffs back the tears looking at me when she sweetly asks, "eally, my mummy umming home?"

"Yes, sweetie. Really soon."

Stepping back she giggles excitedly and then breaks my heart with her words, "N Kent too?"

Again I gulp, looking at my son as well, who loves his Uncle Quentin so much that I know telling the truth is the right thing to do but also the absolutely wrong thing to do as well.

"Yes, sweetie and Quentin as well."

"Ood, I luv Kent. I want im oo be my daddy."

Tickling her playfully I reply, "I think Quentin would love to be your daddy sweetie."

River lets out a huff, folding his arms over his chest. "If Unci Kent is Em's daddy he not ine anymore."

"That's not true River. You can share him with Ember. You have your own Daddy and you know Ember's daddy has gone to sleep forever." He squeaks, reaching out awkwardly to hug Ember as though he's trying to not touch their private parts together.

"I can are Unci Kent ith oo Em."

They both giggle, their sweet innocent laughter infectious, making me laugh.

"Okay, little ones it's bath time," I announce, stretching up on my knees a little to turn on the taps, adjusting the temperature before putting the bath plug in.

Once there is enough water in the bath, I lean in checking the temperature with my elbow before I lift both River and Ember in, sitting one up each end. They playfully splash each other and I wash their faces with the flannel.

They're only in the water for a few minutes when a sharp pain stabs me in the belly. I can't help but curse out loud, clapping a hand to my mouth when I realise I just said, *'Fuck'* in front of my son who repeats every word he hears.

"Mummy, oo aid bad erd."

"Yes, sweet boy I did, but oh..." I reply biting my lip when another rush of pain hits.

River looks at me with the same worried look from earlier. This time I'm worried myself, feeling the warm liquid gush down my legs.

Awkwardly standing up, River looks at the wet patch at the front of my trackies and on the floor.

"Mummy oo pee peed." He laughs.

I nod at him but scowl to make him stop laughing.

"Pull the plug please River. Time to get out."

"But Mummy, want oo ay in!" he protests.

"Not now River!"

He huffs, reaching behind into the water, pulling the plug, watching the water gurgling down the plughole with glee on his face. Ember shrinks back scared, so I grab her out first, wrapping her swiftly in a towel and drying her off.

As she pulls on her knickers again I grab River out, wrapping him in a towel when another surge of pain rushes through me. He hugs my belly, asking, "Mummy, ins ok?"

"Yes, sweetie, but I think they might be coming."

"Eally Mummy?"

"Yes, sweetie." I nod. "Can you go get Mummy's phone from the coffee table?"

He doesn't reply, instead rushes out of the bathroom still completely naked. He's back clutching my phone in his hand before I can even think about what to do.

I think about messaging Hunter again, but don't want him to rush back or even just worry.

Instead, when River hands me my phone I dial Addison's number.

She answers almost straight away.

"Hi Savannah, everything ok?"

"No, Addison. My water just broke and I'm having pains."

"Oh no. Um...are you home alone?"

"Yeah, I'm...at," I say when another rush of pain hits. "Quentin's."

"Oh yes, right. River and Ember are with you, yeah?"

"Yes," I hiss, trying to fight the urge to scream out in pain.

"Ok, I'm going to call Zane to send the ambulance right over."

"I can't leave the kids here," I hiss again.
"I know. I'm coming over now. I'll stay with them."
"Thank you, Addison. I owe you."
"No worries, and you don't owe me anything Savannah. I'll see you in ten minutes."

૫

Just as she said ten minutes later Addison bursts into the house, straight into the bathroom. River jumps up excitedly to give her a hug.
"Hey Unty Ad, what oo oing here?"
"Hi, River. I'm here to look after you. Mummy has to go to the hospital."
"Why?"
"So your siblings can be born sweetie."
"Eally unty Ad?"
"Yes, sweetie. You go help Ember into some pj's while I help Mummy for a minute ok?"
"Ok unty Ad," he coos at her, making her smile when he grabs Ember's hand and they run out of the bathroom giggling.
Addison holds out her hand to me, helping me stand up.
"Thanks, Addison."
"It's nothing."
"You're going to be such a good mother in a couple of months," I suggest, looking at her seven-month rounded belly.
"Yeah, I hope so."
"You will be." I smile at her. "I'm jealous that you look so good pregnant."
"You're carrying twins Savannah." She laughs and we walk out of the bathroom.
"Yeah, and I can't wait until they are out." I laugh gripping my stomach when another rush of pain surges through me.
Addison takes my hand. "Breathe, in...out...stay calm," she suggests softly. "Do you have a hospital bag here?"
"Yeah, it's by the door," I inform her, listening to the approaching sirens of the ambulance.

Unlawful Attachment

"Great, sounds like the ambo's are here," she replies when Mark pushes the ajar front door open.

He doesn't even say anything whilst he helps me outside and onto the stretcher, the other officer has waiting by the front door.

Addison kisses my cheek. "Let me know when you've got twins and don't worry about anything here."

"Thanks, Addison," I reply lying down on the stretcher before they wheel it inside the ambulance.

Closing my eyes, I try to block out the pain by thinking about the names Hunter and I have discussed for our babies.

❧

The next few hours are a complete blur, a whirlwind of emotions as I'm rushed into the emergency department and straight into the delivery ward for a c-section. Zane is a dutiful doctor, guiding me through the delivery of my two beautiful babies.

He places the first one on my chest, heartily congratulating me when he announces, "Congrats Savannah you're doing well, baby one is a little girl!"

I look down at her delicate features, my heart instantly swelling with love. "Hi, Sienna Rae."

Her little fingers grip mine, just as Zane announces, "And baby number two is a boy!"

He's placed on my chest and he gives me the same look like his sister. Again I know his name instantly. "Hi, Forrest Sawyer."

Staring at my two babies for a moment, I feel empty when they're taken from my arms for their newborn checks.

My eyes close, I feel myself slipping away. I can hear Zane's voice in my head.

'Savannah, Savannah, stay with me.'

My heart is pounding, and I try to focus my mind on Hunter, on River and my two sweet babies who can't be without me, but the world slips away into darkness.

(64) Emilie

My whole body aches, inside and out. Hearing of Quentin's accident had ripped my heart out, but thankfully he's alive because losing him would've been even worse than death.

My feelings on death have changed since crashing into Ridgehope six months ago.

At first, facing Caleb's death was torture but made me realise that I'd never loved him and was only with him because of the support he tried to desperately give me and Ember.

It wasn't that I wanted him to die, because he was a good person, but I'd learnt that we have no control over when our time is up.

Watching Alec die in my arms, knowing that his life was taken by Vlad had changed my perspective on everything in my life.

I want to start anew in my life now, never afraid to put myself out there in positive ways. The last week had been like a cyclone, tearing down everything in its path.

The only good thing being that Vlad was behind bars, finally about to confront a trial to pay for his crimes. He was up for eliciting prostitution, statutory rape, fraud, money laundering, drug trafficking and murder.

There's so much evidence against him, he's likely to be in jail for the rest of his life. I'm kinda hoping though that someone will get to him in jail though. He'd taken so much from me, my brother's life and now two of my children's lives before they even had a chance to live.

There's nothing—no words—that could describe the emptiness I felt waking up in the hospital bed, having passed out from the shock.

The doctors clinically told me I was no longer pregnant and the tears I cried were wretched, uncontrollable and barely left my eyes.

Having the Sergeant come in later that evening broke my heart more, because he spoke of Quentin's car accident like it happened every day.

Unlawful Attachment

I'm still not supposed to be up, but I need to see Quentin, to tell him again that I love him and hope it isn't the last time he'll possibly hear it.

Dragging my I.V drip down the hallway to the nurses' station I stop at the desk a little breathless to ask, "Hi, I um, was wondering if you knew which area Quentin Mackenney is in?"

The nurse looks at me like I'm asking her something obscure, and she taps away on the keyboard.

"And who are you?" she asks coldly.

"I'm...um...I'm his girlfriend," I reply meekly, thinking I should have said I'm engaged to him instead as it might have held more weight.

"Oh right, well normally we only let family in to see people in the ICU."

"Right, family ok? Are they here?"

"As far as I know. Please go back to your own bed, Miss."

Not replying I shuffle down the hallway, pretending to head back to my room. Watching her, making sure her gaze is turned I shuffle awkwardly to the elevator, giggling that she'd been stupid enough to admit that Quentin is in the ICU.

Riding the elevator up to level four I think about the last six months with Quentin, how quickly I fell in love with him and how sweet he has been with Ember.

The elevators spring open to a wide foyer with a nurses desk at the end. This time I don't bother to ask which room he's in, instead, shuffling along the rooms on one side.

Luckily I only have gone past two when I see Quentin in the bed, his body lifeless with monitors showing a steady heartbeat.

Next to the bed, an older woman is seated clutching his hand in hers. Sensing my presence she gets up, a little shaky on her feet when she comes to open the door.

At first, she doesn't say a word but pulls me into a tight hug.

"You must be Emilie?"

"Yes, and your Quentin's Mum?"

"Yes, you can call me Grace dear," she informs me, sitting back down whilst I drag my I.V in and shut the door behind me.

"Is he, is he going to be ok?"

"Yes, dear, they think he'll wake up soon. Thankfully they don't think there's any lasting internal bleeding or brain injury."

Shuffling over to the other side of the bed, I grab his hand in mine. It feels warm, which gives me hope.

"I'm really glad to hear that. He wouldn't even be here if it wasn't for me."

Grace shakes her head. "Don't blame yourself, dear."

"But I do. I dragged him back into my world, into the past and he could have died."

"But he didn't dear, plus I know my boy and he definitely doesn't do anything he doesn't want to."

"I don't understand what you mean?"

"He's a Mackenney man dear, they fall hard and fast for those they are meant to be with. And dear he's in love with you and your sweet little girl."

My heart swells, knowing that he'd confided in his Mother about his feelings for me.

"He told you that?"

"Not in so many words, but I know my baby boy."

"Yeah, I really love him, Grace. I was so afraid I'd never get to see him again."

"As I said, he's a Mackenney man. They don't give up on those that they love without a fight. Why do you still have the drip dear?"

"Pain meds," I reply, tapping the clear bag at the top. "I had some internal bleeding, extensive bruising and I um..."

"My goodness dear, whatever from?"

"From being with the most heinous man ever. I can't say any more than that, but I was also..." I try to say the words but they freeze on my tongue, my eyes stinging with tears.

"That sounds horrible dear. Is there something else that's bugging you?"

I smile at her, loving that she has the proper motherly instinct that my Mother never did.

"Yes...I was...um...pregnant..." I stutter, letting the words sink in.

"Was dear?"

I sniff back the tears. "Yes...was...he caused my miscarriage."

Grace's breath hitches a moment when she replies, "Whose baby was it?"

Squeezing Quentin's hand I look down at him when I reply, "Quentin's...I think the baby was Quentin's."

"Oh dear, I'm so sorry."

"Me too," I mutter, leaning down to kiss Quentin's forehead.

Silence engulfs the room then, a sense of overwhelming love filling the room. A knock on the door a few minutes later startles me.

Grace stands up to let Hunter in. "Emilie! How are you?" he asks eagerly, but also as though he's a little agitated.

"I'm ok considering everything. Are you ok?"

He takes his Mum's hand.

"Um, no not exactly," he states. "Mum are you ok to stay here? I need to head home immediately."

"Why dear?"

"Savannah had the twins. She lost a lot of blood from the c-section and they nearly lost her. I just need to get home."

Grace hugs him tightly, enveloping him with her love for him.

"Go, Hunter. Your beautiful wife needs you and you have twins to meet."

"Thanks, Mum," he coos, turning to look at me. "Will you let me know if he wakes up Emilie?"

"Yes, Hunter I will. I'm not going anywhere."

Caz May

"Thanks," he replies kissing my cheek before he leaves.
Smiling at Grace I softly say, "I wish I was a Mackenney."

She lets out a lighthearted laugh that warms my heart.
"I don't doubt that when my baby boy wakes up he'll make that wish come true Emilie. You're already a Mackenney because he loves you."
For a moment I ponder what that means, thinking about my name being, *'Emilie Jade Mackenney'*.
It has a nice ring to it and I really hope that Grace is right.
There's nothing I want more than to be Quentin's wife, to be a part of the Mackenney family and add to the growing clan of Mackenney's.
He just has to wake up.

(65) Quentin

Hearing Emilie's sweet voice in my head even though I can't open my eyes to see her beautiful face is like coming home.
Knowing she's alive and safe is everything.
Snippets of her conversation with Mum had floated into my head, words that momentarily made my heart swell before shattering.
I want to embrace her so tightly to take the pain away, from losing our baby.

The only thing I need to do is open my eyes, but they won't open.
Instead—after Hunter had rushed in and out of the room announcing that he was going home to be with Savannah and his newborn twins—I gently squeeze Emilie's hand that she's holding with mine.

She lets out a little screech. "Grace, he...he...squeezed my hand!"
"Really dear?"
"Yes, I swear," Emilie replies before brushing her other hand down my cheek. "Quentin, babe, please wake up. I love you."
Again I squeeze her hand—harder this time—my heart beating a little more rapidly at hearing her say she loves me again.
I never thought I'd hear those words again.

They're both silent, the room deathly silent. The breathing mask I know is on my face feels all of a sudden suffocating, so reaching up to my face I pull it away when other unfamiliar voices enter the room.

"What happened?" A strong male voice asks.
"He squeezed my hand before just now he pulled the mask off."

"Well, looks like it's time to get all these machines unhooked to let him wake up. He appears to be breathing on his own and his heartbeat has normalised."

"Thank you, doctor," Emilie replies, meekly.

"Who are you, Miss? You're not family?" The doctor asks when he appears to shuffle around the room.

"Well, I'm not family yet. I'm his fiancée."

"Oh right ok, well your arrival even though it wasn't protocol has been for the better."

The room is again silent, before the doctor speaks again.

"Ok everything is unhooked now. It may be a little longer until he regains full consciousness but you're both welcome to stay until he does. Press the buzzer when he opens his eyes please."

"Thank you, doctor, we will."

He leaves the room and I feel the bed shift when someone sits awkwardly on the edge.

Time seems to stop then, and I know it's my Emilie when she sighs.

"Babe, I'm here. Please open your eyes."

Taking a deep breath in, I will my eyes to open but they still feel glued shut. It's a nightmarish torture, like being trapped.

"Quentin, I love you, please babe," she pleads desperately, starting to sob.

I feel Mum grab my hand when she reassuringly says, "Emilie dear, he will wake up. The doctor said it may still take some time."

"I...I...know..but I..." Emilie stutters, her head falling against my chest when she starts to sob more.

"Dear, I'm going to go get a coffee. Stay here with him, keep telling him you love him."

"Ok Mum," Emilie mumbles, making my heart skip a beat at her referring to my Mum as hers.

It seems like ages have passed when I feel Emilie lift her head up, hear her intake of a shaky breath and feel her plump lips press against mine.

Even though I'm not able to open my eyes, I find my lips tingling, responding to her kiss.

It's a desperate kiss—but loving—her pouring her heart out to me, our very own Sleeping beauty moment.

She pulls back from the kiss. Taking a deep breath, her lips leave mine and I find my eyes fluttering open to look up at her.

She squeals in delight. "Oh my god, babe! Quentin!"

"Hey, Emi."

"I...I can't believe you're awake...you're alive."

"I couldn't leave you, babe."

"I'm sorry Quentin...for everything."

I reach a hand up to brush her cheek.

"You have nothing to be sorry about, babe. Nothing at all."

"I love you, Quentin."

"I love you too, my beautiful fiancée."

Her mouth drops open.

"Are you serious, babe?"

"Yes, Emilie, marry me?"

"Yes, a thousand times yes," she squeals kissing me, reaching behind to press the call button for the doctors to come in.

"Why'd you press that for?" I laugh. "I wanted more time with you, babe."

"I know babe, but I need to head back to my room. We have the rest of our lives to be together."

"God Emi, I love you so fucking much," I reply smashing my lips to hers for a desire filled kiss when the door opens and the doctor enters.

"Well, it looks like someone's awake," he says with laugh making Emilie pull back from the kiss and stand up from the bed.

"I'll see you later babe, love you."

"Love you to babe," I reply blowing her kiss when she walks out.

The doctor busies himself, checking me over. "How's the pain?"

"My leg is caining but all good otherwise."

"Great, great, I'll get some painkillers for you."

"Thanks, doctor, can I ask what happened to Emilie?"

"Your fiancé?"

"Yes, it's a long story but she had the I.V and I'm worried."

"Well, you're not her emergency contact but in the circumstances, I'll overlook that."

"Thank you, so?"

"Were you aware she was pregnant?"

"No, well yes I heard her talking before I woke up."

"Yes, well, she was only a few weeks along but lost the baby due to the trauma of her injuries. She was brought in with severe shock, extensive bruising and internal bleeding. We believe she was punched hard in the stomach causing the bleeding and her miscarriage."

Tears start to sting my eyes. "Do you know who caused the injuries?"

"You will need to speak to the police about that. I will let them know you're awake and they will come in to speak to you both before we clear you for discharge."

"Ok doctor, thanks," I reply a little angry that he won't tell me any more.

It's not like I really need him to tell me anyway, because I know only one person would've harmed Emilie—the one person she feared the most—Vladimir Manning.

I need to know the truth, need to know if the fucker is dead and out of our lives for good. It's the only way Emilie will ever be able to move on from her past and completely let go.

Closing my eyes when the doctor leaves the room I think about the past, how it collides with the present.

I think about love too, finally understanding how Hunter feels about Savannah.

Finally understanding my Mum's words about Mackenney men always falling hard and fast with the woman they're meant to be with.

It might have taken Emilie and I longer to find each other, but I don't doubt for a second that she's meant to be mine.

Unlawful Attachment

Emilie Mackenney has a nice ring to it and as I slip away into sleep I think about how I'm going to officially propose to her.

She deserves nothing less than perfect, because Emilie is perfect for me in every way.

Emilie is my light, able to deal with my darkness and bring me the light I need.

(Epilogue)

Emilie

Six months later

Waking up beside Quentin in his four-poster bed is a feeling I don't think I'll ever get used to. Most mornings I wake before him, the minute any sunlight peeks through the crack in the curtains.
I lie in bed just watching him sleep, bathing in the sunlight washing over me.
Waking up this morning is particularly special. I've been waiting six months for this day since the day Quentin officially proposed in his family's old farmhouse.
He'd faced his past to help clean it up, so the farm hands could stay in there when needed. His speech was perfect, about how loving me had helped him confront his past. I'd already said, 'yes' the day he woke up in the hospital but when he actually slipped the ring on my finger I knew I'd never felt more love than I did in that moment.

Murmuring he wakes up, his eyes blinking a few times when he looks at me. "Good morning Emi," he purrs huskily.
"Morning babe," I reply, kissing him quickly when the pitter patter of feet enters the bedroom.
The bed shifts when Ember jumps on the end.
"Mummy, Papa, is it wedding day?"
"Yes, sweetie, today is our wedding day. I'll officially be your Papa."
She squeals excitedly when Quentin hugs her.
Smiling at him, I'm caught in the moment, completely startled when my phone starts ringing on the bedside table.

Unlawful Attachment

Grabbing it I look at the number, a little worried seeing it's possibly a city number.

Jumping out of bed, I step out of the bedroom to answer it.

"Hello," I say tentatively, walking out into the kitchen.

"Hello ma'am, am I speaking to Emilie Buccianti?"

"Yes, speaking."

"Great, great," the male voice on the end of the line repeats.

"It's Sergeant Maxwell from the Adelaide CBD. I'm calling you as we've heard some news from the jail that you may be interested in."

"Oh," I gasp, swallowing a lump that has risen in my throat.

"What news is that Sergeant?"

"A Mr Vladimir Manning has been killed by another inmate."

"I'm sorry, what? He is dead? Like actually dead?"

"Yes, Emilie, his death has been confirmed."

"Thank you for calling me. That's amazing news."

He laughs. "The really bad ones don't last long in jail."

I laugh then. "Yeah, thanks again for the call."

"No problems, have a good day now Emilie."

"Oh I will, thanks again Sergeant Maxwell," I reply hanging up and racing down the hallway.

Stopping in the bedroom door I'm completely breathless, tongue-tied.

"Emi? Babe, what's wrong?"

I take a deep breath to try and calm myself.

"Vlad...Vlad...is...dead."

Quentin sits bolt upright, shrieking, "What?"

"He's dead. Another inmate killed him."

"Oh my god Emi! That's...that's horrible but kinda awesome."

"I know right? And hearing about it today."

"Double cause for celebration most definitely. Come here, babe."

Sitting back down on the bed, he kisses me quickly.

"Eww, Mummy. You kiss Papa on ips." Ember giggles.

"Yeah, I love your Papa, sweetie. Do you love him?"

"Yes!" she squeals when Quentin grabs her around her tiny waist to start tickling her.

"Do you love me Ember?" Quentin asks her, tickling her, making her giggle excitedly.

"Es, Es, Papa I wuv oo!"

Quentin ceases tickling her, kissing her forehead.

"Good to know Ember, because I love you so much, sweetie."

My heart swells with love for them both. "Babe, you should probably get ready to head to Hunter's."

"Yeah, I know," he smiles, getting out of bed. "I can't wait to see you in your wedding gown, babe."

"And I can't wait to see you in your black suit, babe."

He presses a kiss to my lips, and one to Ember's forehead.

"I'll see you soon to sweetie ok. Help Mummy look beautiful?"

"Es Papa!" Ember squeals when Quentin leaves the room, pulling on his clothes as he stumbles out.

In mere hours I'm going to be walking down the aisle to become his wife.

I've never been more excited and happier than I am in that moment.

Quentin

Arriving at the farmhouse I'm greeted by River running down the driveway with Blitz at his side.

"Unci Kent, it's wedding day!" he screams whilst I get out of my new purple XR6. It's a huge upgrade from my Kingswood and it feels a little odd driving it sometimes.

River wraps his arms around my legs and I scoop him up to hold him against my hip, ruffling his hair.

"Hey River. Yeah, it's my wedding day. Do you want to know a secret Riv?"

"Yes, Unci Kent."

Unlawful Attachment

"I'm really scared."

"Why Unci Kent?" he asks as we walk onto the verandah.

"It's a pretty big deal to be getting married. I remember when your Mummy and Daddy got married."

"Eally? Was Daddy ared like you?"

"Yeah he was sweet boy." I smile at him, putting him down inside the front door.

He calls out loudly, "Daddy! Unci Kent here!"

Hunter slides around the corner, only wearing his pants and socks.

"Oh hey little brother." He smiles. "You ready to get married?"

"Not really, but I love Emilie more than anything so..."

"Yeah I know," he replies, picking River up. "We need to hurry up and get ready if we're going to be out under the arch when the girls arrive."

"Yeah," I muse, following him down the hallway to the spare room to get into my suit.

ꝫ

Standing under the same arch where Hunter had married Savannah a few years earlier my heart is pounding hard in my chest. I look to the seats in front to see everyone who matters to me, Addison and Zane, holding their newborn baby girl Alexis, and my Mum next to her holding one of the twins, the other in a pram in front of her.

Savannah is standing on the other side of the arch in a simple purple gown.

Next to me, under the arch is my older brother.

He grabs my hand and I turn to look at him.

"You ready Quent?"

I sigh. "Yeah I'm ready," I reply when the music starts, *'I love you, I want you, I need you' by Tenth Avenue North,* summing up how I feel about Emilie.

At the end of the aisle, two little figures start the short walk down, holding hands and smiling sweetly. I smile wide at how sweet my nephew and stepdaughter look as my page boy and flower girl.

When they reach the front, I scoop Ember up, kissing her cheek. River stands by Hunter's legs and I put Ember back down to stand next to him when Emilie appears at the end of the aisle.
She looks absolutely stunning, beyond beautiful. Her brown hair is up, her eyes painted blue-green with her lips stained a soft pink.
Her dress is breathtaking, a strapless lace dress that hugs her tiny waist, flaring out into a wide skirt with a billowing train that follows her.
A captivating smile is plastered on her face as she steps up to me, taking my hand with hers, after she hands Savannah her bouquet.
"Emi, you look phenomenal."
"You look incredible, Quentin. I love you."
"I love you too Emilie," I reply when the celebrant starts the ceremony.

The ceremony is short, sweet and a complete blur until the kiss.
With Emilie's hand in mine, we walk down the aisle—as husband and wife—our first steps together as one.
Hugging Mum I freeze, dropping Emilie's hand when Mum feels weak in my arms, falling to the ground, her whole body shaking.
Hunter comes rushing over, telling me to go spend time with Emilie.
He ushers the guests away, all except for Mark who's by Mum's side checking her.
My heart shatters, feeling like this is a goodbye and even though it's been the best day of my life I can't help but think the worst.

"I love you, Quentin," Emilie whispers in my ear. "It will be ok."
"I hope so Emilie. I'm scared to say goodbye to her."
"I know babe," she replies when we get into the decked out police car to head off for photos.
Emilie kisses me softly, and I let my mind try to focus on her and the fact that she's now my wife. She's now a Mackenney and my life with her is just beginning, maybe as my Mum's is ending.
Life and love really do come full circle.

The End (for now)

Caz May

Playlist

Below is the playlist of songs for this story and the associated chapter if applicable. They are not in order. <u>Spotify Link</u>

1. Let You Down-NF (Prologue)
2. Not meant to be- Theory of a Deadman (Ch 1)
3. Code Name Vivaldi-The Piano Guys (Ch 2)
4. Paradise-George Ezra (Ch
5. Want you back-5SOS (Ch 27)
6. Don't Give In-Snow Patrol (Ch
7. Boys from the bush-Lee Kernaghan (Ch 18)
8. The Outback Club-Lee Kernaghan (Ch 17)
9. Next to me-Imagine Dragons
10. Chemicals-Dean Lewis
11. Broken Arrows-Avicii
12. Ride-Chase Rice ft Macy Maloy
13. Battlefield-Lea Michele (Ch 23)
14. Craving You-Travis Atreo, Colton Haynes (Ch 34)
15. The Dark of you-Breaking Benjamin
16. The Diary of Jane-Breaking Benjamin (Ch 8)
17. Self Control-DallasK (Ch 31)
18. Beautifully broken-Plumb (Ch 36)
19. Together Again-Evanesence (Ch 58)
20. Watch over you-Alter Bridge (Ch 3)
21. Climax-Usher (Ch 24)
22. Bloom-Troye Sivan
23. Hold me-Savage Garden (Ch 32)
24. Waking up with you-Shannon Curtis (Ch 35)
25. Can you hold me-NF (Ch 40)
26. 50 shades of crazy-Chase Rice
27. Call out my name-The Weekend
28. Save me-My Darkest Days
29. You & Me-James TW
30. Broken-Seether ft Amy Lee
31. I found-Amber Run (Ch)
32. Come away with me-Norah Jones (Ch 20)
33. My Way-Limp Bizkit (Ch 37)
34. Slow me down-Emmy Rossum (Ch 39)
35. Run to you-Lea Michele (Ch 41)
36. Beneath your beautiful-labrinth feat Emili Sandé (Ch 45)
37. For your entertainment-Adam Lambert (Ch 48)

38. Stay with me-Ironik feat Alex Sparks (Ch 50)

39. Forever-Rascal Flatts (Ch 54)

40. Get away with murder-Jeffree Star (Ch 59)

41. Bleed Out-Blue October (Ch 61)

42. I need you, I love you, I want you-Tenth Avenue North (Epilogue)

About the Author

Caz May is a librarian/teacher by trade, but was always destined to be an author from a young age. In her spare time, she can be found devouring books or writing her own stories with characters that may not be the typical romance heroes but are loveable just as much.

Caz is married to her own real-life bearded hero and has two fur babies.

She lives for Iced coffee, especially from Gloria Jeans or a Farmers Union but pretty much just loves food in general.

When she's not writing, or reading a book most likely she can probably be found asleep or binge-watching shows on Netflix and Stan. And probably also drooling over her character inspiration on Instagram as well.

Check out her Instagram or other socials to get in touch. She loves chatting with her readers whilst they're reading her books and after as well.

Instagram- @cazmayauthor

BookBub-Caz May https://www.bookbub.com/profile/caz-may

Goodreads-https://www.goodreads.com/cazmay

Facebook- @CazMayAuthor

Spotify- cazcat25

TAKE FLIGHT

A Christmas Romance Preview

One

Kaiya

Shuffling the papers on her desk, Kaiya sighs deeply hearing her phone buzzing somewhere on the melamine desk. She curses under her breath, wondering who would be calling so late on a Friday afternoon.

The buzzing stops just as her fingers brush against the screen of her phone, it displaying one missed call from 'Mom'. She knew better than to call back, as it would only be a game of phone tag if she did. Her Mom never called once, it was repeated until Kaiya answered.

Flicking her phone off silent, she drops it in her handbag on the swivel chair pulled out from her desk and she continues tidying up all the papers. Her desk needed to be pristine, ready for the Christmas holiday period. She didn't want to be thinking about what she'd left behind on her desk whilst enduring the torture of a Palmieri family Christmas. It was bad enough that her wound tight boss had delivered a rather large manuscript to her email inbox mere hours ago, with the instruction that it needed to be read by the time she came back to work on January third or she could kiss her job as a copy editor for Mon Amour Publishing goodbye.

Losing her job was the last thing Kaiya needed, as her roommate had just up and left, no warning whatsoever and she was now going to have to pay double rent on her Manhattan apartment, as well as have enough money to not have to eat Strawberry Poptarts for every meal.

Picking up one of the many coffee cups strewn across the melamine, she sniffs it, screwing up her nose at the putrid smell of week-old coffee and creamer. Grabbing as many as she can, she awkwardly carries them to the kitchen throwing them haphazardly in the sink before squeezing in too much detergent.

Starting to clean out the cups, she starts humming 'Silent Night' completely oblivious that anyone else was still in the office until the chief editor Baxter Manson steps up behind her leaning on the door frame. His voice is gruff when he speaks, "Kai, girl what are you still doing here?"

Carnality laces his words as his eyes scan her ass in the tight black pencil skirt. Kaiya swallows the lump in her throat at the words, dropping the cups in the soapy water and turning to face him.

"I...um...was just...cleaning up," she mutters, not able to meet Baxter's gaze that wanders her body.

"Forget that girl, there's no one else here."

She wants to spit words at him, vicious words to make Baxter; the only male employee of Mon Amour Publishing; back off and leave her alone to finish up her holiday preparations. But Baxter had other plans to take advantage of their time alone in the office.

Further entering the kitchen he steps up behind her, pressing his body against hers. She tenses her body, clenching her thighs together at the unwelcome feeling that pools in her underwear. She hates her body's reaction to having Baxter so close, but she couldn't deny that she was a little bit attracted to him. His dark ash blonde hair was always perfectly styled, stubble always framing his jaw and across the crevice at the top of his lips.

His lips brush against the sensitive skin under her ear, his breath against her ear as he whispers making her temperature rise, "Kai, you taste delicious." She huffs, fighting the feelings she'd felt for so long when it came to sex. Doing anything remotely sexual with the office man-whore was all kind of wrong. Pushing her back against him, he steps back laughing. Kaiya turns to face him, trying not to meet his eyes for fear she would blush from head to toe when his eyes took in her in.

"Oh so it's like that is it?" he asked, smirking at her as he loosens his slinky jet black tie from the collar of his crisp white shirt.

"Please Baxter, just let me finish these dishes."

He steps closer to her, pushing her back against the cold stainless steel sink. His hand brush against the skin of her blouse. It felt cold against her skin.

"Did you realise your blouse is all wet Kai?" he asks teasingly.

Kaiya swallows hard, muttering, "No...no...I..didn't."

"You should take it off," he says again with the teasing tone, running his hands up and down the buttons. She wants to protest as he starts undoing them, but her breathing is unsteady and his eyes locked on hers make her feel like melting. She couldn't deny the attraction she felt to him, like every other girl in the office. Baxter had almost done the rounds of the office, sleeping with everyone except Kaiya and her friend Alice.

Reaching the bottom of her blouse he untucks it from her skirt, undoing the last button and watching as the fabric falls open to expose her creamy white lace bra.

"Mmm, Kai, your tits are perfect girl," Baxter moans grabbing her small perky breast in his palm.

Kaiya gasps at the sensation, trying to not let the whimper of pleasure from his intimate touch escape her lips. She miserably fails, as Baxter kneads her breast in his palm for a moment with his eyes still locked on hers.

"Do you like that Kaiya?"

She's frozen, feeling a mix of fear and lust. A straight jolt of pleasure shot through to her core when Baxter's mouth found the sensitive bud through the lace. She'd never had a man do anything of the sort to her, having only read about such things in the romance books she devoured as part of her job.

Stopping his sweet torture, he looks up at her smirking before smashing his lips against hers in a fierce kiss. His tongue runs along her lower lip, demanding entrance that she wasn't sure she should give him. She'd only ever been kissed once before in her life, by her best friend Eddie and it was sweet, soft and nothing like the kiss she was now getting from Baxter.

Giving in, she opens her mouth, gasping against his lips as he takes her tongue with his. His arms grip her waist, lifting her off the floor and awkwardly moving her across the room.

With their lips still locked Baxter puts Kaiya down, her butt resting on the edge of the small glass dining table in the communal kitchen.

Reaching down his fingers brush her thigh edging her skirt up. He wants to touch her, knowing her underwear would be soaked with want from the hot kiss they'd just shared. About to kiss her again, she turns her head shaking it as she says, "No Baxter, please stop. I...I...can't do this."

"Seriously Kaiya?"

"Yes, I...I...um," she mumbles, pushing her hands against his chest making him stumble backwards.

"Fuck Kaiya, you're a fucking cock-tease!" he screams at her, running a hand through his blonde locks before he turns to leave the room. Kaiya stands up, smoothing her skirt down before she goes back to the sink to finish off the dishes.

Five minutes later when she's drying the last of the cups, she hears her phone trill from in the office. Racing back to her desk, grabbing it out she sees there are now another four missed calls from her Mom.

This time she knew she'd have to call back, and hoped her Mom would answer. Quickly she shuts down her computer and slings her bag over her shoulder. Walking out she flicks off the lights, sets the alarm and dials her Mom's number.

She takes a deep sigh when her Mom answers on the second ring.

"Kaiya darling, I've been trying to call you for the last half hour."

"Hi Mom," Kaiya replies meekly as she steps into the elevator.

She knew from the tone in her Mom's voice that this phone call was the dreaded one, and she wasn't sure if she could keep up the lie any longer.